PRAISE FOR
STRANGE LIES

"Smart, sexy, darker than dark."
—Jeff Zentner,
author of Morris Award winner *The Serpent King*

"Twisty, bawdy, gossipy . . . This is a solid pick for fans of
the TV series *Riverdale* and other dark, campy mysteries."
—*Booklist*

"Thrash's fans will love this."
—*VOYA*

"Fast-paced and suspenseful . . . Thrash's brazen characters
and dark humor will compel readers forward."
—*Kirkus Reviews*

PRAISE FOR
STRANGE TRUTH
(Previously titled *We Know It Was You*)

"A fast-paced, sassy, and sultry whodunit."
—*School Library Journal*

"The definition of a page-turner. Thrash's unique ability to balance humor, mystery, and teen angst blew me away. Hilarious, twisty, and full of unforgettable characters—this is damn good stuff."
—John Corey Whaley,
Printz Award–winning author of *Where Things Come Back* and National Book Award Finalist *Noggin*

"*[Strange Truth]* has all the elements of a great read: mystery, humor, romance, and drama. . . . Thrash's writing is so mesmerizingly good I found myself rereading sentences for the sheer pleasure and surprise of them."
—Cecily von Ziegesar,
New York Times bestselling author of the Gossip Girl series

"A complicated and twisty tale that blends noir mystery, gothic romance, and dark humor."
—VOYA

ALSO BY MAGGIE THRASH

Strange Truth

A *STRANGE* NOVEL

MAGGIE THRASH

Simon Pulse
New York London Toronto Sydney New Delhi

SIMON PULSE

An imprint of Simon & Schuster Children's Publishing Division

1230 Avenue of the Americas, New York, New York 10020

First Simon Pulse paperback edition October 2018

Text copyright © 2017 by Maggie Thrash

Cover title illustration copyright © 2017 by John Harwood

All other cover illustrations copyright © 2017 by Thinkstock

Also available in a Simon Pulse hardcover edition.

All rights reserved, including the right of reproduction in whole or in part in any form.

SIMON PULSE and colophon are registered trademarks of Simon & Schuster, Inc.

For information about special discounts for bulk purchases, please contact Simon & Schuster Special Sales at 1-866-506-1949 or business@simonandschuster.com.

The Simon & Schuster Speakers Bureau can bring authors to your live event.

For more information or to book an event contact the Simon & Schuster Speakers Bureau at 1-866-248-3049 or visit our website at www.simonspeakers.com.

Cover designed by Jessica Handelman

Interior designed by Mike Rosamilia

The text of this book was set in Adobe Garamond Pro.

Manufactured in the United States of America

2 4 6 8 10 9 7 5 3 1

The Library of Congress has cataloged the hardcover edition as follows:

Names: Thrash, Maggie, author.

Title: Strange lies / by Maggie Thrash.

Description: First Simon Pulse hardcover edition. | New York : Simon Pulse, 2017. |

Series: Strange ; 2 | Summary: Benny and Virginia investigate when the student body president is maimed during Winship Academy's science expo in what may have been an accident, while a mystery man was handing out drugs.

Identifiers: LCCN 2017000956 (print) | LCCN 2017030004 (eBook) | ISBN 9781481462037 (hardcover) | ISBN 9781481462051 (eBook)

Subjects: | CYAC: Mystery and detective stories. | Drug abuse—Fiction. | High schools—Fiction. | Schools—Fiction. | Race relations—Fiction.

Classification: LCC PZ7.1.T53 (eBook) | LCC PZ7.1.T53 Wat 2017 (print) | DDC [Fic]—dc23

LC record available at https://lccn.loc.gov/2017000956

ISBN 9781481462044 (pbk)

To Dean, with hatred

What no one realized about life was that every second you weren't free, you were dying. Every breath you breathed was a criminal waste of air if you weren't free.

He stared at the cream-colored horse and carriage stationed anachronistically in the school parking lot. It was quiet now, but in an hour everyone would be crowding outside to wave and cheer as the Homecoming King and Queen took their triumphant ride around the block. It was one of many social customs at Winship Academy that underscored the school's unwritten motto: *Some people are better than others.*

He'd come outside with the vague objective to look at the stars and experience a sublime moment of inner peace. But of course it was the city, and only one star was visible beyond the bruise-colored dome of light pollution. As if the goal of urban existence was to keep everyone looking down instead of up.

He stroked the horse's cheek and golden mane. The horse seemed restless, jostling its head trying to shake off its harness and leather blinders. It, too, was ready to run.

The driver was asleep in his polyester Dickensian costume, the reins lying in his open hand. The horse would be gone if it knew its own power.

He was being followed. He was aware of this, but he wasn't worried. Everything was falling into place; soon escape would be his. He gave the horse a final pat, and then he went back inside, a shadow followed by a shadow.

One week earlier, Thursday
Yasmin Astarabadi's house, 6:00 p.m.

She's gone.

Yasmin Astarabadi's entire body buzzed with megalomaniacal glee. Zaire Bollo was gone. According to Virginia Leeds, who was supposedly there when it happened, she'd run off to Spain and was never coming back. Of course, Virginia was an insane pathological liar and normally Yasmin wouldn't pay attention to anything that girl said, but an entire week had gone by with no sign of Zaire at all. Then a truck had pulled up to the Boarders and hauled all Zaire's stuff away—her gold-and-black wardrobe from Milan, her mountains of books, her imported stationery and tins of tea—everything. She was *gone*.

Carefully, and with great reverence, Yasmin removed Zaire's photo from the large bulletin board on her bedroom wall. A web of ribbons came away with it, leading to index cards with words like "SATs," "Governor's List," *"Summa Cum Laude,"* "clubs," and "yearbook" typed in color-coded ink. She placed the photo faceup in the trash can. The next time she threw away some chewed gum or a Kleenex with a dead bug in it, she wanted it to land right on Zaire's annoying, haughty face.

"Another one bites the fucking dust," she said, delighted by her own corniness. She repositioned the remaining photos on the board, moving each one up a position, like horses in a race: Calvin Harker now at number one, herself at number two, Benny Flax lagging slightly behind her at number three, and DeAndre Bell behind him at a distant fourth. Now that Zaire was gone from the board, its quotient of physical beauty had dipped severely, Yasmin couldn't help but notice. DeAndre was arguably handsome, but his smarmy, politician's perma-grin ruined him in Yasmin's eyes. As for the rest of them, Calvin Harker was lean and grim and ghoulish. Benny Flax was okay-looking, but dopey and distinctly hopeless. And if Yasmin contributed any beauty to the group, it certainly wasn't evident to her. They were three ugly nerds.

Whatever, she thought. Beautiful people were stupid. That was a literal fact. Their brains developed differently, growing larger in the areas dedicated to reinforcing self-worth through the affirmation of others. It's what made people think it was valuable to spend thirty-five minutes on their hair in the morning. That was thirty-five minutes Yasmin could be spending reading Sun Tzu or researching political internships. Time management was the key to life. Yasmin considered any moment in which she was not actively engaged in the advancement of her goals to be a quantifiable loss.

It wasn't a coincidence that the top students in their class were all minorities in some way. The white kids at Winship didn't bother competing academically. They would get whatever they wanted in life whether they had the grades to back it up or not; their fourth-generation country club connections were the only currency they needed. Yasmin felt sorry for them. They would never know the powerful, ecstatic satisfaction that she felt at having to work hard to distinguish herself.

Yasmin gave herself a quick once-over in the mirror. She didn't like her outfit. On non-uniform occasions at Winship, you had basically one option unless you wanted to look like a freak: a cardigan set (color of your choice) with a short black skirt. In the spring and summer you could wear floral, but obviously not past Labor Day. Preppy outfits were always designed to exhibit—never overshadow—the assumed natural radiance of their wearer. On Yasmin, they looked average and drab, but she didn't second-guess her choice. Being different just wasn't worth the hubbub.

She gathered up the materials for her high-voltage electric arc. Tonight was the science expo, which excited Yasmin more than any football game or dance. Academic events were basically popularity contests of the brain. And now that Zaire was gone, Yasmin had a shot at actually winning.

She took a last glance at her newly organized bulletin board. Calvin Harker would be tough to beat. He was almost two years older than everyone else in the sophomore class. He'd had to drop out of school for ten months because he had heart cancer or a brain tumor or something. By all rights he should have been a junior. It wasn't fair.

At least Benny Flax wouldn't be a problem. He was smart and had great grades, but his heart wasn't in the race. All he cared about was his little baby club about *Blue's Clues* or whatever it was. *What a waste of a good mind.*

DeAndre made her nervous. His grades weren't a huge threat, but he was the student body president, which would carry a lot of weight with the cocksuckers at Harvard. She knew for a fact that every decent college had been sniffing around him since ninth grade, when he'd taken the football team to state.

Whatever, she thought again. The word was her talisman. With it she'd surmounted the indignities of ninth grade, which had included an assault of acne and the realization that high school didn't magically make boys interesting— they were the same annoying dipshits they'd been in middle school, only bigger, and if Yasmin ever wanted to have sex with one of them she'd have to dramatically lower her standards. Not that sex was even a remote priority for Yasmin. The only climax that mattered to her was making it to the top of the class—that gleaming, perfect pinnacle—where she'd grin down at everyone she'd crushed to get there.

Outside the gym, 6:30 p.m.

Benny felt like an imposter. He always did on these occasions.

It was the clothes—khaki pants, blue blazer, tie. The outfit wasn't mandatory, technically, but it's what every guy would be wearing. It wasn't what he'd planned to wear. He'd planned to wear his dad's gray wool suit, which had been hanging in the closet since the accident, immaculate and untouched. It was still in the plastic bag from the dry cleaners. The crease in the trousers was as perfect as if it had been ironed yesterday, not eighteen months ago. Seeing it, Benny had stopped. He wasn't really going to wear this, was he? This was a man's suit, and he was just a kid. What if it didn't fit? What if he messed it up or spilled punch on it? What if his dad needed it? That last question was ridiculous, Benny knew. Benny's dad had severe brain damage from a plane crash and wouldn't be needing a suit tonight or possibly ever again. But still, what if he suddenly felt better and wanted to go out for a nice dinner in his suit, and when he went to the closet it was gone and the shock sent his brain back into its foggy maze? The idea was ludicrous, but as soon as it had germinated in Benny's mind, he knew he wouldn't be touching that suit.

He sat on the curb outside the gym, waiting for Virginia Leeds to appear. They were going to the science expo together. It was not a date, as if that needed to be established. He'd never heard of anyone going to a science expo as a date. He wasn't exactly sure why they were going together at all. Ostensibly it was for Mystery Club, but really it was just a habit they'd developed of meeting each other places—in the hall after assemblies, by the apple stand during break, in the cafeteria if they had the same lunch period. They'd report any unusual observations—usually there weren't many—then they'd go their separate ways.

Benny had founded Mystery Club on the basic philosophy that mysteries were everywhere, and that the greatest advantage in solving one was to Be There. Be watching, be a witness. Don't wait for mysteries to come to you, because they won't. Benny had learned this quickly enough. When he'd first created the club, he'd expected to be barraged with inquiries: Who started that rumor that I tongue-kissed a dog? Who put a bag of peanuts on the peanut allergy table in the cafeteria? Weird things were always happening at Winship, but people seemed too self-absorbed to care. Except for Virginia. Virginia cared—cared too much maybe. She was obsessed with other people's business and always had been. Sometimes Benny wondered if she'd only joined Mystery Club as an excuse to spy on people.

"Hey."

Benny twisted around and saw her approaching. She was wearing a soft black sweater and a gold skirt that Benny recognized as having belonged to Zaire Bollo. It looked expensive, and was short enough to glue anyone's eyes to her legs. It was definitely inappropriate for an academic event that was mostly a spectacle for parents. Benny's own mother was already inside, examining every tenth grader's project to assess the competition.

Benny was about to stand up, knowing there was no way Virginia could sit on a street curb in that skirt without flashing the entire world. But Virginia either didn't know or didn't care. She plunked down next to him, immediately scooching away a bit, apparently having misjudged how close to him she'd landed. Benny stared ahead. Just because her underwear was probably showing didn't mean he had to look. In fact, it was his duty not to.

"You look like a calculator salesman," Virginia said.

"I look the same as everyone," Benny said, nodding toward a very athletic, sandy-haired boy climbing out of a blue Mazda who was wearing the same combination of khakis and blue blazer as him.

"Oh yeah, you're clearly twins separated at birth."

Benny gritted his teeth. Virginia always managed to blithely zero in on whatever anyone was insecure about and broadcast it to the world. Did she do it on purpose? Benny didn't know. Perhaps she'd enjoy it if Benny pointed out that she was wearing Zaire Bollo's designer cast-offs and her underwear was showing. *At least I didn't steal my outfit from a murderer,* he imagined saying back. But he knew he wouldn't. It might feel good for a second, but then Virginia would get that crinkled, hurt look on her face, and Benny would be consumed by guilt for days.

Clothes, clothes, clothes, he thought dismally. These events always revolved around clothes. Winship was a uniform school, which meant that on the occasions when people had free reign to wear what they wanted, it became a matter of intense public display and scrutiny. The irony was that everyone ended up dressing the same as one another anyway, but as a collective decision rather than a mandate from above, which seemed to be an important distinction.

Virginia was picking at a large scab on her knee. She'd been picking at it all week. It was never going to heal at this rate, and the skin around the scab was red and infected. Benny was about to say as much when she sat up abruptly and began digging through a small brown bag that didn't match her outfit at all.

"So, um, I got you something." Virginia handed him a small velvet box. Benny examined it warily.

"What is it?" he asked. The last time she'd gotten him a present, it was a bracelet with the letters *W.W.B.D.?* (What Would Benny Do?) sewn onto it, with a matching one for herself. It had been touching but embarrassing.

"Just open it," Virginia insisted.

He snapped open the box. Inside was a silver ring. He turned the ring over in his palm and saw that it was composed of a pair of dials, one engraved with letters and the other engraved with numbers. It looked expensive.

"It's a decoder ring," he said. "Wow, thank you."

"I got us both one!" She held up a second ring. "For writing messages. You're always complaining about the notes I leave on your locker, so . . ." Her voice trailed off, and Benny saw that her cheeks were bright red.

Benny had always found Virginia somewhat irritating-looking: her heart-shaped face prone to flushing, her blank staring eyes, her Afro of blond curls. But in the warm evening light, her features seemed to morph slightly, her face at some middle point between an awkward, chunky cherub and a Renaissance angel. It was an undeniable flash of . . . *cuteness.* Benny didn't like the word—it evoked ponies and puppies and cupcakes—but there it was.

"You need to learn to control that," he said, a little louder than he'd meant to.

"Control what?" Virginia said, turning her face away.

"Your cheeks. You're blushing. If you want to be a great detective, no one should ever be able to tell what you're thinking."

"Oh yeah?" Virginia snapped, looking at him suddenly. "What am I thinking?"

Now Benny was the one blushing. "I . . . I don't know. I'm just saying . . ." He stared down at the decoder ring, pretending to be fascinated by the dials. He could sense that Virginia was glaring at him. Seconds passed.

"So, what's your project?" Virginia asked, back to picking her scab.

"A study of anomalous recoveries from neurological damage. What's yours?"

"'Trees of Georgia.' I dunno. I suck at science."

Virginia's wouldn't even be the worst project, Benny knew. The science expo was mandatory for all students. Winship's science program had recently been called "lacking" in the *Guide to Southern Prep and Boarding Schools*, a slander the administration was obsessed with correcting. But by making the expo mandatory, the result was that people who had no business contributing clogged up the works for the people who were serious. Still, Benny tried not to be bothered. He believed in inclusivity and that everyone deserved a chance. But at the same time, he couldn't help noticing that the chance seemed to be wasted on 99 percent of humanity.

He stood up. "I better go set up my booth. See you later."

"See ya."

"Um, thanks for the ring." Benny made a small show of sliding it onto his finger.

"You're welcome," Virginia said back, not looking up from her scab.

Benny lingered a second, then gave up. He'd screwed up the moment somehow, and now it was over.

Booth 43, 7:15 p.m.

DeAndre's project was the classic volcano. Classic was his thing. He'd seen all the Cary Grant movies as a kid and thought, with profound awe, *That's who I want to be.* Cary Grant encompassed everything suave and cool. He was the ultimate leading man, and DeAndre channeled him in all things. Would Cary Grant go overboard with his science project? Nah, he'd do the bare minimum, but do it perfectly. Would Cary Grant be upset that the entire school was laughing at his uncle? Nah, Cary Grant would grin and brush it off. He'd probably laugh, too!

It was hard to keep grinning, though. The thing with his uncle was getting out of control. His whole family had come up from Lakewood Heights to see the science expo, even though he'd practically begged them not to. His mom had seen Winship before, and she knew how to be cool, but the rest of his family had predictably freaked when they'd seen the facilities—the soaring brick buildings, floor-to-ceiling windows with views of the football field and the river, shining tile floors, bathrooms bigger than their entire house, with automatic toilet-seat covers and mild-smelling foaming soap instead of the standard antibacterial pink goo. It was bad enough that they'd wandered around with their mouths hanging open like they were touring the White House. But then his uncle Jeffrey saw the spread at the refreshments table and exclaimed with loud glee, "They got real ham biscuits!" which had taken approximately five seconds to become a school-wide joke. Ten years from now, people would probably still be ribbing each other and saying, "They got real ham biscuits!" long after DeAndre was gone and the joke's origin was forgotten.

Be glad to have contributed to the school's history, he told himself. Cary Grant was always buoyant in these situations.

He wouldn't let an embarrassing uncle get him down. And if Uncle Jeffrey thought it was weird that about three different kids had come up and asked him if he'd seen that there were real ham biscuits at the refreshments table, he didn't show it. In fact, he seemed delighted that Winship students were such attentive hosts. He slapped their shoulders congenially and said to each one, "You fuckin' bet I did!"

The three judges appeared, and DeAndre got ready to make the volcano erupt. A group of students, mostly girls, were hovering nearby, obviously less interested in his volcano than in gawking at his family. DeAndre pretended not to realize this and greeted them warmly.

"Hey, guys! Come on in!" He was good at bringing people together. As the student body president, it was pretty much his job. A few weeks ago when everyone thought Brittany Montague was dead, it was DeAndre who had stepped up to organize the candlelight vigil, while everyone else was dissolving into despair.

"Come watch!" he said again to the girls.

"Um, okay!" They came forward, everyone smiling now. *If you're nice to people, they'll be nice back,* he thought happily. It was the simplest truth in the world. Why didn't people get it? Sure, it could be hard sometimes. Kids at Winship weren't known for welcoming outsiders. But if you were nice, and you weren't a huge nerd, life at Winship could be pretty all right.

He poured vinegar into the crater and the papier-mâché

mountain overflowed with burbling lava. His parents clapped and his little sister shrieked adorably.

"Great job, D!" Mr. Rashid said. "Wow. What a crowd-pleaser!"

Two girls were whispering to each other next to the volcano. "Omigod, did you hear about Virginia and Skylar?" DeAndre wiped up the table with a paper towel, trying not to look like he was listening. Gossip was in poor taste, but it was important to know what was going on in the lives of his constituents. But then Uncle Jeffrey appeared with a heaping plate from the refreshments table.

"You gotta get some of this shit, D!"

"I sure will, Uncle J," he said, and by then the girls had left.

"Death. Death. Black band leader of endless night."

DeAndre rolled his eyes. It was Calvin Harker again, in the booth across the row. Apparently his project was on morbid poetry or something.

"Hot spewing magma hardens to igneous rock. The blaze of life snuffed by ash."

Oh god, please don't drag me into this, DeAndre pleaded in his mind. Calvin used to be fairly normal, despite being freakishly tall and also the headmaster's son, which was a serious social hurdle. But lately it was like he'd given up completely. DeAndre prided himself on never being cliquish or rude, but people like Calvin got on his nerves.

I can't help you if you insist on being weird.

"No fire is eternal. Even the sun will burn out, our planet left an icy, forgotten globe."

Booth 29, 7:30 p.m.

Why is everyone so willing to be boring?

It was a question Virginia asked herself almost every single day. Why did anyone do homework? Or wear navy? Or date the same person for three years? The other day in Ethics class, they'd gone around the room saying what everyone wanted to be when they grew up, and Corny Davenport said, "A real estate agent, just like my mom!" It was pretty much the most depressing thing Virginia had ever heard.

She'd been looking forward to the science expo all day. In her mind she'd conflated it with a dance somehow, imagining dim lighting and the promise of romance, except with science projects everywhere. Only now was she realizing how non-conducive to romance the science expo environment was. The gym's fluorescent lights assaulted every corner. It was loud, and the roving panel of judges were making everyone uptight. This was going to be as boring as school, wasn't it? Except worse, because at least at school you didn't normally have to be around a hundred million parents.

On the "Trees of Georgia" poster she'd made, several of the dried, crumbling leaves had fallen down, and another was lopsided. She'd known it wasn't a great project, but now it seemed actually pathetic. As she looked around, some of the other projects seemed barely even related to science. A group of juniors were doing a project on *The Fast and the Furious* that was just pictures of exploding cars and Vin Diesel quotes. And Trevor Cheek had a project called, simply, "Hunting," which was showing off all the heads of deer he'd killed. If Virginia had known you could just do whatever you wanted, she would have done a project on classic cocktails, or Body Language of the Rich and Powerful.

In the booth next to her, Yasmin Astarabadi was erecting an immense pair of metal wires, one of which kept drooping perilously toward her. Virginia leaned away, not wanting her outfit to get stabbed. It felt different, wearing expensive clothes. It made her more conscious of her posture and of potentially ruinous stabbing wires. She'd never cared about perfect clothes before, but she loved this outfit and would probably literally cry if anything happened to it. You couldn't find clothes like this in Atlanta. All of Zaire Bollo's clothes had come from Paris and London and Milan. And back to Paris and London and Milan they'd gone after Zaire failed to return from fall break—except this one particular outfit, which Virginia had swiped from her closet and intended to wear as often as possible until she grew up into a person who bought clothes like this all the time.

"What is that?" she asked Yasmin, who was bending the wire back into place.

"A high-voltage traveling arc," Yasmin said, not looking up from her weird equipment.

"What does that mean?"

Yasmin sighed impatiently and gave a long answer involving the words "cathode voltage drop" and "heated ionized air." Virginia wished she hadn't asked.

On the other side of her, Lindsay Bean had a project called "Pudding Inventions," which seemed to involve making pudding out of the grossest flavors imaginable, like seaweed and diet popcorn and lobster. Sophat Tiang and Skylar Jones, the biggest stoners in school, had wandered over to sample them. Virginia tried to look busy putting the falling leaves back on her pathetic poster. Skylar acted like she wasn't even there.

Hello? Virginia thought, getting annoyed. Skylar always ignored her as if they hadn't totally had a thing last year. Not a huge thing, but enough of a thing that she deserved some respect from him. She'd only liked him because he seemed different from everyone else at Winship. He wore *sandals*, and a hemp necklace, and had once said, "I'd rather have a bottle in front of me than a frontal lobotomy," which Virginia had found unbelievably clever until someone told her it was a famous quote.

"Is it going to explode?" Skylar was asking Lindsay. He was grinning and pointing at a cylinder full of white frothy substance.

Lindsay giggled. "Maybe!"

"It looks like jizz. I think it wants to be released." Skylar and Sophat laughed. Skylar reached across the table and rubbed the cylinder up and down obscenely.

"Skylar, stop. Skylar! Don't!" Lindsay squealed. Virginia considered giving Skylar a shove to make him quit, but then decided it was better to remain aloof from his gross immaturity. Lindsay could fend for herself. But then, as she was turning back to her leaf poster, she heard a squishing noise and felt a hot thick liquid all over her neck.

"Ew!" She touched her shoulder and her fingers came away sticky with a white, fishy-smelling goo. Skylar and Sophat were slapping each other's backs and laughing hysterically.

"Skylar, you moron!" Virginia hissed at him.

"Was it good for you, too?" he said, grinning hugely.

Virginia turned to Lindsay and pointed to the nasty white smear covering half her sweater. "What the hell is this?"

"It's lobster paste."

Skylar laughed even harder. "What can I say?"

Virginia grabbed a paper towel from Lindsay's table and started dabbing at the ugly splotch. She felt angry tears sting her eyes. *Does lobster paste stain?* She felt like kicking Skylar in the balls, but what if she didn't kick hard enough and accidentally gave him a boner or something? It was just impossible, trying to get the upper hand with boys.

Skylar and Sophat had moved on to poking Yasmin's

gigantic metal wires. Yasmin was ignoring them and messing with a transformer box. Nerds like Yasmin were used to this kind of thing, Virginia figured. They just conducted their lives as best they could amid constant disruptions from people who couldn't build anything of their own, so they tore everyone else down. She couldn't decide which side of the dynamic was more pathetic. Virginia grabbed more paper towels and started toward the bathroom, dabbing at herself.

"Wait!" Skylar shouted at her, suddenly not laughing anymore. "Are you going to the bathroom?"

Virginia paused. Why did Skylar care if she went to the bathroom or not? Was he going to invite himself along? She glanced at Yasmin, who was giving her a blank, weirdly hostile look, as if to her, she and Skylar and Sophat were all the same. *I'm not with them,* Virginia wanted to tell her.

"You don't wanna go in there," Skylar was saying, his face serious. Sophat and Yasmin looked from him to her, like something was about to happen.

Virginia narrowed her eyes. "Why, did you do something gross?"

"No," Skylar said. "Just trust me, dude. Don't go in there."

Virginia tossed her hair and kept walking. You couldn't take anything that loser said seriously. But then, the second she crossed into the hall, she sensed a shift in the air. It was quieter, and brighter. The hum of four hundred voices was instantly muted. Without daylight streaming through the windows, the fluorescent lights gave the white walls an eerie glow. A group of girls was huddled by the water fountain, talking in urgent whispers. They looked like paint swatches, each with a different vibrantly colored cardigan set. Virginia walked past them and was almost at the bathroom door when she heard her name.

"Virginia," one of them was whispering. "Virginia, don't go in there."

Booth 33, 7:30 p.m.

Benny stood surrounded by brains. His project was called "Mind Over Matter," and it was a case study of brain-damaged patients who had "miraculously" overcome incredibly grim prognoses.

Mrs. Flax was not happy. Benny had been vague about the topic of his project, knowing she would disapprove. Some of his own father's brain scans were mixed among the ones he'd copied from neurological textbooks, and he knew his mother would recognize them. The unique purple splotch representing the damaged area of his cerebrum was distinct. To Benny it resembled a ghost leaning forward against a brutal wind. Mrs. Flax had never expressed precisely what she found objectionable about Benny's interest in his father's recovery. But he'd gotten used to a certain expression on her face: a vague, tired sneer, the face of someone exhausted from dealing with a child who insists on being stupid.

Benny read his concluding thoughts from an index card: "In summation, 'medical miracles' do not exist. This concept is left over from our superstitious past. Advancements in medical science will prove that every 'miracle' has a logical explanation."

No one clapped. His audience included his mother—who had not looked him in the eye once—and the three judges scribbling on their reports. A steady stream of students had walked past, but none seemed to have found fifty pictures of brains sufficiently intriguing to stop and listen. One of the judges, Mr. Rashid, shook Benny's hand.

"Thank you, Benny. Would you make sure everyone in AP Science has the judging schedule?"

He dropped a stack of papers on the table with a thump, and Benny frowned at them. He wasn't even the teacher's assistant, but people just assumed—in a way that felt vaguely anti-Semitic yet annoyingly accurate—that Benny could be always tasked with the business side of things while everyone else goofed off.

"Sure."

"Thanks, Scooby." Benny felt his stomach lurch. Had his mom heard that? He was too afraid to look at her and see. *Scooby.* When were people going to stop calling him that? It was against his philosophy to solve mysteries for personal glory, and it was against his nature to brag. The result was that no one at Winship knew that Mystery Club, mere weeks before, had rooted out a murderer among them: Zaire Bollo.

For a brief, ecstatic moment, the experience had confirmed everything Benny believed about mystery solving—that it expanded the mind, that it made the world a better place, not merely through justice but through knowledge. But then Zaire had fled, and the moment had passed, and the world didn't seem particularly better; it seemed the same. Same world, same Scooby.

"This must have used a hell of a lot of printer ink," Mr. Rashid was saying, gesturing toward the many pictures of brains.

Benny felt annoyed. He'd spent over a month working on this project, and all Mr. Rashid could say was that he must have used a lot of printer ink?

"Sure did," he managed.

"Well, you make sure you get those schedules around. Everyone's project needs to get fair time. That's crucial. It's the American way. Everyone gets their fifteen minutes."

"Okay, Mr. Rashid."

It was absurd, Benny being placed in charge of making sure a bunch of spoiled rich kids got their fifteen minutes. All of life was their fifteen minutes! Winship was the most moneyed school in Atlanta, with only a handful of students there on scholarship. Benny was one of them, a fact he was never allowed to forget.

Mr. Rashid and the other judges left, and Benny's mom announced that she was going to read a magazine in the library. Benny watched her go. He wished the judges had been more complimentary. He'd been counting on impressing her tonight. He sat down in his chair, feeling gloomy and defeated. The decoder ring on his finger was slightly irritating. The metal was thick and substantial, not some cheap thing you'd find in a cereal box. Decoder rings weren't actually very useful—they relied on a Caesar code, which was pretty much the most crackable code ever created. It would have been more practical if Virginia had just gotten herself a cell phone. In their last case, her weird lack of one had been a constant impediment. But Benny believed in personal freedom and didn't want to embarrass her by bringing it up. He didn't know exactly what Virginia's deal was. He knew she was from Florida, or at least went there on vacation a lot. She'd mentioned a stepfather in Cuba once, but it seemed like something she'd made up to sound exotic. Benny didn't feel comfortable prying into her home life, which was probably dysfunctional. All the boarding students had dysfunctional home lives; it's why they didn't live at home.

Benny wandered through the maze of booths, passing out the judging schedules and trying to pick out the obvious winners. He'd assumed he'd be in contention, but based on Mr. Rashid's lackluster response, he wasn't sure now. Some of the projects were ludicrous. There was one project on tanning salons, and another on which was better, chicken wings or pizza. Trevor Cheek had all his grotesque murdered deer heads displayed, which maybe could have worked if the presentation were about taxidermy, but it was just Trevor telling self-mythologizing hunting stories.

Benny located Calvin Harker's booth. Calvin was usually serious competition; he always won almost every academic prize in their grade. But when Benny got to his booth, there was no one there. It was just a table with a bunch of facts printed out on plain paper.

- Every five seconds a child dies of hunger. One just died while you were reading this sentence.
- Tsunamis kill thousands in a single wave.
- Every other day, a coconut falls on someone's head and they die.
- 41 percent of the people in this gym will die of cancer.

Benny leafed through the pieces of paper. Calvin's project seemed to be a collection of random and depressing ways people could die. It certainly didn't look like an award-winning presentation.

- A woman in Ireland beat breast cancer four times before dying from a cow falling through her roof.
- A man who had just received a miracle kidney transplant was discharged from the

hospital and was immediately hit by a truck
and killed.

What the hell is this? Benny knew Calvin fairly well; the two of them were always being thrown together. There seemed to be a persistent expectation that they should be best friends, since they were both loners who got good grades. But the friendship never managed to bloom. Admittedly, Benny was a little jealous of Calvin's undisputed status as the smartest guy in school. But beyond that, there was just something weird about Calvin that Benny could never quite connect with.

At the bottom of the pile, the last paper read:

So what is the point of living, you ask.

Benny flipped back through the papers, wondering if he'd read them out of order. But there didn't seem to be an answer.

The whole thing gave him a chilling feeling, like Calvin was about to run out with a machine gun and shoot up the gym. Benny tried to shrug the thought away. That sort of thing didn't happen at private schools. And besides, Calvin was on track to be valedictorian—not exactly the profile of a mass shooter. But Benny still found himself backing away from Calvin's booth as if a coconut were about to drop from the sky and smash his head. It wasn't even the weirdest project in the expo, but it was definitely the creepiest.

So what is the point of living, you ask.

The lobby, 7:50 p.m.

"Don't go in there."

Virginia whirled around. She squinted at the trio of girls huddled down the hall. In the fluorescent light, the paint-bucket colors of their sweaters looked drained. They stared at her. It was Constance Bouchelle and her friends Yu Yan and Beth. The three of them were always together, attached at the hip in a way that Virginia found annoying and child-ish. This wasn't third grade anymore; it was time to start acting independent. And they did that thing Virginia truly hated, where they bogusly assigned themselves unique per-sonas (Constance was "the smart one," Yu Yan was "the cool one," Beth "the crazy one") when in reality they were interchangeable in every way.

"Why not?" Virginia said. "What's going on?"

"There's a *guy* in there," Yu Yan whispered, scandalized.

Virginia rolled her eyes. Winship was so behind the times. She'd heard of schools that had unisex bathrooms where no one even batted an eye. "So what?" she said, try-ing to sound like she went into bathrooms with guys in them all the time.

"He's giving away drugs!" Constance hissed.

Virginia felt her heart beat a little faster. "Really?" she said, trying to sound nonchalant. Virginia knew Constance—she loved drama and would dangle this over her all night if she knew how badly Virginia wanted to hear more.

"Ew, what is that?" Constance asked, pointing to the white smear on Virginia's sweater.

"It's lobster paste."

"Well, it's all over you."

"Thanks for noticing."

Virginia looked past Constance to Yu Yan and Beth, who were snickering behind their hands. "Hey. Do y'all know who it is? The guy in there? Is it one of Skylar's friends?"

"No one knows," Beth breathed dramatically. Constance shot her a look.

"No one *knows*?" Virginia repeated. How had a dude just walked into the girls' room without anyone noticing?

"He locked himself in a stall, and he won't tell anyone his name. But supposedly if you know the secret password, he'll give you drugs."

"What's the password?" Virginia demanded. "Come on, tell me."

"Jesus, *we* don't know!" Constance said, stepping in front of Beth. "Do we look like the kind of girls who know secret passwords for free drugs?"

Virginia smirked. "You wish you did." She turned and started walking toward the bathroom.

"What are you doing?" Yu Yan whispered.

"I'm going in there."

Wherever you go, something might happen, she told herself. *Don't just be a detective: be a witness.* They were Benny's words. His number one rule for solving mysteries was to Be There. For Benny, it was about wanting to be his own witness and not rely on anyone else. For Virginia, it was something different. She had her own reasons, though she wasn't exactly sure what those reasons were anymore. She'd thought it was about wanting to be mysterious, wanting to know secret things. But ever since the insanity with Zaire Bollo, she and Benny had more secrets than anyone—yet she felt the same. Maybe she just needed more.

She pushed the door open with her foot. Someone had left the water running. That was the only sound. Virginia stepped inside, and the door whooshed closed behind her. She went over to the sink and turned off the faucet. Then it was silent.

She could see his feet under the stall: a pair of plain black loafers and gray wool slacks, the kind with a neat crease running down the front of each leg. *A drug dealer who irons his pants?* The thought made Virginia very conscious of her own legs and feet—the small tear in her stockings and her shitty pleather flats from Target. If she could see his feet, he could probably see hers.

Virginia suddenly couldn't remember what her plan was. She had a plan, right? Surely she hadn't just charged into a spooky, ill-lit bathroom containing an anonymous drug dealer with absolutely zero plan. She'd had a vague notion that she would simply stalk up to the occupied stall, stick her head under the door, and demand that the interloper identify and explain himself. Suddenly that idea seemed foolish. And possibly dangerous.

"Hello?" she said. She'd meant to sound confident, but her voice was barely above a whisper.

There was a pause, and then she heard a voice come from inside the stall: "Do you know the password?" It was a low voice. Purposely low, Virginia thought, like a subtle disguise. *He's worried about being recognized,* she realized. That meant he wasn't a stranger. He could be someone she actually knew. This possibility didn't comfort her. It made a chill run down both her arms.

"Do you know the password?" the voice repeated in the same low, even tone.

Virginia held her breath. What could it be? *Benny could probably guess it,* she thought, annoyed at herself for barging in here without getting him first.

"No," she finally said. Maybe it was a trick, she figured, and "no" actually was the password. But part of her hoped it wasn't. It was one thing to be daring, it was another to be accepting unknown substances in the girls' room at night. She'd be expelled in a second if she got caught.

"Wrong," the voice growled.

Virginia stood motionless for a moment, hovering between disappointment and relief. Then she ran out the door as fast as she could.

Booth 40, 7:54 p.m.

"On her *sweater*. Apparently she's, like, a secret cum queen."

"Omigod. Secret's out now!"

Both girls giggled hysterically behind their hands.

Benny froze, pretending to listen to a ninth grader's presentation about the ripening process of bananas. It was the second group of girls he'd heard talking about Virginia. The story seemed to be that she'd hooked up with Skylar Jones and he'd . . . *released himself* all over her, and that she was walking around with it on her sweater for the world to see. He doubted it was true. Was it possibly true? If he thought about it, he didn't really know Virginia that well. He was aware that she and Skylar had been a thing for like five seconds in ninth grade, but as far as he understood, she basically hated him now. But moments like these always highlighted just how clueless he truly was. Maybe they were back together; maybe they were *sexually active*. The thought dumbfounded him, forming a wall of white noise between him and the world in front of his face.

Stop being immature, he told himself. It probably wasn't true, and even if it was, whatever. Virginia could take care of herself. Except actually that was up for debate. She repeatedly showed poor judgment, doing dumb things like getting into cars with murder suspects. But she'd managed to survive this far. It was her life.

"Bullets don't kill; velocity kills."

Benny halted, as if the word "kill" had been screamed

31

rather than spoken mildly by junior classman Craig Beaver. Benny looked over. A small group of students and teachers was gathered around his booth. Benny knew Craig a little. He was a scrawny and energetic guy who was usually the first in any situation to make an infantile fart joke. But he was smarter than people realized, despite having an immature sense of humor, which he'd probably developed as a defense mechanism from having such a dumb name.

"Watch," Craig was saying. "What happens if I throw this bullet at you?" He held up a small bullet with a gleaming brass shell and threw it at the head of one of his friends, who hammily pretended to have been shot.

"I'm dead! I'm dead! Tell Brittany Montague I love her!"

"Shut up, Jake," Craig said, laughing. "As you can see, Jake will live another day to be rejected by Brittany Montague. But what if I'd shot this bullet at him from a 92 FS Fusion Beretta? Traveling at four hundred and sixty miles per second, this lil bullet would have ripped through his skull and exploded his brain and we'd all be shitting ourselves." He looked at the parents. "Pardon me. Pooping ourselves."

Benny wondered if it was actually legal to throw bullets at people in a school building. The rules were different for private schools. That was the whole point. Winn Davis kept a gun in his car and everyone knew it. Sometimes he even brought it to class. Winn Davis got away with everything; he was the unofficial school mascot, trotted out as a Best-All-Around type because he was handsome yet approachable, played football yet never date-raped, and managed to get B grades while most of the other jocks were flunking. Benny knew more about Winn than most people did; he probably knew more about Winn than Winn knew about himself. The guy was a dim bulb with hidden rage; what was dangerous was that he hid it from himself.

Just then, as if summoned by Benny's thoughts, there he was—Winn Davis. Benny caught only a glimpse of him, past the gym entrance, darting between two rows of booths. Benny kept staring at the hall, though it was empty now. There was something weird about Winn coming out of that door, and it took Benny a minute to realize what it was: it was the door to the *girls' bathroom*. Maybe it wouldn't have seemed that weird if Corny Davenport, his girlfriend, had come sneaking out after him, giggling and adjusting her dress. But she hadn't; Winn was alone. Benny started to get up to follow him, but he had already disappeared, lost in the crowd.

At that second, Benny felt a hand grab his arm. He almost jumped.

"Benny. You have to come with me right now."

The lobby, 8:08 p.m.

"He's right in there," Virginia said, pointing to the girls' bathroom door. She waited for Benny's reaction, but he was just staring at her boob. It was kind of shocking (Benny wasn't usually the slobbering-over-boobs type) until she remembered the gross white stain on her sweater.

"Ugh, it's lobster paste. Whatever. So this guy wouldn't tell anyone his name, but if you said the password, supposedly he'd give you free drugs. It was scary, I'm telling you. And his pants were *ironed*. I could see them under the door. Isn't that weird? A pants-ironing drug dealer?"

"Hm . . . ," Benny said, not seeming as excited as Virginia wanted him to be. Benny was so annoying sometimes. It was like he only cared about a mystery if he found it himself.

"Hello? Why are you spacing out?" Virginia demanded. "Maybe I should be Mystery Club president, and you should be, like, Mystery Club gaping bystander."

"Okay, okay, no need to be insulting," Benny said. "I just saw Winn Davis sneaking out of the girls' room. Maybe it was him?"

Virginia shook her head. "No way!"

"Why not?"

"Because Winn Davis is a football trophy come to life. He doesn't have weird secret passwords for drugs. And besides, whoever he is, he's still in there."

"You're sure?"

"I saw him two seconds ago. His feet anyway."

"Well . . ." Benny stood there thinking for a second. "I guess . . . you stay here and stake out the bathroom. He can't stay in there forever. I'm going to find Winn."

"What do I do if the guy comes out?"

"Just . . . observe."

Virginia rolled her eyes. Benny's reaction to everything was to observe it. He'd probably observe a stampede of elephants and get trampled to death rather than move.

Benny left, and Virginia was alone in the lobby. Constance and her friends were gone, probably to go write in their diaries about the scary man in the bathroom. She frowned at the white splotch on her sweater, which was ruined now. Some of the gunk had even hardened in her hair, making a small blond icicle. Part of her genuinely wanted to cry. Who knew when she'd ever have a sweater this nice again. It was her own fault, she knew, for wearing grown-up clothes around a bunch of high school infants. But it still didn't seem fair.

Get over it, she told herself. There was a mysterious drug dealer in the bathroom, and it wasn't Winn Davis, no matter what Benny said. Winn Davis was a boring lug-head with no imagination. And whoever this guy was, she knew one thing about him: he was interesting.

Booth 40, 8:15 p.m.

Lobster paste. Lobster paste. The words repeated themselves in his mind. What the hell was lobster paste? There was no way it could actually be Skylar's . . . *fluid,* unless he had a medical condition. There was just too much of it. It was even in her hair!

He took out his phone and googled "lobster paste." *A paté formed from puréed lobster meat used in cooking.* Then he googled "lobster paste, sex." But as soon as the results loaded, he jabbed the search window closed. *Get a grip,* he commanded himself, shoving the phone into his pocket.

He scanned the gym for Winn's distinct halo of golden hair. In the back of his mind, Benny wasn't entirely buying the situation. A drug dealer in the girls' room? At *Winship*? Winship was a booze school—even Benny knew that. There were outliers like Skylar and Sophat, but for the most part, drugs were not a part of the upper-crust social scene. And Virginia didn't have the strongest relationship with reality—was this whole scenario one of her flights of fancy?

Benny walked up and down the rows, trying not to draw attention to himself, as if anyone ever paid attention to him anyway. He passed DeAndre Bell's booth (a papier-mâché volcano—was this fourth grade?) and heard the loud, jovial voice of Trevor Cheek's dad.

"Hail to the chief!" he boomed.

"Hail to the chief!" DeAndre boomed back. Someone instantly materialized with a camera, and Mr. Cheek slapped his arm around DeAndre's shoulders to pose for a photo. Benny had witnessed this little bit of theater between them before. DeAndre was the student body president, and Mr. Cheek was the president of the Board of Trustees. Mr. Cheek had a particular fondness for DeAndre, Benny had noticed. Something about it made Benny uncomfortable.

Part of it was the twinge of envy he felt that DeAndre had managed to fit in so well at Winship. But it wasn't just that. Mr. Cheek was a gigantic man, and his thick, hairy hand gripped DeAndre's slim shoulder proprietarily, sinisterly, as if to say, *This black boy is MINE*. DeAndre had run against (and defeated) Mr. Cheek's own son in the school election last spring, making their chumminess even weirder. But if DeAndre was uncomfortable, he didn't show it. His grin was as wide and beaming as Mr. Cheek's, and they laughed loudly together for the camera.

Focus, Benny told himself, looking around for Winn's golden head. The hum of a gym full of people was starting to feel mind-numbing. He turned the corner and walked down the next row, weaving through the slow-moving clumps of students and parents. He saw the judges ooh-ing and ahhing over the little ninth grader's presentation of the ripening process of bananas. That dumb banana project was probably going to win, wasn't it? Normally Benny wasn't competitive—knowledge was its own reward—but for once he'd hoped to get a little recognition, if only for his mother to see.

"Trevor, you're squashing it. Trevor! Give it back."

Benny turned and saw Trevor Cheek with a banana in his hand. He was squeezing it, causing the fruit to ooze out like pus. His face looked twitchy and odd. Something about it made Benny want to steer clear of him.

A flash of blond hair and blue letter jacket appeared

37

and then disappeared amid the crowd. It was Winn. Benny left the banana booth and followed him, but got stalled by a group of people gathered around a project involving taste-testing Coke versus Pepsi. Benny squeezed past them, walking as fast as he could without bumping into people. The blond figure turned the corner. But just as Benny was about to catch up, the lights overhead flickered. There was a brilliant purple streak of light, like neon lightning. It flickered out suddenly, leaving the gym in total blackness. A roar filled Benny's ears.

It was the sound of a hundred people screaming.

The lobby, 8:15 p.m.

Virginia stared at the bathroom door, trying not to even blink. Whoever was in there had to come out at some point, and she was going to catch him. She tried to remember every detail of his feet. Brown shoes. Or were they black? Boys' shoes all looked the same. The ironed pants should have been a giveaway, but it seemed like about one in four boys in the gym had ironed pants. All the teachers did—maybe it was a teacher! The thought made her heart race. Maybe it was someone's *dad*! Or maybe it was a girl, dressed up in boys' pants and shoes. That would explain the cartoonishly low voice, and the fact that no one had seen a guy entering the girls' room.

Oh my god. She wished she'd thought of this back in the bathroom. Benny never asked Virginia what she thought;

it was like he viewed her mind as just an empty receptacle for his own thoughts instead of a living brain that actually produced thoughts of its own. Virginia was used to it, but it was still annoying.

Virginia shifted from one foot to the other. It was starting to get boring, standing there like a statue staring at a bathroom door. She leaned against the wall, wishing the guy would come out already. Then she saw a flash of light in the corner of her eye—a weird purple bolt coming from inside the gym. Instinctively, Virginia turned her head. In an instant, the entire building went black.

Virginia turned around. She couldn't see anything. Someone elbowed her in the back. There were shouts in the darkness. Then Virginia heard a grunt, and a loud crash, and then a scream like she'd never heard before. It sounded like someone having their guts ripped out. A single wild, gurgling howl of pain. The sound was so horrifying it made Virginia want to tear off her own ears.

Then the lights flickered on. Virginia looked around. The purple light appeared again for a single second—a neon ladder in the air that quickly evaporated. Near her, a crowd of people were jumping back, as if to avoid a snaking live wire. They were screaming.

"What's happening?" she shouted. She crouched down and elbowed through the crowd, shoving herself in the middle of the gym. She heard Benny's voice in her mind: *Be There.*

What she saw made her stagger backward.

The breath left her chest.

"DEANDRE!" a girl next to her was howling. "IT'S DEANDRE!"

Between two tables, amid a circle of horrified, frozen bystanders, DeAndre Bell was sputtering on the floor as blood spurted from his chest. He was pinned down by an enormous pair of antlers. A deer—a gigantic, monstrous stag—was bent over him in a deadly pose.

Virginia gasped a breath. *Deer attack people?* For some reason, in the moment, that was the most shocking part. *Deer aren't supposed to attack people.* Then DeAndre's chest convulsed grotesquely, and a fountain of blood spewed out. Virginia jumped, screaming. Everyone around her was screaming too. Parents yanked their children away, covering their eyes. DeAndre moaned loudly.

"Call 911!" Virginia yelled. She couldn't believe she was the first to say it. "Jesus Christ, he's dying!"

There was a guttural retching sound next to Virginia. Someone's mom had pulled out a cell phone, but then started throwing up directly on it before managing to dial a single digit. Virginia reached out and grabbed the phone from the tiny woman, trying not to gag. Touching it as little as possible, she wiped the phone on the woman's back, leaving a brown, repulsive smear on the perfect cream-colored silk blazer. Then she swiped the phone open and dialed 911.

The operator, a woman, had a calm and even voice,

which made Virginia feel calm. She explained that a boy at Winship Academy had been attacked by a deer and was bleeding to death in the gym. The operator asked if the deer was still on the loose. That's when Virginia noticed the stag's feet, which were sticking up stiffly in the air and were attached to a wooden board with wheels.

"No, it's dead," she said. "It's long dead."

The conversation lasted less than a minute. When it was over, Virginia dropped the cell phone and found herself staring at DeAndre, who lay motionless and covered in blood. People were screaming all around her, but the sound of their hysterical voices faded into a dull hum. She felt woozy. Mere feet away, before her eyes, the life was slipping from a human being's grip. Only DeAndre's eyes—still blinking—showed that he was hanging on. His line of vision met the dead, sightless eyes of the stag. The two seemed to stare at each other as if in a battle of wills: will to kill versus will to live. Virginia wished everyone would shut up. *Let him die in peace,* she thought.

Then everything went black again.

The lobby, 8:24 p.m.

There was pandemonium all around. Benny couldn't figure out what was going on. One second he'd been about to catch up with Winn Davis, and the next it was pitch-black, and then people were yelling and everyone was being herded from the gym out the side and back doors.

"What's happening?" he asked the first person he saw. It was Yasmin Astarabadi. Her arms were full of papers and science equipment as if she were fleeing a burning laboratory.

"I dunno. Some kind of animal attack?" Then she hurried away.

A group of sobbing girls passed by, and Benny stepped in front of them. "What's happening?" he asked again. But they just kept crying and ignored him.

He turned around, searching for someone reasonable-looking to ask. He saw Mr. Rashid trying to gather a group of ninth graders together. "Please be calm, everybody. Remain in one place until your parents can locate you."

"What's going on?" Benny asked him, shouting over the din.

"Please be calm," he repeated, not really looking at Benny.

"I am calm."

Across the lobby a girl howled in tears, "WHAT'S GOING ON?" and Mr. Rashid rushed to attend to her. Benny felt a jab of annoyance. He'd asked the exact same question, except in a normal tone of voice instead of freaking out, and Mr. Rashid had completely ignored him. Meanwhile, this hysterical girl was getting fussed over by three teachers, including Mr. Rashid, plus the school nurse. How were they supposed to grow into rational, levelheaded adults if hysterical behavior got validated at every turn?

"Everyone out of the way! Everyone outside!" a man's voice shouted.

What is happening? Benny thought. He ducked behind a column, trying not to get funneled outside with everyone else. He wanted to stay as close to the scene as possible.

"Out! Everyone out! Everyone on the courtyard, now!"

Benny watched as the sea of confused students, teachers, and parents poured out of the lobby into the darkness outside. There was the sound of a siren, but it wasn't getting closer, it was getting farther away. Its tone grew distorted and eerie.

Within minutes, everything was quiet. His heart pounding, Benny darted across the lobby and peered into the gym, which was now empty and too silent. He saw evidence of some kind of crash. Several of the exhibits were knocked down and stuff was strewn everywhere on the floor. In the center of the disarray, a massive dead animal was lying in a pool of blood. It was a deer. Its antlers had been sawed off. The sight chilled Benny to the core. It wasn't just the visceral shock of seeing so much blood; it was the animal's eyes, which were frozen in an expression of utter anguish. Not the anguish of the dead, but of the maimed. Its once-great antlers mutilated into pitiful stubs.

Benny felt his lip trembling, and he stamped his foot. It was a habit from childhood, stamping his foot in frustration whenever he felt like he was about to cry.

Then he noticed that the deer was attached to a board with wheels. *It's taxidermied,* he realized. It wasn't the deer's blood. So whose was it? A person's? Benny felt slightly sick, imagining that much blood seeping from someone's body.

A pair of long, red smears led away from the puddle. Someone had obviously been dragged away from the scene. A small shoe had been left behind, like a grisly Cinderella story. It was ugly fake leather, dotted with sparkling plastic jewels meant to distract from the cheapness of the material. It was covered in blood.

I know that shoe.

It was Virginia's.

The football field, 8:30 p.m.

"I love you. I love you."

Why had the words been so hard to say before now? He loved her. She was so nice, and so pretty, and she loved him and he loved her. He wanted to say it five thousand times.

"I love you too!" Corny squealed. The sound of her laugh made Winn feel like he was going insane. He kissed her lips and wished the kiss could last five thousand years.

"Let me feel your skin. Oh my god." He reached under her pink sweater. Her skin was so soft it was unbelievable. It was like being five years old and touching a kitten. It was like going back in time, before his hands had grown into the rough hands of a man. He lay down on the grass and pulled Corny down next to him.

"What's gotten into you?" Corny giggled. It was dark, and Winn wished he had a flashlight so he could see her smile. He *ached* to see her smile. To see her face, her eyes, her lips, her breasts.

"Come here, sugarplum." *Sugarplum*. It was a gay word, but it felt good coming out of his mouth. He made a mental note to call her sugarplum for the rest of their lives. He kissed her, pressing himself against her with a pure desire he hadn't felt since they first started dating in eighth grade, back when Corny could just look at him and he'd have a boner for three days.

"I love you," he breathed into her hair.

"Oh my god. I so totally love you too, Winn."

She loves me. She loves me. Nothing else would ever matter again. Why had he been so scared before? Corny had told him she loved him about a million times before, but Winn had never said it back. Corny had never pressured him or made him feel bad about it, but he'd known that the day would come he'd have to say it back, and he'd dreaded that day with a dread that made his stomach hurt. But now that day was here, and it was amazing; there was nothing to dread or fear. A wall had come down between himself and his own heart. *This is exactly what I needed,* he thought ecstatically, inhaling the peachy scent of Corny's hair.

Winn had been feeling stressed for weeks. He didn't know why. It was like being smothered by a dark, random cloud. He was tired all the time; food tasted like shit; he sucked balls at football practice; Corny irritated him when she was around, but when she wasn't, he felt so lonely he couldn't stand it. He could barely even jerk off anymore without wishing he could disappear into oblivion afterward.

Then tonight Trevor Cheek had told him there was a random guy in the girls' bathroom, and he had some drugs or whatever, and he was just giving them away for free if you had the secret password. And the password was either "blue pill" or "red pill," which seemed sort of gay.

"It's from *The Matrix*!" Trevor had said. But it still seemed gay. And besides, Winn wasn't interested in drugs, and he hadn't thought Trevor was either. Drugs were for white trash and smelly hippies like Skylar Jones. Couldn't they just get a beer? But Trevor kept saying they had to do it, and suddenly Winn didn't care if drugs were trashy. The science expo was suffocating—everyone's projects made him feel like an underachieving moron. He needed to get out of there. So whatever, he did it.

Trevor had called "red." So Winn took "blue." He didn't know if there was supposed to be a difference. He'd felt like the hugest idiot standing in the girls' room saying "blue pill" to a mystery dude who wouldn't show his face. But it was worth it. For the first time in weeks—in *years*—he felt like a real person. He felt actually alive, being alone with Corny right now on the empty football field. She was so beautiful. He needed to fuck her immediately.

"Wait, get a condom!" Corny squealed.

"No. I want to have a baby." He surprised himself saying it, but as soon as he did, he knew that he meant it. He wanted to have a baby. He wanted a little baby girl who looked exactly like Corny, and they would call her Little Corny, and they'd live in a cabin in the mountains, and Winn would take care of his little Cornys and protect them till the end of time.

"Winn! You're so silly."

"I'm serious! Please let me cum in you and have a baby," Winn begged.

"Um . . . okay!" Corny giggled, and Winn kissed her ferociously. She belonged to him forever. He wanted to mix his DNA with hers, and create a new tiny life that would glue them together forever.

"I love you," he repeated. "I love you."

Her body felt like heaven. Love *was* heaven.

The middle school basketball court, 8:45 p.m.

Virginia found herself lying on a rickety gurney with a thick pillow under her head. Some lady handed her an Advil, and Virginia washed it down with a swig of Gatorade. She rubbed her temples, feeling drained and disoriented. A boy was crying softly on the bleachers. A family was sitting together, the mom giving the daughter a back rub and the son playing a game on his phone. Everyone else was either sitting quietly or lying down on yoga mats. Apparently the middle school basketball court had been designated the recuperative area for overwhelmed people. At least it was quiet and the lights were low. She didn't know how she'd gotten there. Someone must have wheeled her in while she was unconscious.

Five people had fainted, including Virginia. Five people! The number irritated her. If she was going to faint, she wanted to be the only one. She didn't want to be one of *five people*. It made her feel average and lame. And what was Benny going to think? She'd been at the very center of the action and passed out like a dainty maiden in need of smelling salts.

She sat up, but then the image of blood spewing out of DeAndre's chest hit her like a baseball bat to the head, and she lay back down on the gurney.

Get a grip, she ordered herself. She didn't want to be a wimp. But she couldn't bring herself to sit up again.

"Can I ask you something?"

Virginia turned her head. Someone was sitting in shadow on the bleachers. She couldn't tell who it was. Then he stood up, his body elongating as if in slow motion, getting taller and taller until he finally reached his full, looming height.

"Oh, hey, Calvin," she said. "Sure."

He paused, apparently wording the question in his mind. "Did you see it happen?"

Virginia groaned. "Ugh, yeah. It was horrible. . . . Did you faint too?"

Calvin shook his head. "Nah. I just needed a place to calm down. It's a zoo out there."

Virginia closed her eyes. She was glad she was in here, then. She lifted her head and took another sip of Gatorade.

"Is DeAndre dead?" she whispered, not wanting anyone to overhear and start weeping or something.

Calvin shrugged. "No one knows yet. I think they took him in an ambulance. . . . I like your outfit."

"Hm? Oh, thank you." She pinched her sweater. "It's cashmere. Too bad it's ruined." She scowled at the huge white stain.

"The stain is my favorite part. It's like . . . you were too beautiful, so they had to throw garbage at you. To bring you down to their level."

Whoa. Virginia gawked at him. *Where the hell did that come from?* Calvin Harker was someone she could barely remember having ever talked to. They knew each other, but only because everyone in a small school knew each other. She struggled for something to say. She couldn't say "thank you," because she'd just said that five seconds ago. And besides, "thank you" wasn't exactly a sufficient response to the most amazing compliment she'd ever heard in her life. Before she could think of anything, Calvin said, "Can I sit with you?"

"Um, yeah. Sure." Virginia scooched over a bit, unsure of how to situate herself. Calvin half sat, half stood at the very edge of the gurney, making a small gesture with his hands to suggest she should stay lying down. Virginia tried to relax. But this was weird. Did Calvin Harker *like* her? How incredibly random was that? She looked at him, trying to figure out how she felt about it. She couldn't decide if he was good-looking or not. He was certainly . . . *interesting*-looking. His features were all slightly distorted, the result of some congenital disease; Virginia couldn't remember what it was called. Something related to aliens, because in middle school everyone called him Martian Boy. But then he'd gotten a heart transplant and spent a year in the hospital, and people stopped making fun of him after that.

"Can I show you a poem?"

Virginia blinked. "Sure. . . ." She liked that Calvin asked her permission before doing anything. It made her feel important. He handed her a folded piece of paper. Virginia took it, almost afraid to open it.

If the poem is good, I'll like him. If it's bad, I won't.

She opened it.

The fountain, 8:55 p.m.

"Mom, I'm fine. I'm *fine*." Yasmin squirmed out of her mother's death grip of a hug. All around her, mothers were hugging their kids and people were crying and looking for one another and asking what was going on. The splashing water from the fountain, usually so peaceful, seemed overly loud and contributed to the stress of the environment. Yasmin wanted to go home, but a policewoman in a tight ponytail was interviewing everyone and asking what they'd seen. Yasmin barely knew what she'd seen. She knew what she *hadn't* seen, which was the freaking judges. She'd been robbed of her fifteen minutes by a deer that had apparently killed DeAndre Bell.

Supposedly, it was moments like these that made people realize what really mattered in life. What was a science expo prize worth when DeAndre Bell was now dead?

Everything. To Yasmin, it was still worth everything. People died every single day. It was literally the only thing you could count on in life, which is exactly why you couldn't waste a single moment being distracted from your goals. Yasmin had to stay focused. Except her brain was reeling—she'd never personally known someone who'd died before, especially not someone young. Even last month when the whole school had thought Brittany was dead for five seconds, it hadn't hit Yasmin personally. Brittany Montague was so unreal—so perfect, so blond, so far out of Yasmin's social orbit. But Yasmin had almost all her classes with DeAndre. They were doing a Civics project together! Yasmin felt ill. She thought about her Civics project, and then thought about DeAndre being dead. Then her Civics project, then DeAndre being dead.

Am I losing my mind? Maybe I'm not processing this, she thought. *DeAndre is dead. DeAndre is dead. DeAndre is dead.*

She waited for the reality to hit her. But it was too scary to let her feelings in. It was like her brain had short-circuited and wouldn't give her emotions any space. She just wanted to go home and take a shower and watch *True*

Blood in her room. Yasmin hardly ever allowed herself to watch TV—it was a waste of time—but this whole day was fucked, and she didn't have the energy to salvage it. She just wanted to throw it in the garbage and move on.

Yasmin's mom was saying something about the dog-faced policewoman wanting to talk to her. She always spoke Persian when she was upset, even though she knew Yasmin only understood about half of it.

"No one talks to her without Bruce," her dad said. "He'll be here in fifteen minutes."

Bruce Sherazi was the family lawyer, whom Yasmin's father dragged into everything. Mr. Astarabadi understood America. He understood that rewards weren't given to the good-hearted; they were given to the mercilessly litigious.

"There was a purple light," the policewoman was saying. She had a tight ponytail and a face that indeed resembled a Schnauzer. "That was your project, Yasmin?"

Yasmin scowled at her. *A purple light?* People were such morons.

"We think your project caused the power outage," the officer said. "You need to answer some questions."

"Is this a homicide investigation?" Mr. Astarabadi asked, his Persian accent almost imperceptible.

"I'm unable to give information at this time."

"Daddy, I want to go home," Yasmin whined. She pouted at her dad, knowing he couldn't resist her puppy-dog eyes.

Mr. Astarabadi looked at her, deciding. Then he produced an immaculate, cream-colored business card from his Yves Saint Laurent wallet and handed it to the policewoman.

"You will not contact my daughter," he said, hardly making eye contact. It was his signature power move, making people feel like they barely registered with him. "Everything goes through me."

Five minutes later the Astarabadi family was cruising down Peachtree Street toward their Italian-inspired manse in Brookhaven. Riding in the Lexus always felt smooth and deluxe. Yasmin rolled down the window and stuck her head out like a little kid. The autumn air was crisp and cool, and made her feel better. She realized she hadn't been fully breathing for the last twenty minutes, as if avoiding inhaling the fact of DeAndre's death. She didn't want to think about it. So she focused on herself, because everything else was too overwhelming. DeAndre was gone, but she was still here.

She was alive.

The courtyard, 9:00 p.m.

Benny asked every adult he could find if they had seen Virginia Leeds. Most of them didn't know who she was, which made Benny want to throttle them. *Virginia Leeds!* he wanted to yell. *She's been at this school for five years.* But he knew from experience that if you weren't in their country-club crowd, it was like you didn't exist. Weaving through the hubbub, he heard DeAndre's name about a hundred times, but not once did he hear Virginia's. Finally he found a teacher who said there were some people with the EMTs on the middle school basketball court.

The hallway to the gym was ill-lit. This wasn't an area were people were supposed to be tonight. The doors to the basketball court opened, and a pair of men came out—one man, actually, and a boy. The leather soles of their shoes echoed on the tile floor. It was Headmaster Harker and his son. It was always strange to see the two side by side. They were both unnaturally tall; they had the same thin, grim faces; the same vivid green eyes and pale skin. They resembled a pair of vampires: the headmaster an old-school Dracula with white-streaked hair receding sharply at the temples; Calvin his young and hungry scion. The headmaster led him sternly down the hall, a long, white hand gripping his shoulder.

As they passed each other, Calvin shot Benny a long, pained look:

Help.

Benny stopped. But the headmaster and Calvin kept walking, and Calvin didn't look back at him. They turned the dark corner and were gone.

Benny entered the gym. It was dark around the edges, the basketball court lit up in the center. The school nurse was fluttering around, attending to a small collection of students and parents. There, sitting up on a gurney, was Virginia. Benny half walked, half ran over to her.

"Virginia, I've been looking everywhere for you. . . . You're okay?" He looked down at her shoeless foot. Her stocking had blood on it.

"Ugh, I fainted," Virginia said, rolling her eyes. "Did you see what happened?"

"No," Benny said. "I saw the blood . . ."

"It was *awful*. People were, like, throwing their guts up. It was me who called 911." She smiled, obviously expecting to be praised.

"Well, who else was there? What happened? The deer was on wheels; obviously someone pushed it."

"Um . . . I don't know. It was really chaotic. The lights were out, and then they came back on. Someone's mom was next to me . . . and that girl with ten thousand freckles . . ."

"Think hard. Close your eyes and see the scene in your mind."

Virginia closed her eyes. Then she shuddered. "God, all I can see is blood everywhere."

Benny tried not to get frustrated. Of course Virginia had no choice but to jump in and call 911. It was the right thing to do. But he wished she could have stepped back and observed the scene. Who knew the number of details she'd missed.

"Have you seen Trevor Cheek anywhere?" Virginia asked. "It must have been his deer. He had that idiotic project."

"No," Benny said. "I've just been looking for you. I saw your shoe in the blood. . . . I was worried." A feeling of dejection washed over him. Virginia's testimony was useless, and he'd spent the last critical half hour looking all over for her instead of gathering information. Everyone was probably leaving by now. The gym doors had been locked and draped with DO NOT ENTER tape. The scene was dead.

"What should we do?" Virginia hopped off the gurney and then touched her head, seeming dizzy.

"You should go home," Benny said. "I mean, to your room. Do you want a ride to the Boarders?"

"No, I'll walk," she said, to Benny's relief. His mother tended to be less than subtle about her distaste for the yellow-haired, leg-showing *shiksa* in Benny's life, and he wasn't eager to be stuck in a car with them for any length of time.

"We'll talk tomorrow. . . . At morning assembly? Assuming school isn't canceled."

"Okay! See ya." Virginia waved tiredly. Benny noticed a piece of paper folded in her hand. He almost asked her what it was, but then decided not to. He didn't want to seem nosy. Which was ironic because Virginia was the nosiest person on the planet and would not likely have paid him the same courtesy.

They parted ways at the gym doors. Benny watched her walk away, her shoeless left foot splattered with blood. That was so Virginia, to just leave on a pair of blood-splattered stockings; a normal person would have ripped them off immediately. She really creeped him out sometimes.

Benny stood there until she was gone, postponing the

moment when he'd have to go to the library and find his mom and explain that there'd been an accident, and that the prizes wouldn't be handed out tonight after all. Mrs. Flax was impervious to the chaos of life, and expected everyone else to be as well. It was unacceptable to be impaled by a taxidermied deer in the middle of a science expo. She'd look at Benny like it was somehow his fault.

He leaned against the wall, trying to organize his mind. A deer. A student body president. A drug dealer in the bathroom, something Benny had almost forgotten about in the pandemonium. Two football players (Trevor Cheek and Winn Davis—three if you counted DeAndre). This was going to be tricky. He'd been on the wrong side of the gym when it happened. He'd have to depend on other people for the facts, which he hated doing. Other people were flaky and unreliable and stupid. But it was his own fault—he'd failed to fulfill the number one tenet of his own club: above all else, Be There.

Benny's house, 10:30 p.m.

He couldn't stop seeing the deer's face. Its agony was imprinted on his mind: mouth open in a mute scream, eyes searing with futile rage. Benny was a logical person; he didn't believe in New Age mumbo jumbo. But he couldn't help feeling that some spiritual crime had been committed when they sawed off that deer's antlers, leaving the stiff carcass on the floor like a piece of garbage. It seemed you could be anything in this world—a person, a deer—and life would find a way to mar your dignity.

Stop thinking about it. He shook the image of the deer from his mind. He took out his many printouts of brains and spread them on the dining room table, feeling calmed by the array. One good thing had come out of the disastrous evening: the judges hadn't gotten around to announcing the winners, so at least Benny was spared the embarrassment of being passed over in front of his mother.

"THANK YOU FOR BEIN' A FRIEEEND!"

Benny's grandma was watching *The Golden Girls* in the next room, with Mr. Flax next to her in a large leather easy chair. You'd think he was watching too, but if you looked closely, you'd see that his eyes were fixed at a point slightly below the TV.

"Can you put on the news for him?" Benny asked his grandma.

"It's good for his mind to hear happy people chatting! Who wants to hear a bunch of sad news. Not us!" She patted her son-in-law's knee. Benny gritted his teeth. In no universe was it good for anyone's mind to watch *The Golden Girls*. He looked back to his array of brains, wishing his dad could have seen his project tonight. *He* would have appreciated it. *He* would have thought it was brilliant. And they would have gone to the kosher diner in Midtown together and ordered steaks and discussed Benny's bright and promising future.

Stop, he told himself. This had been happening more

and more lately—Benny romanticizing his dad and indulging in unrealistic fantasies about how magical his life would be if the plane crash had never happened, if the test flight for the AeroStream V4 *Spinetail*—his father's baby—had successfully landed. But truthfully, before the accident, Mr. Flax had been a remote and somber workaholic who was rarely around. In all likelihood he wouldn't have gone to the science expo at all, and if he had, it would have been for fifteen minutes and he would have been distracted the whole time. The evening would probably have ended the exact same way: Benny alone and vaguely depressed, the sounds of gabbling old ladies blaring from the TV to mock him. Life's dismal plan trudged on, unaffected by whatever accidents happened along the way.

Except Tank would still be here.

Benny was good at mental compartmentalization—stowing some thoughts deep in the recesses of his consciousness, where they had few opportunities to surface. Probably a psychologist would say it was unhealthy, but Benny didn't know how else he was supposed to survive in his own mind. If he had to think about Tank every day, he'd never get out of bed in the morning.

Benny went to his room and shut the door. Then he pulled out last year's yearbook and flipped to the index in the back: *Bell, DeAndre.* The list of pages featuring DeAndre took up five entire lines. He started going through them one by one: his class portrait, various club pictures, student government, candids from the spring formal. In each photo DeAndre had the same exact pose: a wide "Mentos: the Freshmaker" smile, his arm draped chummily around whoever happened to be standing next to him. Benny couldn't quite picture DeAndre's face without his signature grin; he certainly couldn't picture it contorted in horrible pain.

He flipped to the *C*'s: *Cheek, Trevor.* Trevor had famously run for student body president last spring as a joke. His platform had been "School sucks, but I don't!" Trevor was a buffoon who loved making a mockery of anything anyone took seriously. Benny remembered him giving up on his speech halfway through and spending the rest of his allotted ten minutes leading the assembly hall in a thumping chant of "TRE-VOR, TRE-VOR, TRE-VOR!" People liked that stuff but not in their school president. In the end, DeAndre had won the election. This was particularly impressive considering that DeAndre was only a sophomore while Trevor was a junior; it was rare for underclassmen to achieve the coveted title of student body president. Trevor had made a dumb spectacle of claiming the election was rigged and threatening to "succeed from the Union," which everyone laughed about even though it really wasn't funny considering the historical context. But even DeAndre had laughed, and soon the joke lost steam and died.

Now Benny wondered: Was it possible Trevor actually *cared* about student government? Enough to *kill* his opponent?

Trevor was from an old Southern plantation family; he bragged about it all the time. Maybe he was secretly infuriated that a black student—possibly descended from slaves—had taken a leadership role Trevor felt entitled to. Maybe his "joke" platform had disguised serious ambition. Benny considered it, then shook his head. It was an interesting idea but one that failed to light. If Trevor had really wanted the position, he could have had it. He could have taken his speech seriously, and maybe even asked his dad (the president of the Board) to pull some strings for him. Besides, there wasn't much that Trevor would gain from DeAndre vacating his seat. Trevor wasn't the next in line; the vice president was, and that was Yasmin Astarabadi. If Trevor had pushed the deer, his motive hadn't been ambition but *revenge*. Which seemed a little dramatic.

Benny closed the yearbook. He knew he should get some sleep. He'd been reading a lot lately on how lack of sleep affected mental cognition. A series of tests on sleep-deprived people showed that without sufficient sleep, the body would siphon energy from the brain to power corporeal functions, which shut down creative thought like a zombie. To Benny, this was a reminder that the human capability for brilliance was a gift, not a given; the body would take any opportunity to become a mindless animal again.

He changed into his pajamas and turned out the light. As soon as he closed his eyes, the image of the deer assaulted his mind. *Stop!* he ordered himself. If he wanted to solve mysteries, it would involve seeing disturbing things from time to time. It was part of the job. He couldn't wince and shudder his way though a case like a weenie.

Dewdrop, let me cleanse in your brief sweet waters . . . These dark hands of life. It was a four-hundred-year-old Matsuo Bashō haiku that Benny found relaxing. Half of Bashō's poems were about dew: pearls of dew, chrysanthemum's dew, dew that cleansed, dew that symbolized the swiftly evaporating beauty of life. It seemed like such an ancient thing, dew. Yet it was a simple function of nature that not even the stamping foot of suburbia could obstruct. Benny made a mental note to take a moment in the morning to reach down and touch the dew of the grass in the front lawn. Had he ever intentionally, *meaningfully*, touched a dewdrop? Suddenly it was clear that this was what his life was missing: a daily touch of dew. . . .

And then he was asleep, his resolution to touch some dew relegated to the realm of midnight flights of fancy that by the morning are forgotten.

The Boarders, 1:02 a.m.

FREEDOM!
(is an illusion)
Carpe diem?
NO!

The day has seized you and me
Its grip will never tire
All are prisoners of time
Even beauty
Even the stars

Virginia lay in her bed reading the words for the five hundredth time. She wasn't sure exactly what they meant, but that didn't matter. Obviously it wouldn't be a poem if it were just a bunch of normal sentences saying stuff.

She loved it. If a better poem existed, she couldn't think of it off the top of her head. Granted, she never paid much attention in English class, which was just a boring lady insisting that some boring old book was important. But *this* was actually important.

She jumped out of bed and crept down the dark hall to the common room. After eleven o'clock they were supposed to stay in their rooms. But gradually every boarding student came to the independent realization that they had been abandoned. The house mom, Mrs. Morehouse, appeared less and less frequently, making up for long stretches of absence with spit-spraying, Miss Trunchbull–esque tirades whenever she randomly appeared. But other than that, the Boarders was always quiet, especially at night. Every semester fewer overnight students returned, leaving the house increasingly deserted. At this point less than half the rooms were filled. The room across from Virginia's had been Zaire Bollo's; now it was just another set of beige walls containing a bare mattress and empty drawers. The room would remain vacant forever. The Boarders was famously haunted, and it was known that territory ceded to the ghost would never be restored to the living.

She turned on a lamp, half expecting to find Gottfried the German exchange student sprawled out on the sofa. Gottfried was an insomniac and hung out in the common room at all hours eating junk food and staring at the ceiling fan. He wasn't there now, though Virginia wished he was. It was spooky being alone in the common room. Huge, curtainless windows exposed her to the outside world, the black silhouettes of trees and the ill-lit street ideal for lurkers. She considered turning off the lamp to make herself less visible, but the idea of sitting alone in the dark was even creepier.

The ancient desktop computer hummed awake. She pulled up the browser and typed in "best poetry." A list of the "10 Best Poems" popped up, and she scanned them. They seemed to be mostly about farms and walking in the woods and describing daffodils. *Boring!* Virginia thought, excited by the confirmation that Calvin's poem was better.

She logged into her Winship e-mail account. Her plan was to send Calvin a short but intriguing e-mail and see how he responded. She still wasn't 100 percent sure she liked him, but she didn't want him to get taken by some other girl either. Her in-box was a slew of junk that she deleted without reading: inspirational Christian forwards by the Montague twins (and more from Chrissie White, who copied whatever the twins did); gobbledygook from her mother's personal accountant in Boca Raton (why was Virginia always cc'd on this crap?); repeated memos from Mrs. Jewel, the new upper-school principal who had made it her mission to stop the girls from wearing their skirts so short ("Expose your *minds*, ladies, not your panties!!!"), and reminders to vote for Homecoming King and Queen.

Then she noticed an e-mail from an address she didn't recognize. She opened it.

> To: v.leeds@winship.edu
> From: mjtheman678@gmail.com
> Subject: Your the boss
>
> I can't use this with my network. The whole point is their supposed to be virgins. But if u want to work with me we can expand. ($$$) Obviously i am shit at this, need a camera man (or GIRL, haha). Let me know cutie

The message wasn't signed, and at first Virginia was confused. She didn't know anyone who called her "cutie." Then her heart slammed in her chest. It was Min-Jun, the guy from Mr. Choi's sordid jazz band/cheerleader porn ring. He was one of the creepiest people Virginia had ever met. Why was he contacting her? Was he a complete moron? The police had picked him up at the bonfire a few weeks ago after he'd gotten into a bloody fistfight with Winn Davis. They'd let him go, and as far as she and Benny understood, the guy's low-rent production company, *Locker Room Wildcats*, was over, and remained a secret. They'd both figured Min-Jun's brush with the law was enough to scare him off the Winship campus forever. Evidently they'd been wrong.

At the bottom of the e-mail there was a file attached. She hit download and watched the little wheel spin. Finally the file opened, and Virginia winced and held her hand up preemptively, in case it was a penis or something gross. Then she lowered her hand. The image was grainy, of a dark field lit by a single, faraway stadium light. Two people were rolling around on the short-clipped grass. Not rolling, really—*undulating*. It was people having sex! And Virginia knew immediately who they were.

She looked over her shoulder to make sure she was still alone. Then she turned back at the screen. Corny Davenport's huge, overflowing boob was pressed under Winn's chest. Half their clothes were strewn around them, and their bodies were tangled and intertwined. Virginia had walked in on Chrissie White having sex once, and it had been completely gross and disturbing. She'd only witnessed about two seconds of it, but the image was burned into her brain: a guy in plaid boxers pounding Chrissie like a pumpjack while she lay there motionless with her mouth gaping open. It had been pretty much the least romantic scene in history. But what Corny and Winn were doing was nothing like that.

They moved together rhythmically, Winn touching Corny's head like it was a precious artifact. He was on top of her, but seemed considerate of her smaller body, careful not to crush it with his manly weight. Corny's soft, naked legs pointed gracefully toward the black sky. The image of them was so intimate that it felt wrong to be watching. But Virginia couldn't look away. They were gorgeous.

Then a new message appeared in her in-box. It was from mjtheman. Virginia stiffened. The timing was freaky, like he knew she was online. Maybe he *did* know! Obviously he'd been skulking around campus taking videos of people. For all she knew, he was outside watching her right now. She glanced out the window, but all she could see was her own scared-looking reflection.

Be cool, she commanded herself. If he was watching, she didn't want him to see her acting scared. She sat up straighter, taking a deep breath.

To: v.leeds@winship.edu
From: mjtheman678@gmail.com
Subject: Your the boss

if u don't want a piece of the business, i need that $400 back. No joke

Now her heart was truly pounding. The four hundred dollars was gone. She'd spent it on the palladium silver decoder rings, which now seemed like a completely stupid and childish thing to have done. *Why won't this loser leave me alone?* True, she'd basically stolen four hundred dollars from him, but after everything that went down at the bonfire (getting pummeled by Winn and then picked up by the police), she hadn't expected him to be crazy enough to try to get it back. Maybe she could return the rings? She dismissed the idea immediately. The idea of explaining it to Benny, and Benny looking at her like she was an utter fool—no way. She could just call the police and give them Min-Jun's name, but that felt like the reaction of a little kid. It definitely wasn't what Benny would do.

She glanced down at her wrist. *W.W.B.D.?* Benny hated the police; Virginia didn't know exactly why—something involving a dog a long time ago? All she knew was that if two paths diverged in life, and one path was to ask for help and the other was to take care of the thing himself, Benny would choose the second one. It was one of the few things she and Benny actually agreed on: you can't count on anyone besides yourself.

She looked out the window again, half expecting to see Min-Jun waving hello to her. But there was only the reflection of herself looking like her own ghost, white-faced and semitransparent against the backdrop of dark trees outside.

Another message appeared. Virginia was tempted to just delete it. But she opened it and scanned it quickly. It contained two lines:

btw your legs looked amazing tonight

Hott

Virginia yanked the power cable out of the wall. The light from the lamp and the computer screen went black. Virginia froze in the darkness for a minute, barely breathing.

Tonight.

It was him. Min-Jun was the drug dealer in the bathroom. Virginia felt a shiver, realizing he'd been looking at her legs under the stall door. What did he think he was doing? Had he switched from porn to drugs? Or were the drugs a ruse, and he was just in there to spy on girls while they peed?

Wait, she thought. Min-Jun with ironed pants? She couldn't picture it. Unless he'd done it on purpose to divert suspicion. But she couldn't picture him doing that, either. He struck her as fairly . . . lazy.

Christ, calm down. She refused to be scared by that creepy loser. She got that *Locker Room Wildcats* was extra gross and illegal because high schoolers were underage. But somehow she still found the whole thing more insulting than scary. Virginia didn't think of herself as underage. She didn't think of herself as a child. She was fifteen years old and had been taking care of herself since the eighth grade. Winn and Corny weren't *children.* They were sexual beings who obviously enjoyed having sex with each other. They weren't playing house; they were . . . *fucking.* The thought was unbearably exciting but also filled Virginia with quea-siness. It was a private thing that she shouldn't have seen.

Virginia was annoyed now that she'd killed the com-puter before writing her e-mail to Calvin. It would take five minutes for the old geezer to boot up again, and she couldn't deal with sitting exposed in front of that window anymore. She got up and snuck back to her room, locking the deadbolt from Home Depot that Benny had especially installed on her door.

She got in bed with her purple cat-shaped pillow named Puffy that she'd had since she was ten, feeling increasingly stupid for letting Min-Jun's e-mails freak her out. She'd handle the money situation; it wasn't a big deal. And she wasn't some baby who ran and hid from an e-mail. Now that she was safe under the covers, Min-Jun's words took on a different flavor—a flattering one. Min-Jun was a creep, but still—out of all the girls at Winship, he'd noticed *her*.

Hott.

Three announcements were made in succession, each seeming unrelated to the others. The first: DeAndre Bell was alive. He'd been in surgery for twelve hours and was now in stable condition. A crippled condition, but a stable one. The second: Craig Beaver was being suspended for two weeks due to a disciplinary infraction. No details were given. The third: the governor of Georgia would be inviting the top two students from each grade to a special leadership luncheon at the Governor's Mansion—invitees TBA.

The second two announcements were barely heard, because the whole assembly hall burst into relieved applause at the news that DeAndre was alive. It wasn't like a few weeks ago, Benny noted, when Brittany Montague turned out to be alive. At that announcement, the joy had been so boisterous and out of control, it was like all the angels in heaven cheering the victory of God. This was more like a collective sigh: *Thank god we don't have to deal with this.* Maybe Brittany's close call with death had inoculated the student body against future close calls. Or maybe it was just because DeAndre, though popular and beloved, was fundamentally not one of their own. He was from Lakewood Heights; he took a public bus to school; if he went to Harvard for college, it would be as a scholarship student, not a legacy. And he was black. Winship Academy had been the last private school in Atlanta to desegregate in the '60s. The depressing truth was that DeAndre could win student body president and *still* be regarded as an outsider. He would have been mourned but ultimately forgotten, whereas for Brittany they would have built immortal statues.

"Many of you will be called to answer some questions in the library conference room today. The police are here, and I have assured them that our students will be cooperating one hundred percent."

People were murmuring and not really paying attention. Mrs. Jewel had not managed to command much respect at Winship in the two weeks since her arrival. Maybe it was her diminutive height, or her Barbie-ish surname, or her obsession with the girls' skirt length ("two inches above the knee!"), or the fact that she constantly corrected people for calling her "Mrs. Jewel" instead of "Principal Jewel," which only made everyone double down on calling her the former. She just didn't seem to understand how things worked at Winship.

The bell rang, and the assembly hall began emptying out, everyone talking loudly and squeezing into the aisles like herded animals. Benny always stayed seated after assembly so he could leave in a more civilized manner once the crowd thinned out.

"So, apparently, when the lights went out, Trevor slipped on a banana peel. Can you believe that? A *banana peel*. Is life an insane cartoon or what?"

Benny turned to look at Virginia. She was slumped in her seat with her legs sticking completely out, forcing everyone to step over them on their way out.

"Wait, what are you talking about?" Benny asked.

"Trevor was next to his dumb deer in the gym, and when the lights went out, he slipped on a banana peel and fell on the deer, and it launched into DeAndre's chest." Virginia shuddered. "It'd be hilarious if it weren't so horrible."

"Wait, where did you hear that?"

"I dunno. It's just what everyone's saying."

How come I didn't hear it, then? But he already knew the answer to that question. He always managed to be in the same place at the same time with the same people as Virginia, yet he may as well have been on Mars, socially-speaking.

"Surely that's a joke," he said. "A banana peel? Did you see it?"

"No. I was kind of distracted by the fountain of blood and everyone freaking out."

"All right, all right. . . . Well, Trevor *was* holding a banana. That much is true. I saw it myself. There was a ninth grader doing a project on the banana-ripening process. Did you see her?"

"Yancey Kemper?"

"Yeah. Does she have any connection to DeAndre?"

"Probably. I mean, we're all connected."

Benny knew she wasn't speaking in a hippie-dippy collective soul kind of way, just that it was a small school, and most everyone had been cooped up together since they were five. You could probably take any two students at random and come up with a plausible reason why they'd want to kill each other.

"Did you see that purple light?" Benny asked.

"Yeah, it was Yasmin's crazy project. It caused the power outage. Did you ever find Winn?"

"Hm?"

"Remember? The drug dealer in the bathroom?"

Benny nodded. "Oh yeah. Let's give that case second priority for the moment. I want to concentrate on DeAndre."

"Trevor's saying it was an accident," Virginia said. "But I guess if that were true, the police wouldn't be here."

"I don't believe in accidents anyway."

The assembly hall was mostly quiet now, the outpouring of four hundred people reduced to a trickle of dawdlers.

"Your *Highness*," a guy said to Virginia, bowing affectedly as he passed down the aisle. Then another guy did the same thing, and the two of them went off snickering together.

Benny looked at her. "What was that about?"

Virginia shrugged. "No idea. Guys have been doing that to me all morning. People are freaks."

People are freaks. It was statements like these that made Benny realize that Virginia didn't really understand what Mystery Club was about. Life wasn't "an insane cartoon." People weren't simply "freaks." Everything had an explanation. And the entire point of the club was figuring out what it was.

"Okay, well . . . who was around the booth when the lights went out? Besides Trevor."

"Um, it was so chaotic. . . . I think Constance and Beth were there. A bunch of parents. Oh my god, did I tell you about the lady who barfed everywhere?"

"Mm-hm. . . . Why is Craig Beaver being suspended? Have you heard anything about that?"

Virginia shook her head. "Not really. Apparently he brought a bunch of bullets to the science expo and was throwing them at people. Did you see it?"

"Yeah, I saw it," Benny said. "But Winn Davis keeps an entire gun in his car all the time, and he never gets suspended. Something else must be going on. . . . Craig isn't on the football team, is he? Or student government?"

Virginia shook her head again. "I think he just does golf. But so does Trevor. All those preppy guys do. DeAndre doesn't."

Benny realized he was biting his lip. There were too many threads here, and he didn't know where to begin. It wasn't like his other mysteries, where the path had been very clear. He pulled out a notebook.

INCIDENT:
1) Deer in the Blackout
2) Drug Dealer in the Bathroom

SUSPECTS:
Yasmin Astarabadi
Winn Davis
Trevor Cheek   ?
Craig Beaver

"Let's take this one by one," he said. "Process of elimination. Starting with Yasmin."

"Why Yasmin?"

"With any odd occurrence, begin at the most basic point. If the power hadn't gone out, none of this could have happened. Think about how forcefully Trevor must have pushed that deer to be able to pierce DeAndre's organs. You'd have to be a professional stuntman to finagle an assault like that while making it look like an accident in view of a hundred people. But in the darkness, you could just stab away. And when the lights came on, pretend you slipped on a banana."

Virginia looked skeptical. "You're saying Yasmin Astarabadi and Trevor Cheek were, like, coordinating? She and Trevor barely live in the same universe."

"Exactly. That's why they would be the perfect co-conspirators. But it's far too early to get attached to a particular narrative. Keep your mind open."

"Okay. . . . Why is Craig a suspect? Just because he's being suspended for some mystery reason?"

"Yes, that," Benny allowed. "But also his presentation at the science expo. Did you hear it? It was about how, like, bullets are just small bits of metal alloy. There's nothing inherently *deadly* about them. It's the act of propelling them, forcing them, *exploding* them at 1,700 miles per hour—that's what kills. And the same could be said of a taxidermied deer. It's just skin and stuffing, an inanimate object. A grotesque trophy. But *shoved* into someone's chest with enough force? Suddenly it's a deadly weapon. Any object is a weapon if you use it like a weapon."

"Huh . . ." Virginia was picking at the scab on her leg again. Benny wondered how much she'd absorbed of what he'd just said.

"Anyway. I want a list of witnesses. People in the blackout who were near Trevor when he supposedly slipped on this alleged banana."

Virginia said nothing for a moment, then sat up. "Wait, myself? Make the list myself?"

"Yes. What, are you not equal to the task?"

"No, I am, I totally am," Virginia said quickly. "I was just—you usually do everything yourself. But I can do it!"

Virginia's excited grin made Benny feel deceitful. The

truth was, Benny had no idea how to find out who was around Trevor when the lights went out. The idea of going up to people like a clueless fool and grilling them for details made him want to crawl into a hole. But Virginia didn't care. She'd go up to anyone and say exactly what she wanted. It was one of her more annoying qualities, but in this case it would actually be useful.

"Min-Jun e-mailed me last night."

"*What?*"

"He sent me a sex tape of Corny and Winn. Can you believe it? After everything that happened, he's still skulking around trying to make *Locker Room Wildcats* happen. Dude needs to learn when to fold."

Benny looked around. No one was listening and the assembly hall had almost entirely emptied out. But Virginia was still talking way too loud.

"Shhh!" He leaned in. "What did he want?"

"Just . . . same thing. An inside man to replace Choi. Inside *girl*. Obviously I'm not going to do it."

"Did he threaten you?"

"No, no. He's not like that. I think it's just business for him."

Benny squinted, examining her face. "How did he know your e-mail address?"

"Um, I dunno. I guess he just figured out the formula for Winship accounts. Last name, first initial."

"You hadn't contacted him before?"

"No! Of course not."

Benny didn't say anything.

"What, you think I'm lying?"

Benny shrugged. He knew it was a sore spot with her, not being trusted. But it was hard to trust her when sometimes it seemed like she operated with a slightly frayed tether to reality. "I don't think you're *lying*," he said carefully. "I just wonder . . . what the facts are."

"I just *told* you the facts. You are so annoying! It's like a fact isn't a fact unless Benny Flax saw it with his own eyes. God! If I tell you something, it's a *fact*!"

"Okay, sorry!" Benny said.

Virginia folded her arms. "So should I call the police on him or what?"

"The police? Of course not."

"Well, why not? He's still out there. Apparently getting his face bashed in by Winn Davis didn't hamper his ambition to creep on every cheerleader in America. I mean, come on. Let's just turn him in and be done with it."

"You can do what you want," Benny said tersely. "But if you call the police, don't expect me to back you up."

"Oh my god. What is your angst about cops? Were you a donut in a past life or something?"

"A cop shot my dog right in front of me." Benny didn't look at Virginia but sensed her shock.

"Whoa. Jesus . . . I mean, I heard there was something with a dog. Was it attacking someone? Was it justified?"

"No. It was not justified." Benny punctuated the words with steely silence.

"Well, what happened? Tell me the whole story."

"It's not a *story*," Benny said. He wished he hadn't mentioned Tank at all. It was a weird effect Virginia had on him sometimes—he opened up and things slipped out. But he couldn't explain what happened to his dog without explaining his father's accident. And Virginia had that look in her eyes—that *tell me tell me tell me* look that made him snap closed again like a clam.

"I didn't mean it like that," she was saying. "Just tell me what happened. I'm sure I'll be on your side."

Benny stood up abruptly. "It was . . . whatever. It wasn't a big thing."

"Obviously it was, or it wouldn't have formed your entire attitude toward police officers."

"Just drop it, please," Benny said firmly. "And get me the list of witnesses by lunch."

"Okay, fine." Virginia didn't look at him, making a show of getting her backpack together.

Benny turned to leave. Then he turned back. "Thank you. For making the list."

Virginia looked up, meeting his eyes with such open blankness that Benny felt suddenly flustered. *Thank you?* What an awkward thing to say. She wasn't doing him a favor, she was doing her job. He was about to retract it, but then she said, "You're welcome."

They left the assembly hall through separate exits. Benny went through the lobby, where the Fellowship of Christian Athletes had already produced a poster-size "Get Well" card for DeAndre. A group of people were huddled around with brightly colored markers.

"Everyone sign!" Corny Davenport called out in her tinkling, Bambi-ish voice. Benny tried to pass, but she caught him by the arm. "You don't have to be a Christian, and you don't have to be an athlete!" The FCA people were constantly saying that. It always made Benny want to scream at them, *Then get a different name!*

"Let me see that," Benny said, picking up the giant card. About a hundred people had already signed it. He looked for Yasmin Astarabadi's signature. He was familiar with her perfect, tiny handwriting. He didn't see it anywhere.

"Has Trevor signed it yet?"

Corny nodded gravely. "He feels awful. He's the one who bought the poster! Wasn't that nice?"

Wow, a forty-five-cent piece of cardboard. What a guy.

"Show me where he signed."

Corny pointed to a spot in the corner where some scrawled words to "DeBalls" were made out in green marker. What was it with boys having the handwriting of serial killers? Benny read the message, feeling his mouth twitch with anger:

SORRY MY DEER HATES YOU. HE DIDN'T MEAN IT! GET WELL SOON . . .

The library conference room, 9:20 a.m.

The detective had a smooth, deep voice, like those commercials where they make it seem like diet margarine will give you an orgasm. Yasmin felt smug that they'd sent the man detective instead of the dog-faced lady one; it meant they didn't think she'd be easy to intimidate. She sat in the middle of the conference table, flanked by her father on one side, and on the other side Bruce Sherazi, a lawyer so notorious that in Yasmin's family they called him the Shark.

"Are you friends with Trevor Cheek?" the detective asked. His last name was Disco. Yasmin wondered if that was Italian, or if it was just a stereotype that all cops were Italian. She leaned over to Bruce and whispered, "No." Bruce nodded, and only then did Yasmin turn to the detective.

"No."

Detective Disco narrowed his eyes at her. "We have a court order for your phone records. If you have ever had direct contact with Trevor Cheek, we will know about it within the next twelve hours. Better get it out in the open now. I don't like surprises. Do you like surprises, Yasmin?"

"Do not answer that question!" Bruce shouted. Unlike Mr. Astarabadi, his Persian accent was perceptible.

Mr. Astarabadi growled, "You say you have the phone records? Then do your job. Find out for yourself. You Americans. You want everything handed to you."

The detective folded his arms. "I grew up in the American

foster care system, sir. Some days, lunch was a spoonful of ketchup. Nothing has ever been handed to me."

Yasmin smiled to herself. Her dad was winning. Detective Disco's hard-scrapple orphan ketchup story was pathetic and wouldn't make Mr. Astarabadi respect him. All he'd done was brand himself the ketchup-eating cop in Mr. Astarabadi's eyes forever.

"Tell me about your project, Yasmin," the detective said, changing course. "It's called"—he looked at his notes—"a Jacob's Ladder?"

Yasmin looked at Bruce, who gave a terse nod. Yasmin recited her lines: "It's a high-voltage climbing arc. It's an electric spark that jumps between two parallel wires. I tested it in our home one hundred times and it never once caused any power problems. In a gym with the electrical support to power four-hundred-watt metal halide fixtures, the idea that my simple project caused a minute-long blackout is preposterous."

For a moment the detective just stared at her. "Would you like to repeat that in your own words?"

Yasmin scowled. Her own words? Just because she was a teen girl, he expected her to talk like an idiot?

"Like, omigod," she squealed mockingly. "The gym is like, bananas huge. My project used, like, a lip gloss amount of power. If you think this was me, you're like totally buggin'."

Unexpectedly the detective smiled—a long, slow smile

that changed the entire look of his face. Then it disappeared. "You're a good student, Yasmin," he said. "I understand you have your sights set on Harvard?"

Yasmin looked at Bruce, who nodded.

Yasmin also nodded.

"How many students does Harvard typically accept from Winship each year?"

"Typically?" Yasmin shrugged. "A few."

"Hm. A few. You sure about that? When I looked into it, it seemed more like . . . *one*. One student from each graduating class. And I understand they've already expressed interest in DeAndre Bell. Have they expressed interest in . . . you?"

The word was loaded with contempt. *You*. Small, ugly, unpopular, Middle Eastern *you*. Yasmin wanted to throw his cup of coffee in his face.

"This is outrageous! We're finished here!" Bruce yelled loudly. He slammed his fist on the table, providing the violent counterpart to Mr. Astarabadi's silent, brooding glare. Bruce stood up so aggressively that his chair fell over. Then he did his signature move, which was to snap his fingers and then point them like pistols at whoever was offending him, in this case the detective.

"*Pow,*" he said. "Watch your step, detective. I'll shoot so many holes in your case, your pants will fall down."

The detective smiled again, almost a laugh. "Guess I better buy some nicer underwear, then."

Fuck you and your sad, cheap underwear! Yasmin screamed

at him in her mind. But on the surface she stayed glassy and cool, a trick she'd learned from her dad. She followed Bruce out of the conference room, and Yasmin could feel the detective watching her as they left. His eyes drew hers like a pair of magnets, and she looked at him, not meaning to. For a second it felt like he could see every secret thing about her. He could see her soul, and he found it . . . unbeautiful.

Yasmin looked away, wishing she could disappear. There was no protection from what other people decided to think about you. Not even her dad and the Shark could protect her from that.

The gym, 9:45 a.m.

The yellow DO NOT ENTER tape drooped, flagging in its cautionary duty. Benny gave the doors a slight push. They were unlocked. He looked over his shoulder to make sure no one was there, then slipped inside.

His whole body felt tense. He was already wincing, dreading seeing the mangled deer again. But when he arrived at the scene, the deer was gone. The blood had been cleaned up, and the floor shined brightly from bleach. DeAndre's volcano had fallen off the table and lay upside-down on the floor. The gym was quiet and empty. It felt like a science expo from a ghost town; Benny half expected to see a tumbleweed blowing past the rows of abandoned booths.

He looked around quickly, having only ten minutes until fruit break was over. Benny had a free period later, but by then the scene could be even further corrupted. He examined the area from every angle. He looked for a banana peel or any sign of one, but was unsurprised not to find one. If there had been a banana, it would have been cleaned up with the blood, or taken by the police as evidence of Trevor's supposed fall. Benny felt a surge of irritation at the thought of the police having a leg up on him.

He moved on to the next row of booths, looking for the spot where the purple light had come from. He found Yasmin's presentation, which she'd called, straightforwardly: HIGH-VOLTAGE TRAVELING ARC. It was a tall pair of attached copper wires sticking in the air. Benny found the switch on the transformer that powered the apparatus. He looked around again, making absolutely sure that he was alone. Then he turned it on.

A flash of purple light traveled quickly from the bottom of the wires to the top, over and over again. Benny had seen this experiment before in science videos online. It was also called a Jacob's Ladder, named after a scene in the Torah where Jacob dreams of God. Benny pulled up the verse on his phone, Genesis 28:10–19:

> *Jacob dreamed, and behold, there was a ladder*
> *set up on the earth, and the top of it reached*
> *to heaven; and behold, the angels of God were*

ascending and descending on it! And behold,
the Lord stood above it and said, "I am the
Lord, the God of Abraham your father and the
God of Isaac; the land on which you lie I will
give to you and to your descendants."

Benny remembered the passage from Hebrew School. It
was an important moment in the Torah, one that could be
cited as the very formation of the Jewish people. In it, Jacob
is chosen over his twin brother, Esau, and shown a ladder
to Heaven by which he and his descendants would climb to
meet God, while the descendants of Esau would be left to
rot. All Jews were supposedly the descendants of Jacob, and
thus chosen by God. Benny stared at the swiftly moving
purple light, feeling slightly mesmerized. When he died,
would he climb a high-voltage traveling arc to Heaven?

Benny turned it off. Heaven was a ludicrous fiction, quite
literally a dream. If a man in modern times claimed God
chose him in a dream, he'd probably be institutionalized.

He switched the apparatus on again, then off again.
Three more times he turned it on and off. The lights overhead didn't so much as flicker.

The bell rang. Benny knew he needed to leave. He
cracked open the gym doors and peered out between the
pieces of DO NOT ENTER tape. Across the lobby a door was
open. Inside was a tiny room filled with circuit breakers
and transformers. Benny had passed that door a thousand

times and had never seen it open. It was an electrical closet. And Benny immediately recognized the man and woman inside: they were detectives.

Benny had seen this pair before. They'd investigated the "suicide" of Mr. Choi a few weeks ago. The woman had a sharp, cold face; of the two of them, you'd assume she was the smart one. But it was the man, the handsome and muscle-bound Detective Disco, who'd suspected that Benny and Virginia were involved in the strange case. Benny knew that if he were caught lurking around the crime scene right now, Detective Disco's internal alert would go haywire.

He watched them from the tiny crack in the gym doors. He couldn't hear their voices, but they were discussing something and shining their flashlights at a particular electrical panel. Rick the janitor stood by, holding the keys. Then the two detectives did something odd: they began circling the entire lobby, seeming to be examining the walls.

They're looking for power outlets, Benny realized. When they didn't find any, they talked for another minute. Then they took some notes, and Rick shut and locked the closet door. Then they all left.

Benny waited a beat before slipping into the lobby. He went to the door and turned the door handle, hoping by some stroke of luck that Rick hadn't locked it properly. It didn't open. Benny stepped back and surveyed the area. That's when he suddenly understood:

The girls' bathroom.

It was directly next to the electrical closet. They shared a wall.

The second bell rang. Benny was now officially late for Chemistry. He stood for a second, deciding whether to go to class or pursue his line of thought. Benny hated being late. It was rude and attracted unwanted attention. But he couldn't leave now.

He pushed the door to the girls' room open with his foot. It didn't sound like anyone was inside. The anxiety of getting caught—the scream of girls, being labeled a pervert forever—made his stomach hurt.

Go, he commanded himself. He opened the door, his heart pounding. The bathroom was empty. He remembered how it had seemed last night—dark and dingy, the lair of a mysterious drug dealer. Now it seemed bright and clean and normal. A place girls went to brush their hair. Benny wasn't sure exactly what he was looking for. He quickly scanned all the walls, searching for power outlets. There weren't any.

The fluorescent light in the ceiling caught his eye. It seemed a little dim. He squinted at it. Under the plastic shield it appeared that one of the long, tubular bulbs was missing.

There.

Benny jumped onto the sink. He wasn't strong, but he was nimble and had excellent balance from his aikido training. He swiftly pushed the large, rectangular piece of plastic from the ceiling. Peering into the exposed fixture, he saw that where the second bulb should be, there was a homemade outlet with a pair of wires sticking out. And plugged into it was a little white square.

Benny reached and grabbed it. He hastily returned the plastic shield to its place and hopped down, then bolted out of the bathroom. He instantly realized he should have looked first. The detectives were standing right outside. He tried to hide behind a trophy case, but they'd already spotted him through the lobby's immense windows.

Idiot! he yelled at himself. Trying to hide had just made him look ten times more suspicious.

"Well, hi!" Detective Disco said, swaggering through the lobby doors. "I was wondering when I'd bump into the Mysterious Club."

"*Mystery* Club," Benny corrected him.

"Of course, of course. Because where there's crime . . ." He let the words dangle, as if they were the first half of an expression that he expected Benny to complete.

Benny clutched the plastic square in his right hand. He tried to relax his fingers so it wouldn't be so obvious that he was holding something. But he was afraid he would drop it.

"I'm just on my way to class," he said.

"Well, you're late, son! Want us to write you a note? We can say you were helping us. It doesn't even have to be a lie. Do you want to help us?" While Detective Disco spoke, his partner looked Benny up and down.

Don't look at my hand. Don't look at my hand.

"I-I don't have any help to be," Benny said ineptly.

For a long, torturous moment, the detectives stared at him.

"Well!" Detective Disco said finally. "Let us know if you want to combine efforts this time, son."

Stop calling me "son"! Benny yelled in his mind. He'd disliked Detective Disco since the moment they'd met during the investigation of Mr. Choi. Detective Disco had the same smarmy demeanor as the officer who'd shot Tank. The same impenetrable wall of smugness. The kind of man who'd never admitted that he'd done anything wrong in his life.

"Here's my card." Detective Disco reached inside his pocket. It was obvious he was right-handed; he removed the card with his right hand, and presented it unconsciously (or possibly consciously) toward Benny's right hand, which was clutching the white square. Awkwardly Benny extended his left hand to take it. The detective clearly perceived the awkwardness of the handoff. He narrowed his eyes, then gave Benny's shoulder a weird squeeze.

"Do you work out, son?"

"Excuse me?"

"You should work out. I used to be a scrawny guy like you. Felt like a stranger in my own body. Now I feel great!"

"Great."

The woman detective's cell phone rang. "We gotta go, Mitch," she said.

Detective Disco gave Benny a final look. "Well, I'm sure we'll meet again."

"Where there's crime . . . ," Benny replied weakly. The detectives both laughed. Their laughter was fake and hollow. Benny didn't like it.

As soon as the detectives were gone, Benny exhaled and looked at his watch. He was now ten minutes late for chemistry. But he couldn't go to class without taking a closer look at the thing he'd found plugged in the bathroom. He moved to an empty hallway in case the detectives came back. Then he opened his hand.

He was pretty sure he already knew what it was. He'd have to google it to be certain, but it looked like an X10 controller. When plugged into an outlet, it could be linked to a smartphone and used to control the electricity on that particular circuit. Which meant Yasmin Astarabadi hadn't caused the power to go out. It was the drug dealer in the bathroom.

Benny took photos of the device from every angle. Then he snuck back into the girls' room and returned it to the hidden outlet in the ceiling. Whoever had put it there would have to come back for it eventually. If Benny could figure out a way to sneak a motion-sensitive camera into the light fixture, all he'd have to do is wait for the drug dealer to show up and expose himself.

Benny grinned at the photos on his phone, feeling creepily like Gollum with the Precious. The proof was his and his alone. The detectives were idiots. They should have looked in the bathroom immediately. But their minds were limited and full of walls.

It was the drug dealer, Benny thought triumphantly. And now all that was left was to find out who he was.

The library, 11:31 a.m.

Virginia felt very Benny-ish and smart, sitting in the empty upstairs part of the library drawing a diagram onto graph paper. She'd spent every minute between classes plus her free period tracking down who had seen Trevor slip on the banana. The information had been pretty easy to get. Everyone was talking about DeAndre and eager to spill their guts to anyone who would listen. From what Virginia had gathered, there'd been a number of people near Trevor and DeAndre's booths at the moment of the blackout, but only three people had actually heard Trevor slip. Two were Constance Bouchelle and Yu Yan. And the third person— Benny was going to *freak*—was Craig Beaver.

"Isn't there some guy who solves mysteries?"

"Like Sherlock Holmes?"

"No . . . Scooby-Doo."

"Winn, you're so silly! Scooby-Doo is a *dog*!"

Virginia twisted around in her chair. In the corner, half obscured by a bookshelf, Winn Davis and Corny Davenport were making out in a fake leather armchair. Corny's shirt was unbuttoned, and Winn's hand was practically on her boob. Virginia felt her face flushing hot. The video flashed in her mind: Winn's ecstatic expression, Corny's legs in the air. *Stop being perverted,* she told herself.

"Benny Flax solves mysteries," she said loudly.

Corny and Winn looked up from their make-out session. Winn seemed embarrassed, and Corny squealed. She fell off Winn's lap, giggling.

"What did you say?" Winn asked.

"Benny Flax solves mysteries," Virginia repeated, leaning back in her chair.

"Shhh!" the witchy upstairs librarian hissed at them.

Corny was quickly buttoning herself up. She yanked Winn's arm and skipped out of the library, giggling and dragging Winn behind her. Winn seemed slightly dazed, looking over his shoulder at Virginia as he clumped down the stairs. Then they both disappeared.

What was that about? Virginia thought. Maybe Winn *was* the drug dealer in the bathroom, and he knew Mystery Club would be on his trail. She thought about the suspect list: Winn Davis and a question mark. She knew she should have told Benny to add Min-Jun, but he'd been so annoying when she'd mentioned his e-mails. It was obvious that Benny didn't think Virginia could handle herself around Min-Jun, which was totally unfair. She'd handled herself fine—*twice*—once in his car and once on the bridge. Benny was just a control freak who didn't want her to do anything besides make dumb diagrams. He wouldn't even tell her what happened to his dog. But it was hard for Virginia to feel too indignant when she knew there were things Benny didn't know about her, either. Things she wasn't eager for him to find out.

She went back to the diagram, drawing an *X* on the graph paper to represent the deer, a *T* for Trevor, a *D* for DeAndre, and three *W*'s indicating the three witnesses. The *W*'s formed almost a perfect triangle around the *X* and *T*.

"What's that?"

Virginia whirled around, instinctively covering the graph paper with her hand. At the height where a normal person's head would be, there was a pair of shoulders. Virginia raised her eyes higher. It was Calvin Harker.

"Oh, hi," she said. "Um, it's for Mystery Club."

"Cool. Can you show me?"

"Uhh . . . sure." Virginia knew Benny hated it when she showed Mystery Club stuff to random people. But it's not like the diagram showed anything other than public information. Calvin sat down in the plastic chair across from her, which made her feel unsure of him. If he liked her, wouldn't he have chosen the seat next to her?

"So, we're trying to figure out if Trevor slipped on purpose or not. The W's are the three people who saw it happen. That's Constance, that's Yu Yan, and that's Craig Beaver."

Virginia watched Calvin squint at the diagram. She'd been thinking about him all night, but now she realized she'd mentally Photoshopped his face a bit—warmed up the pallor of his skin, plumped the hollows of his cheeks. Now faced with his real-life gauntness, she wasn't certain if he was good-looking anymore. One thing she hadn't exaggerated were his eyes, which were a crazy green, the green of emeralds and leprechauns. Virginia had green eyes too, but not like Calvin's; hers were murky and speckled, like a pond covered in gross algae. She decided to focus on Calvin's eyes until she figured out if she liked the rest of him.

"What?" Calvin said suddenly, startling her.

"What . . . what?"

"You're looking at me weird."

Virginia tried to think of something to say. But before she could, Calvin said, "How do you know Craig Beaver was there?"

"Constance and Yu Yan said he was. Apparently he tried to grab Trevor, but then he slipped on the banana too."

"Wow, that is one banana on a mission."

Virginia laughed, and Calvin looked surprised, like he'd been telling that banana joke all day but this was the first time anyone had actually laughed. Virginia's mind raced, trying to think of something smart to say. What would Benny say? Something cynical and skeptical that showed he didn't think the same way as everyone else.

"I don't think Craig was suspended for the bullets," she said breezily, as if the idea had been hers and not Benny's. "There must be something else going on. . . ."

"Oh, I know what's going on."

Virginia cocked her eyebrow at him. He'd said it so casually—surely he was joking. "Oh yeah?"

"I'm serious. I know why Craig was expelled."

"Well . . . tell me!"

"I can't." He shrugged and grinned as he said it.

Virginia didn't like being teased. She didn't think it was cute. "Shut up," she said. "Are you screwing with me or what?"

"I swear to God—I swear to the *universe*—I'm not screwing with you. I seriously cannot tell you. I signed a nondisclosure agreement, and if I tell you, there will be a court order. I will immediately be expelled and then sued in civil court."

Virginia's mouth fell open. "*What?* You can't possibly be serious."

Calvin pressed his abnormally long fingers to his chest. "Virginia Forsythia Leeds, I swear upon my own eternal soul that I am serious."

"Okaaay . . . ," Virginia said, feeling half thrilled and half weirded out that he knew her middle name.

Calvin leaned across the table. The collar of his shirt shifted, showing a small purple bruise on his neck. *Is that a hickey?* Virginia thought, feeling curious and also faintly jealous. Who was giving Calvin Harker hickeys? But on closer look, Virginia didn't think it was. It looked more like . . . a fingerprint.

At that second, Calvin swiftly adjusted his collar to cover

the bruise. The motion was so casual, Virginia couldn't be sure if he'd done it unconsciously, or if he'd noticed her noticing. He lowered his voice to a whisper and said, "Listen. You can figure this out yourself. All you need is Trevor Cheek's cell phone."

"His phone," Virginia repeated.

"Don't. Get. Caught," Calvin said seriously. "If you're caught, they'll know I tipped you off. And then I'll be expelled, along with about ten other guys."

"How would they know it was you who tipped me off, then? If there are ten other guys?"

Calvin leaned back. "Because it's obvious that I like you."

Virginia inhaled sharply. So he did like her—unless he was teasing her. She didn't think he was, though. He was reminding her of Min-Jun right now. This seemed to be the kind of guy she attracted: older, slightly weird-looking ones who didn't bother hiding the fact that they liked her. Calvin was 100 percent better than Min-Jun, though; he was smarter and more interesting, and hopefully he wasn't an icky pervert.

"I better go," Calvin said, standing up. "I have Calculus next. I'm not gonna make it without some sativa."

Virginia nodded vaguely, not wanting Calvin to know she was in remedial math and didn't know what "sativa" was. She assumed it was some kind of study guide.

"Hey, did you like my poem?"

Virginia let him dangle for a second. "It was very . . .

stimulating." She'd pulled the word out of thin air, but was pleased with how it sounded. *Stimulating.*

Calvin's face brightened. "Stimulating! Really!"

"Do you have any other poems?"

"For you? A million."

"Shut up," she said, her mouth twisting as she tried not to smile.

"Good luck with your case. Maybe we'll meet again once you figure it out."

"Maybe," Virginia said coolly. She went back to her graph paper. When she was sure Calvin was walking away, she snuck a look at him over her shoulder. She liked the way he walked, and the way his nose looked in profile. Suddenly she wanted him to come back. Had she been too chilly toward him? Would he find a nicer girl to send poems to?

You did fine, she assured herself. She'd lived with Chrissie White long enough to know that throwing yourself at guys only worked in the short term. It was better to play the field and stay in the power position until you were really sure about somebody.

Stop thinking about boys. Virginia took a deep breath to clear her head. There was fifteen minutes of her free period left, and if she worked quickly, she could have a whole dossier of information to present to Benny at lunch. She felt as hyper as a dog chasing a squirrel. Maybe Benny would be so impressed with her dirt that he'd make her co-president of Mystery Club!

She swept her pens and graph paper into her backpack. A little folded note slipped out and dropped to the floor. Virginia picked it up and slowly opened it.

> THE FAINTING GIRL
> When she went out
> Like a light
> So did the light
> Of her consciousness
> And for a moment
> All the world
> Sucked

The cafeteria, 12:21 p.m.

"I wonder whose blood it was."

"Omigod, remember that episode of *Seinfeld* where he gets a blood transfusion from Newman?"

"Helloooo, Newman!"

"NO SOUP FOR YOU!"

How come everyone loved *Seinfeld* but still hated Jews? It was something Benny wondered about a lot. He presumed it was the same cognitive glitch that caused people to love rap music while hating black people. He sat alone at a table for four eating his standard lunch, which was a turkey sandwich and two cartons of 2 percent milk. He tucked an earbud in each ear so people would think he was listening to music instead of to their conversations. Most people were discussing DeAndre. Someone had gotten in contact with the hospital, and it seemed the situation was worse than Mrs. Jewel had made it out to be in the assembly. Multiple vital organs had been punctured, and he'd required a massive blood transfusion. The main headline was that his football days were almost certainly over. There was much moaning over the fact that he'd miss the wonderful joy of the Homecoming game next Friday. People seemed very unaware that for DeAndre, football might be more than a *game*. That he'd probably been hoping to land an athletic scholarship somewhere, a hope that was now down the drain. Nothing in life was secure. No matter what you had, you could lose it in a second. That was the lesson life seemed intent on teaching over and over. *I get it!* Benny felt like screaming sometimes. *I get it.*

"Are you Scooby-Doo?"

"Hm?" Benny took the earbuds out of his ears.

"Scooby-Doo? That's you?" It was Winn Davis. He looked tired and frazzled. There were deep circles under his eyes, and his hair lacked its usual Ken-doll shape.

"Yes. I mean, I'm Benny."

Winn plunked down in the chair next to him and set down his lunch tray, which was piled with enough food to feed a family of four. Benny glanced around. People were looking at them, obviously wondering why in hell Winn Davis was choosing to eat lunch with Benny Flax.

"I need help," Winn said in a low voice.

"Um, of course. What can I do for you?"

Winn didn't look Benny in the eye. Instead he stared somewhat vacantly at his pile of food. "Last night . . . there was a . . . *guy*. In the *girls'* bathroom . . ."

"Yes, I'm aware of that," Benny said.

This seemed to perk Winn up a little. "Oh, really? Okay, cool. I need to know who it was."

"Well, I'm afraid I don't know at this time. But I can assure you that Mystery Club is working on it."

"Cool . . . Okay . . . Well, I need to know as soon as you know. How much do you charge?"

"Charge? Oh, nothing. No charge," Benny said. "We're a nonprofit club."

"Cool . . ."

Benny narrowed his eyes, appraising him. Was it possible that Winn was the drug dealer, and he was just doing this to throw Benny off? Benny didn't think that was a likely scenario. Winn wasn't that clever, and he seemed genuine.

"Listen, um . . . Hey, do you have a pen?" he was saying. "I think it would be better if I wrote this down."

"Of course," Benny replied, quickly pulling a pen and a small notepad out of his pocket. Winn took them, pushing away his tray of untouched food. He paused, apparently deciding what to say. Then he wrote in sloppy capital letters:

IF YOU DON'T FIND HIM I
THINK I MIGHT DIE.

Whoa, Benny thought. But he tried to look unfazed. It was unprofessional to seem freaked out by your clients.

Abruptly, without saying another word, Winn picked up his tray and walked away. Benny watched him join his football player friends at a faraway table. Benny looked at the note again.

If you don't find him I think I might die.

Suddenly he felt a pair of hands closing around his throat.

"BENNY."

Benny jumped and almost toppled over in his chair. He swatted the hands away. They were Virginia's.

"Geez, don't do that."

"Omigod. Omigod. Omigod." Virginia crashed into the chair next to him. "You won't believe the dirt I got."

"What? What is it?"

She slammed a piece of graph paper onto the table and then proceeded to talk a hundred miles an hour about Calvin Harker and Craig Beaver and a conspiracy and nondisclosure agreements and golf-related Satanic orgies. *Christ,* Benny thought. Give Virginia an hour and who knew what kind of crap she'd dig up.

"Stop, stop," Benny said. "Please speak in a linear manner. You sound like you're on crack."

Virginia raced on, "It has to be the golf team. *Ten* guys? And there's no other group in school that has Trevor, Craig, *and* Calvin in it. I checked." She slammed a yearbook on top of the graph paper. "And they do blood-letting ceremonies on the golf course to appease the gods of victory. Did you know the golf team hasn't lost a tournament in *four years*? I checked that, too."

"Hang on. Calvin Harker told you this? That the golf team are Satanists?"

"No, Calvin wouldn't say anything! That's just my theory."

Benny gritted his teeth. "Virginia. Tell me exactly what happened. Do not embellish a single detail or inject any theories about Satanism."

Virginia took a breath and started over. Benny listened, feeling only slightly less overwhelmed by her second recitation. What was with this case? Everything seemed to be happening around Virginia, with a complete lack of regard for the fact that it was *Benny's* club. And what was with Virginia "checking" stuff without him? Research was his thing!

"So what do we do?" Virginia asked breathlessly. "We get the phone, right?"

Benny tried to think quickly. Virginia was leagues ahead of him on this one. How was he supposed to judge the proper course of action relying entirely on her reporting? He wished he could have seen Calvin's face, observed his posture, heard his exact words. Maybe he was trying to trick them. Benny just had no idea, because he hadn't been there.

"I . . . I don't think so. I think we should stick to the plan. Interview the witnesses near Trevor when he fell."

"Constance and Yu Yan? Come on, they're idiots. They don't know anything."

"Then we should focus on the drug dealer in the bathroom. I have new information. It wasn't Winn Davis. Look what I found." He pulled out his phone and discreetly showed Virginia the pictures of the X10 device he'd found in the bathroom ceiling. "It's what the drug dealer used to control the power. It was *him*. We can cross Yasmin off the suspect list."

"Okay, fine! Then we move on to the next person, which is *Trevor*!" Virginia hissed excitedly. "So we have to get his phone!"

"Okay, well . . . except how would we even do that?"

Virginia grabbed half of his turkey sandwich and helped herself to it. She took a large bite and said, "I haf de puffak pwan."

Benny sighed. "Chew, swallow, then speak."

Virginia swallowed hard. "I have the perfect plan. You're gonna love it because it's simple and classic. It's *textbook*."

Benny narrowed his eyes. Was she calling him boring? Virginia had clasped her hands together and was making a pathetic "pleeeease" face. He had a feeling that if he didn't say yes, she would just go behind his back and do it anyway. Better to maintain some semblance of control over the situation.

"Fine, we'll get the phone."

Virginia clapped her hands like a five-year-old and took another huge bite of his sandwich.

"You'll choke one day if you don't learn to take smaller bites," Benny said.

"Fanks, Dad."

"You're lucky I know the Heimlich maneuver."

Virginia swallowed. "Gee, I'm the luckiest girl in the world!"

Benny frowned. He was not enjoying being the Watson in this situation. He was almost afraid to ask what Virginia's "simple and classic" plan entailed.

"I'll do most of it," Virginia assured him, as if reading his mind. "All you have to do is one tiny, tiny thing."

The second-floor hall, 1:15 p.m.

I can't do this.

It wasn't a tiny thing. It was a huge thing. It was the very entry point of juvenile delinquency. All the atoms of Benny's being begged him not to do this.

Every child in America was acquainted with the terrible temptation of the fire alarm. It was bright red, every kid's favorite color. It had a handle that pretty much screamed "PULL ME!" It promised instant chaos: the power to upend an entire school, the power to create deafening noise and fear and disorder. All within your reach.

It was the first thing they learned in kindergarten, drilled into their skulls over and over: *never pull the fire alarm.* If you pull the fire alarm, you are a worthless, selfish, evil miscreant. If you pull the fire alarm, your life will be over. You will never become the president; you'll become a garbage collector on minimum wage, surrounded by garbage and smelling like garbage, because if you pull the fire alarm, you will *be* garbage.

Benny's heart was pounding in time with his thoughts: *I can't DO this, I can't DO this, I can't DO this.* His palms were clammy and cold. He was clutching a paper towel to avoid leaving fingerprints on the handle; already the brown sheet was damp with sweat.

Logically, he understood why it had to be him. If Virginia was going to do the dirty work of stealing the phone, it made sense for her to have an alibi when the alarm went off. She was in class right now with fifteen people around her; even if she got caught stealing the phone, no one could accuse her of having pulled the alarm. And no one would accuse Benny, either, if no one saw him. He'd be one of twenty to thirty unaccounted-for students with free periods right now—not a huge pool of suspects, but few with Benny's 100 percent spotless disciplinary record. In his five years at Winship, he'd never received so much as a uniform infraction. No one would ever imagine Benny Flax pulling a fire alarm—Benny could barely imagine it himself. And yet here he was, standing in the empty hallway, willing himself to yank down that forbidden handle.

The longer I stand here, the more I'm putting myself at risk.

He was starting to feel queasy and ill. He reviewed his

plan in his mind. Brisk walk along the wall, hand outstretched and ready. A single, swift, forceful pull. Keep moving, duck into the boys' restroom as quickly as possible. He'd already checked to make sure the restroom was empty. Everything was going to be fine. He wouldn't be caught, as long as he did it *right now.*

Seconds passed. Benny felt paralyzed.

Do it. Do it, you coward!

He took a deep breath, willing himself to move. If he wimped out on this, Virginia would never let him live it down. *Who cares?* a little voice inside his head demanded. *Virginia's a weird, annoying ditz! She can't judge you!* But it wasn't just Virginia's judgment he'd have to face; it was his own. Why did this feel like the defining moment of his life? Who *was* Benny Flax? Someone who could pull a fire alarm? Or someone who couldn't?

Either way, there would be consequences.

Room 202, 1:15 p.m.

Skylar Jones read the poem in a flat, monotonous voice:

". . . toward heaven till the tree could bear no more. But dipped its top and set me down again. That would be good both going and coming back. One could do worse than be a swinger of birches." He slammed the book closed and slumped back down in his desk.

"Thank you, Skylar!" Mrs. Hope said. "That was wonderful."

Virginia rolled her eyes. It definitely had *not* been wonderful. But Mrs. Hope was one of those teachers who believed that even morons should have self-esteem.

"So what is Robert Frost saying in this poem? What is a 'swinger of birches'?"

Her question was met by a long, customary silence. None of them ever knew what the hell any of these old cheeseballs from a century ago were talking about. It wasn't like Calvin's poems, where maybe they weren't traditional, but at least you could see the passion and pizzazz.

"The birch is a tree that grows in New England," Mrs. Hope explained. "And children would *swing* on the long, white branches. It represents escapism, and the poet's lost sense of childlike wonder."

"Why do we have to read about a Yankee tree?" Big Gabe piped up. "Why can't we read about a Southern tree?"

There was a smattering of agreement: "Yeah!" "Why not!" "Why not a Southern tree?"

Mrs. Hope tried to suppress the revolt: "I'm afraid the great movements in American poetry all occurred in New England. The Fireside Poets, the Transcendentalists, the Romantics . . ."

Virginia was barely listening. Every minute that passed, she felt more and more tense. At any second, the fire alarm would start blaring its deafening, high-pitched tone. It was like waiting for a jack-in-the-box to pop.

What are you waiting for, Benny?

The debate about Yankee trees versus Southern trees was heating up. Mrs. Hope always let her classes get hijacked by dumb discussions. "Let's hear some different voices," she was saying. "Virginia?"

"Hm? What?"

"Would you like the poem better if it were about a Southern tree?"

"Um, I guess . . ." In a halfway decent world, the alarm would have gone off right then. But it didn't, so Virginia was forced to go on, "I mean, it's hard to relate to some old dude's nostalgia for a tree that we don't even have down here."

Mrs. Hope's face looked like she'd been electrocuted by happiness. "Virginia, what an astute point!" She immediately told everyone to get out a piece of paper and rewrite the poem by replacing the birch tree with something precious from their own childhood. Virginia stared at her desk, praying the alarm would go off before her turn to share.

"One could do worse than be a watcher of NASCAR."

"Excellent, Gabe!"

One could do worse than be . . . Virginia didn't know. It was dumb to dwell on your childhood. As her stepdad Esteban always said, "He who looks behind him gets a crick in his neck."

"One could do worse than go to Disney World the same week Kylie Jenner was there!"

"Very poignant, Beth! Virginia? Your turn."

Virginia took a slow breath. "One could do worse than be . . . a . . ." *Come on, Benny!*

BEEEEP. BEEEEP. BEEEEP.

"Walk calmly! You know the drill!" Mrs. Hope was shouting. "No stopping, leave everything!"

Virginia covered her ears. *Christ.* She'd forgotten just how hellishly loud these alarms were. She stood up and maneuvered herself to the end of the line out the door. When Mrs. Hope's back was turned, she slipped into the river of students away from her class. She knew exactly where to go: first floor, room 114. Trevor had Marine Biology (the "dumb" class). It would be easy because she could just flow down the stairs with everyone else; it would be hard because once she ducked into the classroom, the huge windows would expose her to anyone walking past outside. She'd have to work very quickly.

BEEEEP. BEEEEP. BEEEEP.

Virginia covered her ears as she snuck into the room. Most teachers at Winship made everyone drop their phones into a basket at the beginning of class. Sure enough, a large plastic bowl with cartoons of fish and dolphins sat on Mr. Howe's desk, full of sleek black phones. Then Virginia felt her stomach sink.

Shit.

She hadn't thought about how she would actually determine which phone was Trevor's. This wasn't fifth grade; no one used cute name labels anymore. Outside, a group of students led by a frantic-looking teacher passed. Virginia crouched behind Mr. Howe's desk. She picked up a random phone and pushed the button on the front. She'd never had a cell phone, but she'd seen other kids using them.

ENTER PASSCODE.

Shit!

She threw it down and picked up another. It also had a passcode. The earsplitting tone of the fire alarm made her feel like she was going insane. Maybe she could just take all the phones and figure out which was Trevor's later. No, Benny would hate that, she knew. Fifteen vanished phones would be a huge deal, and make it immediately obvious that the fire alarm had been a ploy.

BEEEEP. BEEEEP. BEEEEP.

It felt like the alarm was personally attacking her. She went through six more phones until she finally found one without a passcode. She swiped it open and went through the contacts. *Please have Trevor's number. Please have Trevor's number.*

"Yes!" She pressed and waited. After an agonizing moment, one of the phones lit up—a surprisingly crappy one—and she heard the tinny sound of its "Save a Horse, Ride a Cowboy" ringtone. She shoved the phone into her jacket pocket. Then she threw the other phones back into the bowl and put the bowl on the desk. If she heard that obnoxious BEEP one more time, she was going to seriously lose her mind. She covered her ears and ran out into the hall, not even bothering to check if the coast was clear first.

She felt so stressed out and harassed she wanted to explode into a million pieces.

BEEEEP. BEEEEP. BEEEEP.

She burst through the front doors. The second she was outside, the volume of the alarm dropped about a million decibels. She hurried away from the building. A pair of sandy-haired guys saw her and quickly got out of her way.

"Your Highness," one of them said, bowing.

She shot him a sideways look. Why did people keep calling her that?

"Virginia. Virginia!"

She turned and saw Benny. He was standing at the edge of the crowd of students being herded into the courtyard. He looked pale and nervous. Without thinking about it, she ran over to him and flung her arms around his shoulders. An immense wave of relief washed over her. She'd gotten the phone, and no one had seen her.

"Oh my *god*," she said, her voice half muffled by his sweater. She could feel that Benny had stiffened. He patted her shoulder like a humoring grandma. Virginia rolled her eyes. *I need a hug. Deal with it.* Just as she started to detach herself, Benny's arms relaxed and it seemed like he might actually hug her back. But it was too late; she was already pulling away. *Whatever,* she thought. She was way too frazzled to deal with Benny's fraught internal struggle to hug or not to hug.

"Did you get the phone?"

Virginia grinned and patted her pocket. "Yep. God, you look like a ghost. Are you okay?"

"I'm fine. I was just worried."

"About getting caught?"

"About *you* getting caught."

"Oh."

They stood there awkwardly for a moment. Virginia didn't know if Benny expected her to give him the phone, or if she was allowed to hang on to it herself. The last time she'd been responsible for a piece of evidence, Zaire Bollo had managed to steal it from her and destroy it. Now would be the time for Benny to bring that up. But he didn't.

"I better go sign in with my homeroom," she said.

"Yeah. Can I come over later? To your room?"

It was a normal question. Virginia knew he just wanted to look at the phone. But something about the way he'd asked felt . . . different. The fact that he'd asked at all was new. Usually Benny just barked orders and Virginia obeyed.

"Sure," she said. "Come over at four?"

Benny nodded and started walking back to his homeroom. "See ya."

"See ya."

The alarm was still blaring inside the building, screaming of a nonexistent danger. All around Virginia, students were loudly fretting about the school burning down and whether they'd ever see their Michael Kors backpacks again. Virginia looked up at the sky, where a bunch of puffy, slow-moving clouds hung above their heads. It was hard to believe how peaceful the world was up there, when down here it was such a clusterfuck of insanity. Not that she'd prefer to live in the clouds. It was like in Bible class when they learned about Heaven: supposedly it was a bunch of angels sitting around singing God's praise for eternity, which sounded soul-crushingly boring to Virginia. She'd rather have her feet on the ground down here.

What was heavenly about Heaven if you had to miss out on all the action?

The fountain, 1:40 p.m.

Yasmin Astarabadi was slowly going insane. Actually, she was quite quickly going insane. She couldn't tell if the last twenty-four hours were going perfectly or horribly for her. On the one hand, if DeAndre Bell was hurt so badly he had to miss a bunch of school—that wasn't such a bad thing for her. It meant Yasmin would get to fill in and add student body president to her resumé for at least a semester. But on the other hand, if he was only hurt badly enough to be forced to drop his sports teams—well, shit. That just meant he'd use extra time to study harder and possibly surpass her academically.

And now someone had pulled the fire alarm, which also was either a blessing or a curse. Her English class had been scheduled for an in-class essay, which would now be postponed till tomorrow. That meant she'd have a whole evening to improve her answer, but then again, so would everyone else, which would ruin the curve. And besides, every hour of today was already accounted for. She didn't have time to squeeze in extra prep for an essay that was postponed because some fucktard was bored and wanted a break from Remedial Dum-Dum class.

All around her, people were chatting and laughing and wasting their lives. A group of boys were kicking a hacky sack. Though it was chilly out, all the girls were holding their jackets instead of wearing them, and counting all the goose bumps on their arms.

"Every goose bump burns a calorie," Angie Montague informed all her friends. "So we can eat an entire poppy-seed muffin after this!"

Have fun with that! Yasmin thought icily. She grabbed her SAT flash cards from her pocket, refusing to allow her path to glory to be derailed. If she was going to be stuck out here, she was going to use the time to memorize ten new vocabulary terms to have at her fingertips for the leadership luncheon in December. Governor St. Martin was never going to forget Yasmin Astarabadi, the girl with the vocabulary of a PhD candidate.

She wandered to the thicket of bushes and trees at the edge of the courtyard, away from the hubbub of the crowd. She chose an isolated tree and leaned against it. The fire alarm was still beeping faintly from the building. Who knew how long this was going to take.

Chicanery: the use of trickery to achieve a political or legal aim. From the French meaning "to quibble."

She heard a pair of muffled voices behind her. She looked over her shoulder. Two people were standing in the clearing between the trees about twenty feet away. Their tall, matching frames were unmistakable: it was Headmaster Harker and Calvin. And it was immediately obvious that something was off.

There had always been stories that the Harkers were aliens, which everyone pretended to believe as a joke. The alien comparisons came easily: both were freakishly tall, and freakishly smart. Yasmin had never seen either of them laugh. She'd never seen either of them eat. Calvin's long absence from eighth grade had created a stir of jokes that he'd returned to his home planet. But when it turned out he'd been in the hospital and had almost died, the jokes stopped. Yasmin hadn't heard anyone call him "Martian Boy" in years.

But suddenly the alien thing seemed creepily apt. Yasmin found herself staring. They were standing across from each other, about two feet apart. The headmaster was holding Calvin's neck, his long arm outstretched. The scene was tense and silent. It was like they were speaking telepathically, or waiting to be beamed up to an orbiting ship. Yasmin didn't have a brother, so she didn't know much about fathers and sons. But she didn't think fathers went around gripping their sons' necks like that. It was spooky.

Suddenly, as if they'd heard her thoughts, the headmaster and Calvin looked right at her. The headmaster's hand immediately dropped from his son's throat.

"Sorry!" Yasmin called out. "Sorry! I didn't see anything . . ." She held up her flash cards feebly, as if they were an excuse. The Harkers just stared at her. For a second she felt afraid they might actually pull off their faces to reveal green Martian scales and menacing red eyes.

"Sorry!" she said a third time. Then she walked away. *Don't look back,* she commanded herself. Was this going to screw up her goal of getting the headmaster to recommend her for Harvard? Scoring the headmaster was the ultimate prize in teacher recs; she didn't want some stupid thing she accidentally saw during a fucking fire alarm to affect her college ambitions. But then again, maybe this was a good thing. Like everything else lately, it could go either way. Maybe Headmaster Harker would do whatever she asked now, to keep her from telling anyone what she'd seen.

Which was . . . what exactly? She didn't even know. But she didn't think it was normal.

The Boarders, 4:15 p.m.

Trevor Cheek's text history was the most boring reading material in the English language. Virginia scrolled through an endless exchange with Winn Davis that was mostly pictures of dachshunds and GIFs from *The Avengers*. It was kind of cute, actually. Winn and Trevor seemed so huge and intimidating (They were *juniors*! They had *cars*!), but really they were just boys who liked dogs and movies. There was a short conversation with "Crissy" (Chrissie White, Virginia presumed), the extent of which was Trevor asking "can I see yr nips?" followed by a picture of boobs clearly taken in the dingy Boarders bathroom mirror.

"Anything interesting?" Benny asked. He was sitting at her desk and messing with a figurine of a mermaid.

"Chrissie's boobs," she said. "Where's the camera app on these things?" She held out the phone toward him.

Benny averted his eyes. "Can you—please—"

"Oh, sorry." She tried to swipe closed the picture of Chrissie's boobs, but it didn't work. "Ugh, I don't know how to use this."

Benny grabbed the phone and made a big deal of closing his eyes while swiping the photo off the screen. Virginia flopped back on her bed and looked at the ceiling. She wondered if boys would text asking to see her nips if she had a cell phone. *Let me see your dick first,* she imagined saying. Except she didn't actually want to see a dick. Which made sexting kind of a losing proposition.

"I think you're right about the golf team," Benny said.

Virginia sat up. "Oh yeah?"

"I don't know if you want to see this. It's a lot of . . . butts. Boys' butts."

Virginia burst out laughing. "Oh my god! Let me see!"

Benny reluctantly handed her the phone. The first

photo was of a golf tee at night. The sky was black, and the camera flash turned the grass a ghastly shade of green. Virginia assumed it was the Beau Ideal Driving Club, a very exclusive country club in Midtown where the golf team practiced.

"Swipe left to see the rest. No, *left*."

The next photo was of a group of juniors appearing to sword-fight with golf clubs. In the next, they were swigging from a Jack Daniels bottle. And then there was the first butt. It was someone with their pants dropped, mooning the camera. There was nothing sexy or raunchy about it; it may as well have been the butt of a rascally fifth grader. She swiped to the next photo.

"Ew!" she shrieked, though what she saw wasn't *gross*, necessarily—just unexpected. It was a close-up of a butt. A tan, manly butt with tight, sculpted muscles clenching a pristine white golf ball. A golf ball! In his butt! Virginia wondered if the butt was Trevor's. It was a really nice one, she decided. But at the end of the day, you could be a man with the nicest butt in the world and it was still the part of the body you sat on a toilet. It wasn't like women's butts, which somehow managed to be beautiful.

Virginia swiped to the next photo, not wanting Benny to think she was excessively interested in dudes' butts. But the next photo had *three* butts, all clenching golf balls like the first one.

"There's Calvin," she said.

"Wait, where?" Benny leaned in to look.

Virginia pointed to a grainy figure behind the trio of asses. He was hunched over a golf club, fully clothed. "He's golfing."

The rest of the photos were more of the same. The boys—no girls—running around the golf course pantsless, red-faced and laughing in various stages of drunkenness. There were about twenty photos in total, the Jack Daniels bottle becoming increasingly empty in each one. Virginia searched them all for Calvin and found him in four. In three he was golfing—pants on. In one he was looking at the camera, his unsmiling face slightly out of focus.

"Where's Craig?" Virginia said. She went through the photos again, looking for him. "And where's Trevor?"

"Well, obviously Trevor took the pictures, so that explains why he's not in most of them."

Maybe Craig is the amazing butt, Virginia thought. The idea made her laugh. Craig's body type was more like Benny's: thin and kind of scrawny. But then again, that was the thing with boys—you never knew what they were hiding in their pants. Maybe Benny had the butt of an Adonis and an eight-inch sausage in there!

"What's so funny?" Benny asked. "Can we please be adults here?"

"Sorry, sorry," Virginia said, letting out a final peal of laughter and wiping the tears from her eyes.

"This could be Craig," he said, taking the phone and

pulling up a particular photo. It was one of the juniors sword-fighting with their golf clubs. In the foreground were the legs of someone lying facedown on the grass. Benny pointed at them. "This could be Craig. He could be posing. Or maybe he drank himself unconscious. Or maybe they actually *hit* him with their clubs. Do you see the smears on his pants? It could be dirt, or it could be blood."

"Maybe they *are* Satanists!" Virginia said excitedly.

Benny held up his hand. "Please don't corrupt my thought process with hasty narrative-forming."

Virginia rolled her eyes. *Your precious, precious thought process.*

"Did you notice the caddie?"

"Huh?"

Benny pulled up a different photo. "Here." He pointed. "And here."

In two photos there was a man in the background. He was hard to see because the image was so grainy. Virginia squinted. He was a black man, and he was wearing a white polo and a green visor and carrying one of those golf bags.

"This is what's really weird to me," Benny was saying. "Obviously they broke into the golf course to drink and conduct their shenanigans—"

Virginia snickered. *Shenanigans.* Sometimes hanging out with Benny was like hanging out with an eighty-year-old man.

"—which is breaking and entering. It's illegal. Why would the caddie allow them to do this?"

"Maybe they hired him privately?" Virginia suggested. "Maybe he's just some guy who doesn't care."

Benny got out his own phone and pulled up the website for the Beau Ideal Driving Club. "Look," he said, showing it to Virginia. "White polo, green visor. It's the Beau Ideal uniform. Why would a Beau Ideal caddie just stand around watching them debauch the golf course?"

"Maybe he's the cult leader!"

Benny shot her a look. "Stop."

"Fine. Money, then." She made the "money" gesture with her fingers.

Benny shook his head. "Unless he's a moron, he's not going to take some cash from a bunch of children over the prospect of losing his job."

"People *are* morons," Virginia said, shrugging. "It's pretty much the one thing you can count on."

Benny looked out the window, thinking. "We'll go to Beau Ideal tomorrow. I'll pick you up here at eleven?"

"Me and you?" Virginia balked. "At Beau Ideal? You're not a member. I'm not a member."

"It doesn't matter. It's not like they check names at the door. The whole point of a country club is that people pay ninety thousand dollars to feel like they belong. They don't stoop to prove themselves to the staff. We just have to blend in and act like we belong too."

"Um, blend in?" Virginia repeated. Benny was a little delusional if he thought he was going to "blend in" at Beau Ideal. She was pretty sure they didn't have a ton of Jewish people there.

"Don't worry about me," Benny assured her. "Just make sure you look the part—pink and green and all that."

"Okay!" Virginia said, starting to feel excited. Investigating incognito! She only wished her character were more interesting, like an eccentric young widow or a visiting French circus performer instead of a boring and blah preppy girl.

Benny kept staring out the window, appearing deep in thought.

"Do you want to hang out tonight?" she asked him. "Just like, watch a movie?" Did Benny watch movies? Virginia imagined not. He probably spent all his free time reading the *Wall Street Journal*. But she was bored, and there wasn't a football game to go to or anything.

Benny was looking at her like she'd suggested they go to the zoo and set all the animals free. "Hm? Oh, I can't. I need to go to a camera store. I'm installing a motion-sensitive camera in the girls' room to catch the drug dealer when he comes back for his X10 device."

"Oh. . . . Well, what about after that?"

"Um, after? I have to go to temple with my grandma. It's Bingo and Chinese Night."

"Cool! I love Chinese food." She let the words dangle,

leaving a wide opening for Benny to invite her. She'd never been to a temple before, and she was curious to see Benny's other world—his true world. Not to mention it was taco salad night in the cafeteria, a fate she was eager to escape.

"Well . . ." Benny stood up. "I better go. See you tomorrow." He waved, not quite meeting her eyes. Virginia kept looking at him. *Is he seriously not going to invite me?*

He left.

Virginia sighed and flopped back on her bed. She was *not* going to eat gross, soggy two-day-old taco salad. That was just totally out of the question. She racked her brain. *Who has a car. . . .* Impulsively she got up and went to the common room. She turned on the computer and logged into her e-mail.

> To: c.harker@winship.edu
> From: v.leeds@winship.edu
> Subject: hungry
>
>
> Craving Chinese food. Wanna take me out
> to dinner?

She pressed "send."

Oh my god. Maybe she should have thought about that for more than five seconds. What was she doing? There were other ways to get Chinese food. She could have asked Chrissie to order take-out and charge it to her AmEx.

You pretty much just asked Calvin on a date! Her heart was pounding. She was about to turn off the computer and pretend the whole thing hadn't happened when an e-mail popped in her in-box.

> To: v.leeds@winship.edu
> From: c.harker@winship.edu
> Re: hungry
>
> I'm grounded. Parents go to sleep around ten. Come over then if you're still hungry. Back door. ☺

Benny's house, 9:15 p.m.
BANANA PEEL: HISTORY

Benny pulled up a Word doc on his laptop and started typing. He'd been researching the cultural significance of the banana. The yellow fruit (technically a berry!) had a very racially charged history. There were incidents—even recent ones—of bananas being thrown at black athletes, stemming from an age-old idea that Africans were inferior and related to monkeys. It reminded Benny of all the Nazi-era propaganda equating Jews with rats.

And that wasn't all. The classic slip-on-a-banana gag, it turned out, came from minstrel shows in the 1800s, where black characters were portrayed as clumsy, dim-witted, banana-peel-slipping fools for the enjoyment of white audiences. By the time Donald Duck was slipping on banana peels in cartoons on TV, the gag's racist origin had been largely forgotten.

But maybe all that symbolism was a coincidence. Maybe Benny was the racist one for focusing on racial undertones instead of viewing the situation color-blind: a couple of kids, a deer on wheels, a banana. Besides, Benny couldn't imagine Trevor being that subtle. He was the biggest Neanderthal in school, a designation he seemed to wear like a badge of honor. If Trevor wanted to kill DeAndre, he'd probably just get drunk and beat him to death.

Benny sighed and closed the laptop. He was tired and distracted and his stomach was growling. He'd barely eaten dinner, even though he loved Chinese food. Who *didn't* love Chinese food? But he kept picturing Virginia in the dingy Winship cafeteria eating meatloaf resembling roadkill or whatever vile slop the evening staff had uncaringly nuked for the boarding students. Why hadn't he invited her? She had clearly wanted him to. But the proposition had just seemed impossible. He couldn't bring Virginia to his *temple*. With his *grandmother*. Who knew what sort of random things she might have said to people. Her yellow hair would have attracted everyone's attention, and she probably would have worn that way-too-short skirt of Zaire Bollo's. It was better that he didn't invite her, he'd assured himself. But he'd felt so guilty he'd hardly eaten a bite.

He got up from the dining room table and peered in the

refrigerator. Nothing looked appetizing. He poured himself a glass of chocolate milk. In the next room his dad was asleep in the big leather easy chair. His mother and grandmother were watching the TV intently. The volume was very low—unusual for them. When Mrs. Flax noticed Benny, she picked up the remote and changed the channel.

"What are you watching?" he asked her.

"Nothing worth interrupting your studies."

Benny went into the living room and picked up the remote from the side table. He hit the "last" button, bringing the TV to the previous channel.

"Benny, stop. Stop!"

A business-looking man with silvery-blond hair was speaking haltingly to a group of reporters: "The situation is—regrettable, but—I assure the public that—a new plant will be opened in Alabama—"

"What's this?" Benny asked.

His grandma waved her hand dismissively. "Oh, some silliness your mom and I are watching. Just frittering away our brain cells. Not that I was using them! You know what they say, use it or lose it!"

Benny gave his grandma a sideways look. He was pretty sure that saying was about sex, not brain cells. But maybe it applied to both. Mrs. Flax sat stonily while her mother rambled.

Benny watched the TV for another minute, trying to figure out what they were guarding from him. The blond-haired man was "lobbyist Garland White," according to the text on the screen. He looked uncomfortable in front of the microphone. Clearly he was accustomed to machinations that played out behind the scenes, not on national news. He continued to speak awkwardly, while across the bottom of the screen, the news scroll read: *SHUTDOWN OF WAYCROSS PLANT, STATE TO LOSE 4,000 JOBS.*

Then the news switched to a story about a bombing in Indonesia. Benny handed the remote back to his mom. They shared a long, tense look in which Mrs. Flax barely blinked.

"Isn't that the plant where Dad worked?" he asked.

No one answered.

"I'm going to bed."

"Good night, *bubele*!" his grandmother chirped.

In his room Benny got out his laptop and searched "Garland White, plant shutdown." The full story was a lot more interesting than the brief clip on the news had shown. An aerospace engineering plant outside the city was being shut down, disgracing Governor St. Martin with massive job losses. Furthermore, a reporter from the *Atlanta Journal-Constitution* was claiming that the plant closure was due to a personal feud between the governor and an airline lobbyist, Garland White. Leaked e-mails showed the two men engaged in vicious personal attacks: the lobbyist had called the governor a "Jay Leno–faced bastard"; the governor had called the lobbyist a "greedy, money-grubbing cum rag." Each described a desire to crush the other "like a cockroach."

The scandal had reached a national level of interest. People were outraged that four thousand hardworking men and women with families had lost their jobs because two hotheaded alpha males with the maturity level of sixth graders couldn't make a compromise. But the story was confusing; the reporter didn't seem to know exactly what the root of the hatred between the two men was, or how it had escalated into such an extreme political screw-up. The governor's office had released a statement that the plant closure was in no way related to the e-mails, or to the acrimonious relationship between the state executive and the "discontented lobbyist." The lobbyist hadn't commented one way or the other, and seemed mostly focused on bringing attention to the new plant in Alabama.

Benny couldn't figure out why his mother and grand-mother hadn't wanted him to see this. Just because it was an aerospace plant, which would remind him of his dad? He was reminded of his dad every day. His dad was still *there*, for god's sake—a permanent fixture in the living room. Benny wished the women in his household would stop treat-ing him like a neurotic child who couldn't deal with life.

He created a Google alert for himself flagging the following words: *Garland White, Waycross plant, Georgia plant shutdown, Governor St. Martin.* Then he closed the computer.

He felt so tired all of a sudden. He took off his shoes and turned off the lamp, not bothering to change out of his clothes. The second he closed his eyes, the face of the deer and its severed antlers accosted him. *Get out of my head!* he wanted to yell. Why couldn't he stop thinking about it? The deer's eyes seemed to grow angrier every time he pictured it, sometimes morphing with DeAndre's pained face. Benny wondered what had happened to the deer after the science expo. Had Trevor taken it home? Had it ended up in a garbage heap somewhere? He felt haunted by it.

Benny fell asleep and slipped into a dark dream. He was at a dance, but his clothes were wrong. Virginia was laughing at him. He knew he had the right clothes in his bag, but every time he reached inside, he couldn't seem to pull them out. By the refreshments table, the wheel from *Wheel of Fortune* spun around and around. Benny knew that when it stopped, someone somewhere would die. As the spinning slowed down, Benny could see that the deer head had been nailed to the wheel's center, its black eyes staring into a reeling void. Then somehow Benny *was* the deer head, and he felt relieved. *I can't die, I'm already dead.*

He awoke with a jolt, covered in a sheen of cold sweat. It was two a.m. Suddenly he knew what was going on. He knew exactly what was going on.

It was Calvin.

Calvin's house, 9:50 p.m.

It was scary to walk alone at night, a fact Virginia always managed to forget. The rubber soles of her cheap shoes padded quietly on the pavement, but even that sound seemed too loud. The road to the headmaster's house was deserted and silent.

Virginia had seen the house a million times, but never imagined she'd actually go inside it one day. It was technically on-campus, just up the hill and past the tennis courts—a five-minute walk from the Boarders (though in the emptiness of night the walk felt longer). It was a large brick mansion with old-fashioned dormer windows and a grand columned portico framing the front door. The yard was illuminated by floodlights placed strategically in the surrounding trees, creating the effect of supercharged moonlight. Virginia stood in the darkness at the edge of the grass, nervous to set foot on the property. She checked the time on her Indiglo watch. She was early—too early. She'd felt so hyper and restless sitting around in her room waiting for ten o'clock that she'd left at the earliest reasonable moment. And now she was here.

She crept along the trees at the edge of the property toward the back. Around ten. What did that mean? 10:01? 10:15? She guessed she'd knock lightly on the back door. Would Calvin be there waiting? Would there actually be Chinese food? What if as soon as she was alone with him, she didn't like him anymore? It was a pivotal move, going to his house at night. She wasn't sure why she'd put herself in this position. But it felt exciting and daredevilish.

She reached the back of the house. Huge windows revealed a beautiful living room full of dark wood and crimson furniture, and a vaulted ceiling at least twenty-five feet high. There was a fireplace, and an immense leather sofa, and a spotless tile floor covered in Oriental rugs. It looked like a photograph from *Better Homes and Gardens*. Virginia wasn't usually the type to go apeshit over interior design, which in Florida meant making everything look like a hotel. But Calvin's house was spectacular, and she couldn't wait to be inside. There was so much to look at that for a second she didn't notice Calvin and his dad were standing in the middle of the room.

She jumped back into the shadows instinctively, though she knew they probably couldn't see her. They were talking—or rather, Headmaster Harker was talking. And the conversation was obviously not a pleasant one. Virginia watched Calvin, who kept opening his mouth to speak, but his dad wouldn't give him a chance. Suddenly Virginia felt a surge of . . . she didn't know what to call the feeling. Pathos? Was that a word?

Calvin was *crying*. His chin quivered and a tear fell down his cheek. Virginia had never seen a man cry before. She'd seen boys cry, but Calvin was so grown-up-looking, she'd unconsciously categorized him as a man.

What's going on? She couldn't look away.

Calvin was shaking his head. More tears were streaming down his cheeks. He wiped them away with his hand. Virginia couldn't tell what they were talking about at all, but it definitely involved Headmaster Harker saying "yes" and Calvin saying "no."

And then the headmaster did something that chilled Virginia to the core. He grabbed Calvin by the throat. His face was calm but menacing. He leaned toward his son, their faces now inches apart, and stared into his eyes. Just stared at him. They were the same extreme height, almost mirror images, as if Calvin were looking at a projection of himself from the future, hardened and corrupted by time and now turning on his young self. It made Virginia shiver.

At that second, Virginia realized that Calvin could see her through the window. He looked right at her, inching his head to the left as far as the grip of his father's hand would allow.

Go.

He hadn't been saying "no" to his dad. He'd been mouthing the word "Go." *To her.*

Virginia shook her head. She wasn't going to abandon him to be strangled in his own house! Not that his dad was *strangling* him, exactly, he was just . . . *gripping* him. But it was scary.

Go.

Headmaster Harker's eyes cut to the window, following

his son's gaze. Virginia ducked quickly behind a tree. *Oh my god.* She stood frozen, trying not to make a sound even though she knew there was no way they could hear her inside. After a long moment she peeked around the tree. The living room was empty. They were gone.

She stood in the shadows for five entire minutes. Was Calvin coming back? She checked her watch. It was long past ten at this point. A strong gust of wind blew against her face, like it was trying to push her away. But the immaculate living room—warmly and perfectly lit—still seemed to say, *Hello, do come in.*

What would Benny do? Virginia knew what he would do. He would leave, and enter all the data into a color-coded spreadsheet and then stare at it for four hours. But how could she leave Calvin alone with that man? She'd always been scared of Headmaster Harker—everyone was. He was strict and dour and notoriously harsh. But that was like, scared he'd call your parents and give you six hundred detentions, not scared he'd strangle his son to death.

She decided to go. Calvin could take care of himself. *Could he?* She didn't really know him at all. But she liked people who could take care of themselves, and she wanted Calvin to be one. And anyway, he'd told her to go. So what else was she supposed to do? She slipped back into the darkness, away from the house's alluring glow.

Saturday
The Beau Ideal Driving Club, 11:30 a.m.

"Stop looking at me like that."

"What? You look . . . good."

Benny ignored her. His grandma had said the same thing ("handsome" was her word), but he didn't take the compliments seriously. They only showed how conforming to the dominant paradigm created an illusion of attractiveness in people's eyes. He'd blow-dried his hair, mimicking the shiny, Beatles-esque mop that was popular at Winship. He'd put in contacts, which he only owned in the event of his glasses needing to be repaired. And finally, perhaps most importantly, he'd donned the consummate item of preppy attire: a pink Polo shirt.

His mother had not appreciated the transformation. She hadn't said anything, but he knew what she was thinking. That he had violated the unspoken condition of his attendance at Winship: thrive, but *do not assimilate*. In a childish way, it pleased Benny to annoy her. Let her think he was being coopted by the preppy hive-mind. It served her right, making him go to this school full of trad, pink-Polo-wearing lemmings.

To get them to the city, he'd employed his usual tactic: a made-up meeting for the Model UN at the public library. Once Mrs. Flax's car had disappeared down Peachtree Street, he and Virginia had crossed the park to the hill where the sprawling white buildings of the club lorded over Midtown. It was getting easier and easier to lie to his mother, which reduced Benny's stress level but was also slightly alarming. How many lies did it take before you were officially "a liar"?

"So, do we just walk in?" Virginia asked him. They were standing in front of the club entrance, a massive rotunda where a line of sleek-looking cars were being met by energetic valets. Evidently it was not common to approach the club by foot.

Benny smoothed his hair self-consciously. *Be confident,* he told himself. He looked fine, and Virginia looked fine too, though her yellow-and-green dress was too small. Benny had noticed that about a lot of her clothes. It wasn't like Zaire's gold skirt, which was designed to be skimpy. This was more like, someone needed to buy Virginia new clothes, because she'd outgrown everything in her wardrobe. The fabric stretched tight across her shoulders and her chest. Benny averted his eyes. *Don't stare at her breasts.*

He took a breath. "We just walk in."

As Benny predicted, no one tried to stop them from

entering. He perceived a few looks from the valets, which he interpreted not as suspicious but just wondering where their parents were.

The inside wasn't what Benny expected. It was grand but not like a palace or anything. It was just a large room with nice furniture, elegant but muted.

"This way," he said to Virginia. He'd studied the floor plan of the club ahead of time so they wouldn't have to ask directions. The next room was similar to the first but contained a quiet bar. Benny gestured toward a cluster of leather armchairs overlooking the golf course. "Let's sit for a minute. I have to talk to you about something."

"Am I in trouble?" Virginia flopped into one of the chairs. "Mm, comfy." Benny sat down across from her. He crossed his legs one way and then another, trying to fit the role of country-club teen.

"Not like a girl," Virginia told him. "Put your ankle on your knee."

Benny shot her a look but then did it. Instantly he looked completely cool and composed, like he spent every Saturday relaxing in the bar at Atlanta's most exclusive club. Virginia had forgotten he had this weird ability. She'd seen him do this once before, at the Sapphire Lounge, where he'd managed to fit in among the creepy lounge lizards and boozy jazz fiends just by standing in a certain way. It was sort of annoying. It proved that Benny *chose* to be an outsider, which made his victim-y glasses and out-of-style turtlenecks suddenly seem less dweeby and more self-righteous.

She couldn't stop looking at him. He looked hot. Except not really. It was just that the pink shirt brought out a different tone in his normally sallow skin, and without his glasses, he actually seemed smarter for some reason. Maybe because she could see his eyes better, see him thinking. She arranged herself vampishly in the chair, hoping she looked as cool as he did. She suspected she didn't, though. These flowery Lilly Pulitzer getups weren't designed to make girls look cool, they were designed to make them look like pea-brained dolls.

"I know what's going on," Benny was saying, his fingers tented like a Bond villain. "It was Calvin Harker."

"Do you have any money?" Virginia asked. "I want a ginger ale."

"They don't use money here. All the members have accounts. Did you hear what I said? It was Calvin Harker."

"What was Calvin Harker?"

"The person who tried to kill DeAndre Bell."

Virginia snorted. *"What?"*

"He was probably the drug dealer in the bathroom. You said the guy had ironed pants? Calvin's clothes are always perfect. I think he gets them dry-cleaned."

"That's not super unusual," Virginia said, even though it kind of was. The guys at Winship were famous for being unkempt; their uniforms tended to be handed down from older brothers or cousins, full of holes and barely cared for.

"Did you see his project at the science expo?"

Virginia shook her head.

Benny lowered his voice. "It was strange. It was like, a compilation of random deaths. How life is pointless because at any moment you could be hit by a bus, or a possum could fall from the sky."

"A *possum?*"

"Whatever, not a possum. His point was that every day, people die in random and unpredictable ways."

"So?"

"So he designed this insane death scenario for DeAndre to prove his thesis! To win the science expo! But it backfired, because in the chaos the judges never declared a winner."

Virginia gawked at him. Was he serious? "You think Calvin Harker orchestrated *murder*. To win a *science expo*. Don't you think that's a little juvenile?"

Benny waved his hand impatiently. "Well, fine, maybe it's not about winning. But it *is* about proving his philosophy."

Virginia was trying to be open-minded, but the idea was too stupid. Though "stupid" wasn't a word that Benny would react well to. "That's kind of . . . absurd," she said. "Also, it doesn't make sense. If his thing is about death being random, why would he concoct a murder scheme? That's not random. That's on purpose."

"The *victim* was random. I don't think Calvin cared who got killed. In fact, that was the whole point."

Benny's face was triumphant. It was a good look on him. *Stop thinking about his dumb hot glasses-less face!* Virginia yelled at herself.

"So . . . what are you saying? That Calvin planted the banana Trevor slipped on?"

Benny stared out the window at the golf course. "I know it sounds crazy. It *is* crazy. That's the whole point. Maybe Calvin drops banana peels wherever he goes, on the off chance that someone will slip and die. Virginia, I'm serious! Think about it. The banana peel is the perfect instrument of murder—silly and cartoonish but *ruinous*. For Calvin, it probably symbolizes lack of dignity in death. . . . He was in the hospital for a year in eighth grade—remember that? After a year in a hospital, you're not gonna be romanticizing death anymore."

Virginia tried to think. She didn't feel convinced. She thought of Calvin's tearstained face last night. He'd seemed so . . . *sad*. But in an endearing way, not a banana-peel-dropping murderer way.

"Okay, well," she started awkwardly, "I went to his house last night—"

"You went to his *house*?" Benny interrupted. "Why?"

"We were supposed to have dinner."

"Why?"

"Because I asked him."

"*Why?*"

"Oh my god, stop saying *why*. I'm allowed to hang out with people other than you."

Benny bristled. "I didn't—I never—"

"Okay, whatever," Virginia cut him off. "It wasn't a big deal and it didn't even happen. Because when I got to his house, I was standing outside and I saw his dad, like, strangling him."

"Headmaster Harker? *Strangling* him?"

"Sort of. It was like . . . Here, stand up, I'll show you."

Benny stood up and looked around to make sure no one was watching them. The bartender was wiping down wineglasses and didn't seem interested in the two teenagers hanging out at the other end of the room. Benny's mind was whirring. Virginia and Calvin having dinner? What the hell was that about? Was it a *date*?

Stop it, Benny told himself. He didn't support the predominant societal expectation that a guy and a girl couldn't hang out without it being some romantic thing. Girls and guys could be friends. And Virginia could have dinner with whomever she wanted. *Except not a murderer, please.*

"So I'm the dad, and you're Calvin," Virginia was saying. She positioned herself across from him, seeming taller than usual. Benny glanced down; she was wearing heels. She extended her hand and touched Benny's neck, just below the jaw—tentatively at first, and then firmly once she sensed he wasn't going to swat her away. Her hand felt cool and warm at the same time. She squeezed his throat and looked directly in his eyes.

Benny felt a jolt. He wished he had his glasses on. He

felt vulnerable without those little walls standing between him and the world. Virginia's eyes—mere inches from his own—contained chaotic specks of green and brown and gold. He almost expected the colors to move, like stardust swirling in space.

"And then he leaned in like this. . . ."

Benny barely breathed. He felt an urge to hug her, or wishing she would hug him, which was weird. When someone was gripping you by the throat, the normal reaction was to push them away, not pull them closer.

How long is this going to last?

"Then his dad saw me, and I hid behind a tree." Virginia dropped her hand unceremoniously and flopped back down in her chair. Unconsciously Benny touched where her fingers had been.

"Sorry. Did I hurt you?"

"Hm? No, it's fine." Benny sat back down. The temperature of his neck slowly returned to normal. "So wait, what happened after that?"

"After that, they were both gone. And I left."

Benny looked out the window. He didn't see how this new information contradicted his theory. Headmaster Harker being abusive and Calvin being a killer were by no means mutually exclusive.

"I'd like to hit pause on this conversation," Benny declared, standing up again. "Let's focus on the golf team for now, and why Craig Beaver was really expelled. If we can track down the caddie they used—the black guy in the background of Trevor's photos—we can find out what happened that night."

"Okay," Virginia said simply. It's one of the things Benny liked about her. She didn't dwell on things. If you wanted to move on, she moved on too. He glanced at the bartender, who was now eyeing them suspiciously.

"Let's not do anything else weird," Benny said quietly, touching his neck again. The feeling of her fingers was gone now. He looked out the window again. The sky was filled with puffy white clouds, and the grass of the golf course was an unnatural, uniform shade of green. Of all the recreational activities of man, golf had to be the stupidest. The massive effort to beat nature into submission—daily mowing, watering, and dousing of chemicals—so a man could pay ninety thousand dollars to push a ball into a hole. It was like they'd deliberately dreamed up the most expensive and ecologically damaging way to enjoy a day in the sun.

"Hey, look," Virginia said. She was pointing to a spot far out on the green. Benny squinted. His contacts weren't great for long distance. But he could make out a lean figure hunched over a golf club. His too-long arms were bent oddly to maintain the proper golfing stance.

"Is it Calvin?" Benny asked excitedly. "You see? It's not a coincidence that he keeps popping up. It's just like Zaire Bollo. You have a bunch of odd occurrences spinning in the chaos of space. Then you realize it's *not* chaos—it's a *galaxy*, and at the center of the galaxy is a black hole. A *person* who's set everything in motion."

Virginia patted his shoulder patronizingly. "It's his dad. Nice analogy, though."

"Metaphor," Benny corrected. "An analogy would be, 'Clues are to a galaxy as what Calvin is to a black hole.'"

". . . Cool to know."

Benny's jaw tightened. It didn't matter which Harker was golfing. It didn't matter if Virginia was skeptical. Calvin was still the black hole. Benny knew it, the same way he'd known it was Zaire Bollo last time. It was a gift he had, like how dogs could supposedly smell fear; Benny could smell truth. He didn't know what it was exactly, but he could sense that it was there. . . .

"Benny? Hello? You're spacing out."

"Just give me a minute."

He was thinking about the deer. Its maimed, blood-splattered head loomed in his mind, at odds with the perfectly manicured and civilized scene in front of him. But suddenly the golf course didn't seem so civilized—it seemed repulsive. A piece of raped land where men gathered to roll balls around and consolidate power. It wasn't something Benny would ever say out loud—the stereotype about Jews being Socialists made him self-conscious. But he didn't want to be there. He didn't want to be wearing this stupid pink shirt and these sucky contacts, or to be complicit in their endless golf course of a world.

Get a grip, he ordered himself. Just because he'd blow-dried his hair and put on a Polo didn't make him one of these people. In fact, that was the whole point of them: "born, not made." They even had bumper stickers. There was no power in declaring that you didn't want to be one of them. They'd cut you back down to size with a single look:

We didn't want you anyway.

The women's steam room, 12:10 p.m.

Hello baby in my heart!
In the land of the free may you start
To grow in the light of Jesus
And to delight and please us.
Sorry I did not wait for marriage,
But please God fill my baby carriage!

Corny solemnly recited the poem, which she'd written herself. The paper was damp from the thick steam, and a few of the puppy and angel stickers had fallen off and dropped onto the wet tile floor. She took a sip of pink strawberry-kiwi Gatorade in case it was a girl, then one of blue "Glacier Freeze" Gatorade in case it was a boy. She and the Montague twins had created an elaborate conception ritual inspired by witchcraft they'd found on the Internet, taking all the sacrilegious parts and replacing them with Jesus and patriotic references, and substituting the gross potions with pink and blue Gatorade.

"Wait!" Angle Montague gasped as Corny took alternating sips from the pink and blue bottles. "What if they mix in your stomach and turn purple, and then you have a *gay* one!"

She and her twin sister, Brittany, burst into giggles.

"Omigod!" Corny shrieked. She laughed along but was mostly humoring them. The twins were just girls, whereas she was a woman now—a *mother*. At least hopefully she was! The thought made her so excited she wanted to scream. But she needed to remain calm and complete the ritual. She and the twins sat in a triangle in their Kate Spade string bikinis, their knees touching each other. Corny had chosen the club's steam room for the ceremony because it was warm and steamy and safe, just like a womb. She wanted the baby to feel as welcome as possible in this world.

"Okay, now hold Sarah-Ann-Elizabeth-Jane over my head and do the chant."

Sarah-Ann-Elizabeth-Jane was Corny's baby doll from childhood, a peach-colored hunk of plastic dirtied from a decade of love, with a smear of purple marker on its bald head. The twins lifted the doll in the air like Simba from *The Lion King*. Then they shouted together:

"BRING CORNY A CUPID BABY!"

"Five more times," Corny instructed, and the twins obeyed. But by the fourth recitation, they were so tongue-twisted the chant ended up sounding like, "Beep Corby a poop cupid."

All three of them collapsed into giggles, even Corny.

She couldn't help it! She shrieked, "Y'ALL! I don't want a poop cupid!"

Angie dropped the baby doll. It landed smack on its face and then rolled away, making them laugh even harder. Corny took a few deep breaths, trying to stop laughing.

"Okay, do it right this time," she ordered. But the twins completely broke down in hysterics and ended up shouting what sounded like, "Bring Corbin a stupid boopid!"

"And not a gay one!" Angie screamed between laughs.

Corny giggled and swatted her. It was okay. It didn't matter if they'd accidentally asked for a stupid boopid or a poop cupid or a gay one. Jesus knew what they really meant: a perfect angel from heaven who looked just like Winn, and had deep philosophical thoughts like Winn, and played football like Winn—unless it was a girl, and then she could be a Gap Kids model like Corny!

Corny hit "play" on the playlist she'd created of all the Justin Bieber songs containing the word "baby" in the lyrics.

"You should name it Rory like in *Gilmore Girls*," Brittany suggested. "And then you can be best friends!"

"I already have the names picked out." Corny reached under her towel and pulled out an Anne Geddes journal she'd bought especially for baby-related thoughts. The cover had the cutest baby wearing a cabbage on its head and the words *Water daily—with LOVE!* written in pink flowery letters. "Judd Winn Rufus if it's a boy, and Blue Hydrangea if it's a girl."

"Omigod, those are so cute!" Brittany squealed.

"Will you have to drop out of cheerleading?" Angie asked, frowning like a sad puppy.

"Just for basketball season, when I'm all fat," Corny said.

"Oh good," the twins said in unison, sighing. Basketball cheerleading was a joke and didn't matter, especially now that DeAndre Bell wouldn't be able to play.

"Your boobs are going to be gigantic," Brittany said.

"I am soooooo jealous," Angie whined. "I wish Big Gabe wanted to have a baby with me!"

"Dad would kill you! Aren't your parents going to be mad, Corny?"

Corny shrugged. "If they're mad, then me and Winn will just run away to Sea Island and have it be a beach baby!"

"Awwwww! I want a beach baby!"

Corny turned up the volume of the playlist. She lay back on her towel, her body wet and gleaming from the steam. She wished Winn were there to touch her all over and have sex with her and tell her she was the most beautiful girl in the world. Thinking about it made her so horny it was confusing. It didn't seem very maternal or appropriate to be dreaming of a penis when there was a *baby* inside her! But she couldn't stop thinking about him—how passionate and magical he'd been the other night, how his love had felt almost *painful*. She'd had sex with Winn before, but not like *that*. She'd tried to describe it to the twins, but they didn't get it. Brittany was a virgin, and Angie basically was too, except for that one time at church camp that didn't count because the guy had jizzed himself before getting it in.

Poor Angie! Corny thought, feeling grateful she had such a wonderful stud like Winn to have sex with. She wanted to have sex with Winn one hundred million times and have one hundred million babies, each little angel a unique memento of the power of his penis!

Brittany was fishing around in her pink Vera Bradley bag. "I got four different kinds of pregnancy tests. Are you ready?"

I love you. I love you. She heard the words over and over in her mind. He'd finally admitted it. After years of waiting, she'd finally gotten to hear those three exquisite words. He'd said it over and over, as if making up for lost time. And now time was infinite, because they would be together forever. Corny closed her eyes and inhaled the thick, steamy air, giddily aware that every breath was one she shared with the teeny tiny microscopic angel baby inside her.

I love you. I love you. I love you.

The pro shop, 12:20 p.m.

Virginia picked up a plain green visor and looked at the price tag: $88.

"Oh my god. Benny, look at this. Want a visor for eighty-eight dollars?"

"Virginia—" Benny turned to tell her to shut up, but

stopped short. She'd put the visor on her head, and it looked so cute on her that Benny felt disarmed. She looked like a little kid tennis champ, grinning at him like she'd won the big match and expected a cookie. Then she grabbed a pink visor and shoved it on Benny's head.

"I'll give you five hundred dollars if you wear that to school on Monday."

He removed the visor and returned it to the display. "That would be a tremendous waste of money."

"No it wouldn't," Virginia said. "I'd be getting valuable information."

He rolled his eyes. "What information?"

"That your dignity is for sale."

Whoa. He looked at her. Where had that come from? It was one of the most incisive things he'd ever heard her say. But if Virginia realized she'd just said something really smart, she didn't show it. She was posing vapidly in front of a mirror with a sweater around her shoulders like she'd stepped into a Brooks Brothers catalog.

"Come on," he said to her. He led the way to the front desk, where a very tan man in a Beau Ideal uniform grinned at them eagerly. His name tag said "Curly" even though his hair was straight. From across the room he'd seemed young, but up close his face was lined and hallow. It made Benny feel vaguely superior. He did *not* intend to become a forty-year-old man whose entire job was sucking up to rich men while they played the most boring sport ever invented. But Benny's snobbishness quickly melted into self-reproach. It's not like he actually had a better plan. He hated thinking about the future. *What do you want to be when you grow up?* People assumed he had an answer to this question, because he studied and got good grades and seemed forward-thinking in many respects. But when Benny thought about the end of high school, it felt like an edge of a cliff facing an infinity of empty space.

"Can I help you?" Curly practically shouted at them.

"Um, I, um . . ." *Christ, be confident,* Benny commanded himself. "I'd like to arrange a golf match. Golf game. And I was hoping to employ a caddie I used before. But I can't remember his name. Do you have a directory?"

"We sure do!" Curly grinned, showcasing a set of unnaturally white teeth. "But if you give me your account number, I can just look up who you've used in the past."

"Well, it was a friend's account. I'd like to use their caddie."

"Name?"

"Um . . . Cheek? The Cheeks?"

He typed into a computer. "Uh-huh. Looks like Cody MacPhearson is your man! Do you want to check his availability?"

Benny and Virginia exchanged a look. *Cody MacPhearson?* The name sounded very . . . white. "Um, I think it might have been someone else. I'd recognize him if I saw his face. Can I look through the directory?"

"Sure, son." The man reached behind the desk and pulled out a binder. He flipped to a section in the middle and pushed it across the desk.

Benny scanned the names and faces, looking for a thin black man. But the directory was one sandy-haired, suntanned guy after another, with names like Cody and Bradley and Brett. He flipped through twice to make sure he hadn't missed anyone. There was not a single black caddie employed at Beau Ideal. *So who was that man in the pictures?*

Virginia pushed Benny to the side and looked for herself, still wearing the green visor on her head.

"This is all of them?" she asked.

Curly nodded. "Yep." His sparkling grin had dimmed. Virginia could tell he was starting to lose patience with them. He turned back to Benny. "Who did you say your dad was, son?"

Benny seemed startled. "Hm?"

"Your father. Who is your father? I need to know the name on your account."

Virginia gave Benny a kick. She knew there was some weird situation with Benny's father, like he'd been in an accident and was a paraplegic or something. But she hadn't known Benny was *sensitive* about it.

"You don't recognize him?" Virginia jumped in, pointing at Benny. "That's Benjamin Maximilian Coca-Cola the Third!" The words were barely out of her mouth before she'd cracked herself up. She felt a yank on her arm, and she let Benny lead her out of the pro shop. He plucked the green visor from her head and set it on a rack of Polo shirts.

Outside, Virginia stopped laughing and braced herself for a lecture from Benny about goofing off during an investigation. But he just sat down in one of the wicker lawn chairs and pulled out his phone. Virginia sat down too, choosing a spot under a large beige umbrella. The air smelled like mowed grass. She waited a minute, and when Benny still hadn't looked up from his phone, she said, "Um, hello?"

"Hang on. I need to check my Google alerts."

Virginia stretched out her legs and scanned the golf course for Headmaster Harker. It was creepy, knowing that all around you, men who just looked like boring, upstanding, golf-loving citizens could be secretly strangling their own sons at night. She wondered if Calvin was okay. Maybe he was dead. *He's not dead,* she assured herself. She'd seen bruises on his neck in the library the other day; that meant this was probably something his dad did to him often. Which was still disturbing, but at least suggested that the headmaster wasn't trying to *kill* his son, just . . . hurt him. Benny would probably be impressed by her deduction if he weren't so busy obsessing over his Google alerts.

As she waited for Benny to be done, her mind wandered. She thought about Calvin's face and how he'd looked when he was crying. Some people looked ugly and babyish when they cried, but Calvin hadn't. He'd looked . . . beautiful.

Like a slightly distorted angel mourning Christ in a medieval painting. She wished she could have seen him even closer. His eyes already resembled emeralds, and she imagined that tears would make their color gleam even brighter. She tried to picture Calvin evilly dropping banana peels around for people to slip and die on. She could sort of see it, but not really. Was Calvin the *devilish* type? She guessed she didn't really know.

"Do you know if Chrissie White is related to Garland White? The political lobbyist?" Benny asked suddenly.

"Um, I dunno, possibly," Virginia said, wishing she had a pair of sunglasses. The sun was bright, and she felt like a dork squinting and shielding her eyes with her hand. "I know she's from Washington, DC. Her family only lives here part of the year, which is why they dumped her at Winship. Her dad has this gorgeous mansion in Brookhaven, but it just sits there empty. Meanwhile, she has to live in the Boarders. Isn't that totally depressing?"

Benny put his phone into his pocket and sat at the edge of the wicker chair. He looked serious. Benny always looked serious, but was managing to look even more so than usual. Virginia sat up in her chair.

"Okay, listen. We need to change our approach here. I'm giving you lead on this case."

"Huh? What does that mean?"

"It means you're in charge. On a *probational* basis," he stressed. "You've been ahead of me on this from the beginning. Just keep going. Find the caddie. And focus on Calvin. Find out everything about his medical condition. Marfan syndrome, I think it's called?"

"Wait, whoa, hold on. You want me to do this *by myself*?"

"Not by yourself. I'm here for whatever you need. But I have some stuff I need to attend to."

"Stuff like *what*?" Virginia asked incredulously.

"It's . . . a personal thing."

Virginia balked at him. *Personal?* She felt the familiar itch to wrangle the goods from him immediately. In the past, moments like these had been her reason for living. She loved getting juicy stuff out of people. She'd even created an entire website devoted to reporting and discussing Winship goings-on. But at a certain point she'd gotten tired of everyone's business, and tired of herself for being obsessed with it. She'd looked at her life and realized she'd inadvertently developed a reputation as a brainless gossip-mongerer. That's not who she was anymore. Except actually maybe it was. Because right now she wanted to know what Benny's "personal thing" was so badly she thought she might implode.

Benny was rambling on, "Try to get a copy of Calvin's science expo presentation. You'll need to study it. But be careful! If he senses that you're onto him, there could be another 'crazy accident.' Are you paying attention? Do you need to write this down?"

"You seriously think Calvin planted that banana," Virginia said.

"I think it's a strong possibility. He's already demon-strated an ambiguous sense of ethics. He didn't hesitate to lead you to the evidence on Trevor's phone despite being *legally bound* to secrecy. He's playing a game."

"No he's not. He just wanted to help me because—because he *likes* me." She hadn't really intended to tell Benny that part. But he was annoying her, so it served him right. She watched his reaction. He froze for a second, barely perceptively. Then he said, "Well—well, good. Keep him liking you. It'll make it easier to investigate him. In fact"—his voice cracked slightly—"if he really likes you, maybe he'll violate his nondisclosure. Just get him to tell you what happened that night with Craig."

"Shouldn't we figure it out ourselves?" Virginia said.

"This *is* figuring it out ourselves. We use what we can use. Calvin likes you? Use it."

Virginia shook her head. "I don't want to do that."

"Why not?"

She shrugged. "I'm not running to Calvin just because we hit a snag. He'll think I'm an idiot."

Benny shifted uncomfortably. "Okay, well, the goal is to solve the mystery, not to impress Calvin Harker. . . ."

Neither of them looked at each other. The silence between them stretched out awkwardly. Laughter echoed from a distant corner of the club.

"Are you going to the fundraiser tonight?" Virginia finally asked, changing the subject.

"What fundraiser?"

"The one at Trevor's house. It's a silent auction, and all the money goes to help DeAndre with his medical bills. Everyone's gonna be there."

As usual, it seemed Benny was the last to know. He never understood how Virginia magically absorbed this information about where "everyone" was going to be on a given Saturday night.

"Craig Beaver might be there," she was saying, "since it's not on school grounds."

"Do you think Chrissie will be there?"

Virginia snorted.

"I just need to know for my thing," he said defensively.

"Uh-huh . . ." Virginia narrowed her eyes at him. Why wouldn't he tell her what his *thing* was? Was he trying to lose his virginity or something? Chrissie was kind of famous for being a huge slut. Maybe Benny had seen her boobs on Trevor's phone and decided it was time to become a man. Maybe he'd programmed his Google alert for sex tips.

"What's so funny?"

Virginia couldn't stop laughing. "Oh, Benny!" she said, sighing. Then she casually reached out her hand. "Give me your phone and I'll call Chrissie and ask if she's coming tonight."

Benny hesitated. He hated other people touching his phone. "Just give me the number," he said. Virginia gave him a second to realize it was a terrible idea to call Chrissie

White out of nowhere like a fifth grader with a crush. Sure enough, after a moment he passed her the phone.

Virginia knew she had approximately two seconds to do what she needed to do without Benny getting suspicious. And two seconds was already pushing it since she wasn't 100 percent adept with phones. She quickly located his "alerts" app and pressed. She couldn't believe she was doing this. This was so *not* the new and improved Virginia. But whatever, she was doing it. It was driving her insane that Benny wouldn't tell her what his "thing" was. She was vice president of Mystery Club! She was entitled to know! At least that was what she told herself as she quickly scanned the alerts while pretending to dial the number for Chrissie's room.

"It's ringing," she lied. Her heart pounded. The alerts all seemed to be news items involving the governor and some e-mail scandal. *Yawn!* It definitely wasn't worth breaking a six-month streak of minding her own business if the goods were going to be this boring. But what did she expect, really? It was Benny.

Virginia closed the app and handed the phone back to Benny. "She didn't pick up." She made a point of maintaining eye contact with him as he slid the phone back into his pocket. Benny had told her once that people avoided eye contact when they were lying or being devious.

Why was a bunch of political news such a big secret? Virginia felt offended that he didn't think she deserved to know. Though probably not as offended as Benny would be if he ever found out she'd just deliberately invaded his privacy. The idea made her stomach twist with anxiety.

Maybe I shouldn't have done that, she thought. *Oh well, whatever.* There was no point feeling guilty unless she got caught. And she'd been smooth; Benny was gazing at the golf course, being his normal, deep-in-thought self. Virginia still couldn't decide if the gambit had been worth it, though. The alerts weren't about sex or Chrissie or anything remotely juicy. Maybe she'd missed something? She wished she could have his phone back. That was the thing about snooping on people—once you started, it was hard to stop.

"You'll be there tonight? At Trevor's?" Benny asked her.

"Yeah, I'll be there. I'll get a ride with someone. You gonna wear that outfit?"

"If you give me five hundred dollars."

Virginia looked at him. Was he serious? Benny was always serious. But there was the tiniest little grin on his face. He was *joking.* It was such a shock that Virginia almost didn't know how to respond.

"Well, okay!" she said finally. She felt a rush, calling his bluff. "You're on."

Benny scoffed.

"I'm serious! I'll give you five hundred dollars if you wear that tonight. Including the contacts."

Benny narrowed his eyes. "You don't have five hundred dollars."

"You have no idea what I have." As soon as the words were out of her mouth, Virginia was so impressed with herself she wanted to scream. It was probably the sexiest thing she'd ever said in her life. She wanted this weird conversation to go on forever.

Benny's phone buzzed and he fished it out of his pocket. He read the screen. "We have to go meet my mom in ten minutes."

Wow. No sentence in the English language felt more like a bucket of ice water than "We have to go meet my mom in ten minutes." Before leaving the sunny patio, Virginia took a moment to cement the image in her memory—Benny *smiling*—in case it never happened again.

The Harkers' house, 5:30 p.m.

All he wanted to do was to look at something beautiful. But he was trapped in a locked, windowless room with only a calculus textbook, a laptop with no Internet, and a copy of *Moby Dick*.

It wouldn't be so bad if he could escape using his imagination—close his eyes and ascend to some fantasy world like Narnia or the Land of Oz. But Calvin didn't have the greatest imagination. It was something he'd been forced to accept about himself. He envied artists and their power to summon fantastic, alien landscapes to their mind's eye. Calvin had a hard time seeing things that he hadn't actually *seen*. How did they do it? If only he knew their secret.

Calvin had been grounded before, but not to this extreme. At first it had been a normal grounding: no leaving the house, in bed by ten thirty. But when his dad had realized he was just getting stoned and gazing out the window instead of doing homework, he'd locked him in the basement with only his computer and his textbooks. Calvin had happily watched Enya music videos on YouTube for a while—all waterfalls and falling leaves and otherworldly harmonies—until his dad had cut the Internet connection, leaving him with nothing.

"DAD?" Calvin yelled. "MOM?"

No answer.

They were probably at Beau Ideal, where his dad played golf and his mom Zumba'd within an inch of her life every Saturday. He was pretty sure it was illegal to lock your kid in a room and leave the house, but at least his mom had slipped a sandwich under the crack of the door before they'd gone. He wasn't sure what he was supposed to do if he had to go to the bathroom.

"CAMILLAAAA?" he yelled for his sister. But if his parents were at the club, Camilla probably was too. She made no secret that she thought her little brother was weird and difficult and deserved all the maltreatment he got. He'd never counted on her to save him. He jiggled the door handle futilely.

Think, he commanded himself, looking around the room. *How are you going to get out of here?* He was supposedly the smartest kid in the tristate area. That bit of data had been shoved down his throat since the age of seven. He'd aced every test he'd ever been given. Surely he could figure out a way to get out of a locked room. But he felt irritable and short-fused. The pot he'd smoked had worn off hours ago, and he hated being sober. He hated the boring prison of his brain, which was only good for differential calculus and solving stochastic systems.

Most of his stash of mind-altering substances was gone. His dad had hired a former police detective to search Calvin's room and trash everything he found. Calvin had known it was coming, so he'd tried to give some of it away at the science expo; he couldn't bear to see all those stupendous chemicals going to waste. And it had been worth it to see Winn Davis staring into his cheerleader girlfriend's eyes like they contained the secrets of the universe. And seeing what happened to Trevor had been even more fascinating. . . . There was still some pot and some mescaline hidden in an Academic Decathlon trophy in the living room display case, but that may as well be on Mars if he was trapped down here.

Calvin examined the doorknob. It was an old house, and the doorknobs were white marble, with iron locks opened by skeleton keys. He looked around the room for some sort of tool he could use to bash the entire lock off the door. It was a barbaric approach but a potentially effective one. Unfortunately, his copy of *Moby Dick* was a paperback. There was no lamp in the room, only a bare light bulb screwed into the ceiling. The desk chair was large and unwieldy.

His eyes landed on his laptop. It contained his *Moby Dick* essay for AP English, plus about two hundred poems he hadn't backed up yet. If he destroyed the computer, they would all be gone. It made him want to laugh and cry at the same time.

Fuck. You, Calvin said to the universe. But if this was the sacrifice it required, fine. The universe could have his poems. He would do whatever it took to be free.

He grabbed the laptop and brought it crashing down on the lock. The computer cracked, but the lock remained. He slammed it down again and again, until his heart began to pound from the exertion.

Careful, he told himself. He took a breath, waiting for his heart rate to normalize. It was dangerous to overdo physical stuff with his condition. He'd been born with an enlarged aorta that put him at extreme risk for heart failure. The only sport he was allowed to play was golf. Calvin knew his boundaries; he'd spent most of his life testing them. If he pushed too far, it could be deadly. And a second heart transplant was not an option, Calvin had long resolved. The first transplant had saved his life but left him physically weaker. A second would weaken him even further, and not just physically this time—emotionally and psychologically and mentally and spiritually. He could not survive another year spent in beds in and out of hospitals.

He smashed the laptop again. It was falling apart, battered pieces skittering across the floor. Two hundred poems: gone. But the nails of the lock had begun to come loose. A few more whacks, and it fell to the floor with a clang. The door swayed open.

He was free.

The Boarders, 6:30 p.m.

"What do you mean, there's no money?" Virginia smashed the clunky eighties-looking cordless phone to her ear, certain she must have misheard.

On the other end of the line, a crackly voice said, "Your mother hasn't made a deposit in two months. There's barely enough to cover your spring tuition right now. I can't give you anything."

"But I need five hundred dollars!" she shouted into the phone.

"Is it an emergency?"

"Yes! Well, no. But call my mom and tell her to make a deposit!"

"I don't know where she is."

"Then call Esteban!"

"Ginny . . ."

Virginia paced back and forth across the empty common room. She opened the refrigerator, hoping to miraculously find something worth eating in there. But there was only a can of reduced-fat whipped cream and Mrs. Morehouse's gross yellow buttermilk. She slammed the door shut, getting more frustrated by the minute. Daniel Wham, her family's accountant (called Dan-Wam by Virginia since she was ten years old), was being unbelievably annoying. There was no money in the account? Get some! He didn't know where her mother was? Find her! Life wasn't that hard!

"Have you not been getting my e-mails?" Dan asked.

Virginia thought about all the e-mails from him that she'd sent directly to the trash. Why should she have to pay attention to e-mails from an elderly accountant? She was fifteen years old. Adults needed to get their shit together and leave kids out of it.

"If your mother doesn't make a deposit soon . . . Let's just say . . . the bills are . . . mounting."

Virginia hated how Dan couldn't say a sentence without adding ten dramatic pauses. "Well, where the hell is Esteban?"

"Ginny . . . you know I can't tell you that."

"If he knew how badly you were treating me right now, he'd kill you."

There was silence on the other end of the line. Finally Dan said, "If you hear from your mother, please have her contact me. It really is . . . quite urgent."

"Okay, okay. Bye, Dan-Wam."

"Bye-bye, Ginny."

Virginia slammed the phone back on the receiver. This was not good. She actually needed more than five hundred dollars; she needed *nine* hundred dollars. Five hundred for Benny (Would he actually go through with the dare? Virginia didn't know, but it would be incredibly embarrassing if he did and she didn't have the cash), and four hundred to pay back Min-Jun so he couldn't extort her into working for his gross and scary porn ring. Plus a few twenties for whatever crap they'd be auctioning off at the fundraiser tonight. Money hadn't exactly been *flowing* for a while now, but she'd always been able to count on ol' Dan-Wam when she really needed something. Now what was she supposed to do?

I'll think about it later, she decided. Right now she needed to change her clothes. She hadn't done laundry since the science expo, which meant her go-to sweater still had lobster paste all over it. She put on Zaire's gold skirt and paired it with a white Polo, which didn't really work, but whatever. She'd been getting too obsessed with clothes lately anyway. It was important to look like crap every once in a while to make sure your personality was still the best thing about you.

There was a knock on her door. Virginia opened it. It was Chrissie, wearing a tiny black top that made her boobs pop out, and a pink add-a-pearl necklace around her neck. The idea of Benny losing his virginity to her made Virginia want to laugh for ten hours. Benny would probably lose his virginity to a Tibetan monk while checking his Google alerts.

"You ready? Corn Flakes is giving us a ride."

"No, not Corn Flakes!" Virginia moaned. "We'll all smell like pizza if we go in his car!"

Corn Flakes was the Domino's delivery guy. He was pasty white with blond cornrows, and everyone called him Corn Flakes because he had a dandruff problem. He was in love with Lindsay Bean, and always got her free pizza toppings and drove her friends around, even though he was like twenty years old and should have better things to do. He claimed to be pre-med at Georgia State, but it was pretty obvious he was just a townie loser who would probably be delivering Domino's till he died.

Outside, it was already dark. Autumn had not been particularly impressive that year. Most of the leaves had gone straight from ugly yellow to drab brown. Lindsay Bean was being pushed into the front seat of Corn Flakes's run-down delivery car, shooting furious looks at Chrissie that clearly said, *I can't believe you're making me do this.* Virginia piled into the back with Chrissie and two other girls from the Boarders, both wearing tight black skirts and spaghetti strap tops. Virginia used to do this all the time before she joined Mystery Club—cram herself into a car with whoever was going anywhere, usually a squealing group of girls heading to the mall or some church youth group's bowling night. She'd kind of forgotten how fun it was. They pretended Lindsay and Corn Flakes were their mom and dad, and screamed "ARE WE THERE YET?" every two minutes. They made predictions about who would get their

butt squeezed by Trevor's dad, who was a notorious horn-
dog. No one wore seat belts, which felt thrilling, and they
laughed at Corn Flakes's dumb dad jokes ("Don't make me
pull over and spank you!") and screamed whenever they
spotted anyone remotely weird-looking or old in a neigh-
boring car.

The backseat was a tangle of long legs, arms wrapped
around each other, and boobs nearly popping out left and
right. Virginia was half sitting on Chrissie's lap, straddling one of her thighs. *Min-Jun would love this,* she
thought. It made her feel smug, but also sort of gross and
self-conscious.

"Settle down back there, or no dessert!" Lindsay shouted,
making them shriek with laughter.

"I think Mommy and Daddy need a little grown-up
time away from the kids," Corn Flakes said, and they all
groaned.

Cars were lined all the way down Tuxedo Park, the
ritziest and most ostentatiously named neighborhood in
Atlanta. Girls in black dresses and boys in blue blazers
walked from their cars toward Trevor's house, a white mansion at the center of a sprawling green lawn.

"Bye, cupcake!" Corn Flakes called to Lindsay as she
stepped out of the car, clearly way too into the fantasy of
being married.

"Bye, Dad!" Virginia and Chrissie shouted. They
slammed the door shut and waved as Corn Flakes drove

away to deliver shitty Domino's to the people of Atlanta. The girls sniffed each other to make sure they didn't smell like pizza, and Lindsay spritzed everyone with Clinique Happy perfume. Usually Virginia preferred to go to parties alone like a devastating *femme fatale*. But it was fun to be with a group for once and feed off everyone's excitement. She'd almost forgotten the dismal cause of the night, which was that DeAndre was in the hospital and his family couldn't afford to pay for it.

Oh well, she thought. *You can't take the fun out of fundraiser!*

From the outside, the Cheeks' house looked like a palace. Every window was lit, and the driveway was lined with enchanting strings of tiny lights. As they approached the front steps, the door flung open and a trio of girls stumbled out. It was Constance, Yu Yan, and Beth. They looked shaken and slightly hysterical.

"Oh my god, don't go in there!" Constance shouted, slamming the door closed behind her.

Virginia screeched. This night was getting better and better. "Why not? What's happening? Tell me tell me tell me!"

"Fuck you, Virginia."

Whoa. Virginia felt like she'd been slapped. Constance was one of those prissy girls who never cursed. What the hell was up her ass?

"Whatever, go in if you want," Constance was saying. "Actually, you'll probably love it. *Your Highness.*" She curtsied mockingly and then clomped down the steps on her ugly tan high heels. Beth and Yu Yan scurried after her.

Virginia looked at Chrissie. "What is this 'Your Highness' thing?"

Chrissie shrugged but wouldn't look her in the eyes.

Inside the house, there was an enormous roar of shouting. Only the door stood between them and whatever was inside.

Virginia opened it.

Benny's house, 7:30 p.m.

She investigated me. She investigated me. The words played over and over in Benny's mind. His whole body felt wired.

Virginia hadn't called Chrissie at the club. He'd known it the second she'd picked up his phone. It's not that she hadn't been smooth—she'd actually been very smooth. If he hadn't been Benny and she hadn't been Virginia, he never would have known. But she definitely had not called Chrissie. She'd gone into his Google alerts. She'd *investigated* him. The weirdest part was that he didn't even feel angry. He felt . . . impressed.

Focus, he commanded himself. He was on his laptop trying to fill in a spreadsheet of data from his Google alerts. But he could barely concentrate. His mind was going in five thousand directions. Benny wasn't normally prone to hyperbole, but it really felt like five thousand equally urgent thoughts were clamoring for his attention.

Seventeen Google alerts. The aeronautics plant in Waycross. Was Chrissie's father Garland White? Was Virginia serious about the five hundred dollars? Should he really wear this outfit or should he change? How much money did he need for the auction? Hundreds? How much were kids expected to spend on some crappy vase or a steak dinner for two? Benny's mind was chaos, underscored by one incessant thought: *She investigated me. She investigated me.*

"Whatcha doin'?" It was his dad's nurse, Rodrigo. He came to the house every other day to help with Mr. Flax. Benny was so used to his presence that it felt like Rodrigo was almost a member of the household. He pulled up a chair next to Benny at the dining room table. Benny's mom and grandma were running errands, making it one of the rare evenings where he was alone with his dad and Rodrigo, just the men. Mr. Flax was in the living room messing with a plastic piggy bank Rodrigo had brought for his physical therapy. Benny couldn't bear to watch. It was too depressing to see his dad's fingers fumbling with a single coin when once they'd circuited entire aircraft panels.

"I'm trying to get organized," Benny answered tersely, not needing another distraction.

Rodrigo didn't go away. "You okay, man?"

"Mm-hm." The information from the alerts was still in disarray. It seemed that the Waycross plant had actually been slated for closure two years ago, when Mr. Flax was still their principal consultant. But the closure had been delayed, which for some reason had caused the feud between the governor and Garland White to explode. Benny didn't even know why he was obsessing over this. Just because it was tangentially connected to his dad? This was stupid.

"I like your hair," Rodrigo was saying. "Shiny."

"Thanks," Benny said. Then, abruptly, he slammed his laptop shut and dropped his head on the table. "Oh my god," he moaned.

"Whoa, whoa," Rodrigo said. "I think you need to chill a minute."

Benny buried his face in his arm. "I have to go to a party in thirty minutes and I don't know what to wear."

"What's wrong with what you've got on? It's very Ivy League, very Yale Law School."

"It's more complicated than that." Benny sat up. Was he seriously about to unload his girl problems on his dad's in-home nurse? ". . . Okay. So there's this girl. I . . . *like* her. I don't know. She hates me. Whatever. She thinks I'm a nerd. I *am* a nerd. Whatever. I don't know."

"Whoaaaaaa. Here, take a sip of this." Rodrigo held out his bourbon.

Benny balked. "That's illegal. I'm only fifteen."

"It's cool, Ben. Just take a nice sip. I'm not getting you drunk, I promise. I know you're a responsible kid."

Benny eyed the glass, considering. Then he took it. He was so used to the smell of bourbon, he imagined he knew exactly how it would taste. But he hadn't anticipated the warm burn down his throat. It sent an instant buzz to his head—not unpleasant.

"Okay, let's start over," Rodrigo said. "So there's a girl."

Benny nodded. "So I wore this outfit today, sort of as a costume. And the girl said, 'I'll give you five hundred dollars if you wear that for real to the party tonight.' She was *daring* me. And she was serious. I *think* she was serious."

"Well, you should call her bluff! That would be a badass move. Like, James Bond level."

"Okay. Okay. But here's the thing . . ." Benny felt a tad spaced-out from the swig of bourbon—again, not unpleasant. "Earlier in the day, she'd said this little thing about people's dignity being for sale. And I got the impression that she, like, didn't respect people who were 'for sale.' So maybe she's . . . *testing* me."

"Hmmm . . . I see your quandary." Rodrigo tapped his finger on his glass for a minute. Benny glanced at the living room, where his dad appeared to have fallen asleep. It was hard not to feel like this was one of those touching father-son moments from a Folgers commercial, except in a strange casting decision the "father" role was being played by a twenty-eight-year-old Hispanic man.

"Well, Ben, I guess what you have to decide is, are you for sale?"

Benny thought about it. "No. No, I am not."

"Okay, then. There's your answer."

"Well, maybe I am? Just for tonight?"

Rodrigo cocked his eyebrow, and Benny knew exactly what he was saying:

Just for tonight, or just for her?

Trevor's house, 8:00 p.m.

Craig Beaver scanned the room, looking for anything that might be funny to put on his head. It was a skill he had, making ordinary things funny. He even had his own YouTube channel called "U Craig Me Up!" where he comically reviewed everyday objects. "I give 'the tampon' one star. Not a good product," he'd say, pretending to be frustrated while using a tampon to stir coffee. Craig had been a nobody at Winship for years, until one fateful day Trevor Cheek had posted one of his videos on Facebook. Then suddenly everyone was watching them, earning Craig the coveted position of School Funny Guy. At this point, Craig pretty much lived to make Trevor laugh. Trevor dominated the school, especially the guys; if he laughed, all the guys laughed with him.

The chips bowl sort of resembled a Martian's helmet. Craig could definitely work with that. But unfortunately, it was full of chips, and it was way too early in the night to be dumping food around and making a scene. He'd wait till Mr. and Mrs. Cheek went to bed for that one. For now, he grabbed Lindsay Bean from behind and nestled his chin on her shoulder.

"Hey, Trevor! Take our picture! We're a two-headed monster! Three-headed, if ya know what I mean. . . ."

"Ew! Get off me, Craig!" Lindsay screamed, trying to squirm away. But Craig held on to her tightly. Across the room, Trevor shouted back, "Lost my phone, man!"

Lindsay extricated herself from Craig and elbowed him in the ribs.

Bitch, Craig thought as he watched her walk away, her amazing ass jiggling in her tight skirt. He looked around. What else could he do that would be funny? And when were the non-bitchy girls going to get there?

Wait, he thought suddenly. *Trevor lost his phone?*

Craig pushed through the crowded room toward the dining room.

"Trevor," he said, squeezing into the conversation. Trevor had taken Polaroid pictures of all the girls at the party, and was spreading them out on the immense dining room table. "Trevor. You lost your phone?"

"Huh? Yeah. You wanna be in charge of this shit? I need a BEEEEER!" The guys around the table cheered. "Beer" was the magic word.

"Okay, except, well, did you delete the"—Craig leaned in—"*you know what?*"

Trevor shrugged. "Fuck if I know."

"Trevor, seriously—"

But Trevor was ignoring him completely now. That was the thing about Trevor: the guy liked to laugh—the guy *only* liked to laugh. If you tried to get remotely serious with him, he put a wall up and blamed you for being a bummer.

"Trevor, come on—"

"Craig, if you don't get off my dick, I'm gonna take a red pill and kill you."

Take a red pill? What the hell did that mean? Sometimes Craig felt like a long-suffering wife, trying to read her husband's mind so she could kowtow to his moods. He couldn't afford to be on Trevor's bad side; Craig was smart enough to know that he lived or died by Trevor's social patronage.

Shit, Craig thought. Trevor didn't give a fuck about his lost phone. Trevor didn't give a fuck about anything! But Craig gave *quite* the fuck. His mom and dad plus several lawyers had rammed it down his throat that if anyone ever found out what they'd done on that golf course, his life would be over. Hundreds of thousands of dollars had been spent to assure that the matter would never see the light of day. But all the money in the world meant nothing if Trevor had lost his fucking phone!

He went to the kitchen and ladled himself a very full cup of Chatham Artillery Punch, the most diabolical and drunk-making alcoholic concoction ever devised by man.

"Thirsty?" Mrs. Cheek chirped, giggling as she took a tray of hors d'oeuvres out of the oven. Craig considered Trevor's mom to be one of those amazing Southern women who managed to stay completely fuckable without being fake about it. She wasn't face-lifted or Pilates-ified or yoga-fied; she was a pink-cheeked, big-chested, natural woman from whom Craig would definitely accept a hand job if the opportunity ever presented itself. That would show Trevor. *You think you rule this place? I fucked your mom!*

"Yes ma'am," he said, downing his cup and filling it again. "Nectar of the gods!"

"Well, you deserve it, Craigie." She rubbed the peach fuzz on his shaved head. "You've had a bad week."

Yeah, and it just got worse, Craig thought. It wasn't fair that he was getting singled out for what happened. Trevor had been just as much a part of it! The whole team had! But Craig was expected to dutifully fall on his sword for them, like the doomed and barefooted Confederates who sacrificed themselves to the Cause long after they'd known it was lost.

At first it had felt like an honor, being offered up for the good of the team. But suddenly Craig saw himself for who he really was: a patsy sucker. They would destroy his life, buy him a nice "You've been fucked" bottle of Woodford Reserve (which he'd be expected to share with them, of course), and then they'd go on with their lives and never think of him again.

No, Craig decided right then and there. If he went down, he'd take the team with him. He'd take the entire school! Their futures, their dreams, their comfy, consequence-free lives. He'd take their fucking souls.

Trevor's driveway, 8:30 p.m.

Benny and his mother squinted at the house from the car. It was possibly the biggest house Benny had ever seen in real life. It was obscenely large for a family of four. But it was undeniably beautiful.

"These people need your Bar Mitzvah money?" Mrs. Flax said, pursing her lips in that way she had that drove Benny insane.

"Mom, it's not for *them*. It's for DeAndre Bell. He's a scholarship student."

"And you're not?"

"It's different. DeAndre is . . . *black*." Benny felt horrendous saying it, especially given that the richest student to ever attend Winship in history was probably Zaire Bollo, also black. But it was the easiest way to get his mother off his case.

"And he's the one who got impaled by a deer," Benny explained further. "It's for his medical bills."

"Oh," Mrs. Flax said. "Well, you're very generous." She still sounded slightly suspicious.

"I'll call you when it's over." Benny got out of the car and smoothed back his hair. Then he walked up the long driveway. He could hear a lot of noise coming from inside the house. The front door was slightly ajar. He pushed it open.

Oh my god.

Nothing about the scene before him resembled a fundraiser. Benny had expected banquet chairs arranged in rows, a collection of ugly antiques and gift cards for massages, polite chitchat, and sparkling apple cider. But as soon as he stepped inside, he realized this wasn't a "fundraiser." This was . . . *a party*. Benny Flax was at a real-life, boy-girl under-age drinking high school *party*. He looked around, slightly in shock. Where were the chaperones? Where were Trevor's parents?

Mrs. Cheek appeared, as if summoned by Benny's mind. She fluttered across the room to where a group of boys were drinking beer around a table. She snatched up their bottles, and Benny felt relieved. But then it became clear that she wasn't taking their drinks away, merely setting them on coasters! First Rodrigo and now Trevor's mom—what was with these grown-ups aiding and abetting the consumption of alcohol by teenagers?

"SCOOBY'S HERE!" someone in the living room shouted, and soon everyone was shouting, "SCOOBY-DOO! SCOOBY-DOO! SCOOBY-DOO!"

Benny froze in the doorway. Never in his life had he so powerfully wished to disappear into a cloud of atomic dust particles. The chanting lasted about ten excruciating seconds, until thankfully, the door opened behind Benny and a new guest's arrival was raucously heralded. Benny took the opportunity to duck into the hubbub in the dining room. A huge crowd was packed around the table.

"Need a Scooby Snack, Scooby?" Skylar Jones shouted at him, holding up a chip overflowing with dip. Benny took the chip, not knowing what else to do. "Nice hair!"

"Thanks." Benny's hair was still shiny and straight. The rest of him, however, was back to his regularly programmed self: glasses, maroon sweater, plain brown pants. In the end, he'd decided the preppy outfit was too much of a gamble. What if Virginia thought he was a dweeb for taking her dare seriously? What if she thought he was a sellout? There were just too many uncertainties.

He looked around for her fluffy blond head. He was so nervous to see her that his palms were sweating. He'd know instantly whether he'd made the correct choice as soon as he saw her face. *Where is she?* It took Benny a second to realize that the crowd was made up entirely of boys; there were no girls in the room at all. Benny was startled by a huge cheer as Trevor pushed his way through the group.

"Last one, dickheads!" Trevor yelled. He slapped a sheet of paper on the table, which was already filled with sheets, each stapled to a Polaroid picture of a Winship girl. All around Benny, guys were pledging their names and amounts of money, sometimes returning to the same Polaroid over and over to outbid someone else. Some of the pictures had elicited only one or two bids. Others had ten or twelve.

They're auctioning the girls, Benny realized. It felt like the Wall Street trading floor, with numbers being shouted left and right by boys with fistfuls of cash.

And then he saw it. Virginia's face on one of the Polaroids. She'd clearly been taken by surprise by the camera—her expression was amused but slightly bewildered. Under her name at least twenty bids had been placed, and the amount had reached $255.

Jesus. Since when was Virginia so popular? The only other name that had that many bids was Brittany Montague.

"Do the girls know you're doing this?" Benny shouted to Skylar over the noisy din. But Skylar wasn't paying attention. He was in a mock fistfight with Sophat Tiang over Lindsay Bean's bidding sheet, yelling, "Dude, stab me in the face why don't you! You know I only brought sixty bucks!"

Benny scanned Virginia's sheet. Most of the names were guys Benny barely knew—football players and seniors. Why were they interested in Virginia? One name was written six separate times, each time increasing the bid by at least fifty dollars. Calvin Harker.

Calvin's here? Benny looked around, but didn't see his towering figure in the crowd.

A pair of seniors pushed themselves to the table, shoving Benny aside. One of them bent over Virginia's bidding sheet and scrawled his name and raised the amount to $275. Then he high-fived his friend, shouting, "Long live the Queen!"

"CHICK-FIL-A IN THE HOUSE!" a voice boomed from the front door. Trevor Cheek's dad entered with an enormous platter of chicken strips, and was met with a cheer so loud it felt like the voices were inside Benny's own head. Suddenly he felt very overheated. He pulled at the neck of his turtleneck sweater, wishing he could drink a gallon of water. He needed to find Virginia. He needed to escape this den of barbarians.

He squeezed out of the dining room, not knowing where to go. He wanted some air, but he couldn't go outside for fear that when he came back in, everyone would chant "SCOOBY-DOO" at him again.

He went down a wide, dimly lit hallway, peering in the various rooms to see if any were less insane than the living room and dining room. In one room some guys were playing video games on a massive TV. In another, a group of girls were shrieking over photos from the Cheeks' wedding album. Where was Virginia? She really needed to get a cell phone. He resolved to finally broach the awkward subject with her as soon as he located her. But first he needed to collect himself.

Finally Benny found a room that seemed empty. It was dark and quiet and filled with masculine furniture. He closed the heavy door behind him, blocking the noise. Benny chose a leather sofa and sat down gratefully, closing his eyes.

I am calm however and whenever I am attacked. I have no attachment to life or death.

It was an aikido saying that Benny found relaxing. He opened his eyes. As they adjusted to the dim light, he saw that about twenty pairs of dead eyes were staring at him.

Every surface of the wall was covered in taxidermied deer heads. Benny's body went cold. This wasn't a room—it was a tomb.

Then he noticed a languid tendril of smoke curling in the air. Benny followed its trail to a cigarette balanced in an ashtray. He wasn't alone. A low, growling voice spoke:

"Do you have the password?"

The upstairs parlor, 9:20 p.m.

Every surface in the room was covered in lace doilies and porcelain Cinderella figurines. There had to be at least nine hundred. The story was that Trevor's mom was obsessed with Cinderella, because she'd grown up in a trailer park and was so poor her family didn't even have soap. But then she'd met Trevor's dad at a Hooters, and he'd married her and made her the richest woman in Atlanta. A real-life fairy tale! Except Virginia wasn't buying it. The story made her think about all the other girls in the trailer park. Was Mrs. Cheek just going to let them rot?

Virginia pulled out Trevor's phone from her purse. *Did you delete the . . . you know what?* She'd been right behind Craig Beaver when he'd said it. She'd been trailing him from the moment she got in the house until all the girls had been herded upstairs. It hadn't occurred to her to check if any photos had been deleted. She tapped on the camera app. *Recently deleted files.*

"Brittany's up to three hundred dollars!" someone was

squealing. In the corner a group of girls were huddled around a phone.

"Y'all, stop!" Brittany yelled at them. No one was supposed to know how much anyone was going for. The twins had specifically arranged it so that the boys would be downstairs and the girls would be upstairs while the bidding occurred, so that no one would get their feelings hurt by finding out who among them had gotten more bids than others. But Alexis Zeist was making her boyfriend text her photos of the bidding sheets, which she was now showing to everyone.

Virginia suppressed her curiosity over the bidding sheets. She was the *lead* on the golf case now. She needed to focus on her investigative duties, not on which Montague twin was racking up more money downstairs.

Most of the deleted photos were blurry pictures of dogs. Virginia swiped through about twenty of them, which were followed by blurry pictures of gross deer carcasses.

"Virginia, oh my god. Calvin Harker bid on you like eight million times."

Virginia's face instantly grew hot. *Calvin was here?* She wanted to know more, but Brittany snatched Alexis's phone away and threw it in a gold-lacquered bureau. The dozen Cinderella figurines on top quaked as she shoved the drawer shut.

Virginia barely knew what she was doing there, cooped up in a princessy room with a bunch of idiots, allowing herself to be auctioned off like a cow. It was the twins' idea to have all the girls do body shots because they were DeAndre's "favorite thing in the world." Virginia knew what a body shot was; it was when a girl takes her shirt off and lets a guy drink tequila out of her navel. She'd never done it before, partly because it seemed slutty, and partly because no one had ever asked her to. She wasn't sure if body shots matched her idea of herself. Did Virginia Leeds—woman of intrigue—do trashy body shots? But surely it wasn't trashy if it was for charity. And besides, it was her choice and she could do what she wanted. Except Virginia wondered how much that was really true. No one had actually asked her if she wanted to participate. Trevor had just taken her picture and the bidding had started, and now she would look like a prissy loser, like Constance Bouchelle, if she objected. Was it really a choice if you never had the chance to say no?

Virginia didn't feel like agonizing over it. She was having fun. She hadn't been to a decent party in months. She'd forgotten how Lindsay Bean got really mean when she was drunk and made fun of everyone. She'd forgotten how the cheerleaders were obsessed with Madonna, and how at a party even the most boring conversation could seem exciting, like whether pink or red lipstick made your teeth look whiter. And getting to investigate Craig all by herself was the cherry on top.

"You better be careful with Calvin," Chrissie slurred. She was sitting next to Virginia on a pink velvet settee.

Virginia was tired of Chrissie and was ready to hang out with someone else, but Chrissie was always pathetically clingy at parties until she got wasted enough to be an autonomous person.

"Excuse me?" Virginia said.

"His dick won't fit in you."

"Oh my god! Shut up! Ew!"

Chrissie shrugged. "It's gigantoid."

Virginia gaped at her. How the hell did Chrissie know Calvin's *endowment*? Had they hooked up or something? Virginia felt a surge of jealousy and annoyance. Chrissie was the most banal and predictable girl on the planet; why would Calvin hook up with her? Didn't he have standards?

Relax, she told herself. Chrissie was probably just guessing. Calvin was seven feet tall and had hands the size of dinner plates. So it followed that his member would be equally . . . *gigantoid.*

"Chrissie, you look like a booze hound," Lindsay Bean said loudly, and Chrissie's lip twitched like she was about to cry. It was true that Chrissie got the worst drunk eyes and started to resemble a sleepy, droopy-faced dog after about three Jell-O shots. She was definitely an effective advertisement for sobriety; when the tray of shots came Virginia's way, she passed.

"I drink sidecars," she explained. It wasn't exactly true. *One* time she'd had *a* sidecar, but whatever. Jell-O shots were for children, and she wanted the sidecar to be her signature drink.

She went back to Trevor's phone, swiping through more crappy deleted photos. She was starting to get bored, and wished Benny were there to do this part. Then she saw it.

Oh my god.

Virginia quickly covered the screen, glancing at Chrissie to make sure she hadn't seen it. Then she peeked at it again. She couldn't believe what she was seeing. She had to tell Benny. Now.

"Hey, where are you going?" Chrissie whined, grabbing Virginia arm.

Virginia twisted away. "I'll be right back."

She slipped out of the room, closing the door on the babbling chorus of girlish voices. Downstairs the boys were all shouting. Virginia peered over the banister of the immense staircase, searching for Benny, or for his preppy double. She didn't know which one to expect, or which one she wanted. If it was regular Benny, he'd be totally lost and square and she'd have to socially navigate him through the whole evening. She hated babysitting people at parties. But she didn't want to see his double, either, because she didn't have five hundred dollars, which would make her look like a phony bluffer. And because it was confusing. It's not like Virginia was gaga for preppy dudes; in fact, she avoided them. She'd dated *Skylar Jones*, for Christ's sake. Who had a *dreadlock*. But she liked Benny better without his mammoth glasses deflecting the twinkle in his eye that Virginia hadn't realized was there.

She spotted him. He was sort of wandering around in the hallway below, opening and closing doors like someone's lost kid. He looked completely out of place. He was wearing *maroon*.

Great, Virginia thought. She felt a flood of disappointment, but it quickly dissolved. What had she expected? It was Benny.

The parlor bathroom, 9:30 p.m.

Yasmin was hiding from the party and reading Wikipedia articles on her phone. The seat on the toilet was covered in a pink satin cushion, like it was a prissy throne instead of a big shit bowl. It was one of those bathrooms where nothing was functional. Lacy linens hung from the towel rack, which you obviously weren't supposed to touch or they would get wrinkled. The gold soap dish was full of shell-shaped soaps that you obviously weren't supposed to touch either or they would lose their delicate shape. Yasmin felt claustrophobic and oppressed. She wanted to go home. She'd already texted her dad and asked him to come pick her up.

The only reason she'd come to this ludicrous fundraiser at all was because it would look too suspicious if she didn't. She was being more or less investigated for attempted murder by that smarmy, butt-chinned detective, plus she was the *de facto* student body president now, which meant she had to show her face at school-related events. But she didn't feel like a president. She felt like an ugly nanny who'd been banished while the kids had fun.

If Yasmin were honest, the truth was that she'd banished herself. No one at the party had made fun of her or made her feel particularly unwelcome. In fact, everyone had cheered her name as she arrived. But she hadn't let any of the guys near her with that Polaroid camera, and as soon as the girls were herded upstairs, she'd shut herself in the bathroom. The entire scene was sexist and degrading. As if she'd ever let some slobbering guy fish tequila out of her navel with his tongue.

All of a sudden the bathroom door swung open. Brittany Montague sprang inside like a blond bouncy ball.

"Oh, sorry!" she said, realizing Yasmin was there. "Do you mind if I pee?"

Yasmin stood up. "Sure, sorry—"

Before Yasmin had time to even get out the door, Brittany had plopped down on the toilet and was peeing away. Then she started talking.

"Hey, you're super smart," she said. "Can I ask you a question?"

Yasmin stopped. She wasn't sure where to look. The floor? The ceiling? Was she supposed to make eye contact? She'd never had a conversation with someone while they were peeing before. It seemed like something only close friends or siblings did, of which Yasmin had neither.

"Um, okay," she said.

"I'm just sort of confused. Do guys like it better if you wait for marriage to have sex or if you go all the way? It's confusing because it seems like they want both. It's like, they really want you to have sex with them, but if you do, they'll blame you for being dirty and not love you anymore. But if you don't have sex with them, they won't love you either! So what do you do?"

"I'm not that variety of smart," Yasmin said. "I don't know anything about boys."

"Oh, really?" Brittany seemed sincerely surprised. "But you're so pretty."

Yasmin gawked at her. Was Brittany making fun of her? That didn't seem likely. The Montague twins were famously nice, and of the two of them, Brittany was the even nicer one. People didn't see them as individuals, but it was obvious to Yasmin that they were different. Brittany was a little dumber, but also more genuine and incapable of lying. *Brittany Montague thinks I'm pretty?* And on top of that, Brittany thought that being pretty meant you had all the answers about boys? If that were true, Brittany could just look in the mirror and ask herself.

"I'm not pretty," Yasmin said, dumbfounded.

Brittany laughed like Yasmin was crazy. "Yes you are! And you're so lucky to be exotic."

"You can't call people exotic," Yasmin said. "It's racist."

Brittany frowned. "Oh. I'm sorry! You're just so interesting-looking. And your hair is so shiny."

Brittany took a strand of Yasmin's black hair between her fingers. Then, with no warning, she buried her whole face in Yasmin's neck.

"Mmmmm! And you smell so good! Like spices!"

Yasmin froze. Her entire being felt jolted, like the high-voltage electric arc from the science expo was moving through her body. Brittany was inhaling deeply and sort of hugging her. Obviously she was drunk; that was her excuse. But what was Yasmin's?

Then Yasmin's phone buzzed, and Brittany jumped away. "Make room for Jesus!" she chirped, and then laughed at her own random joke.

"My dad's here . . . ," Yasmin said, now wishing she hadn't texted him. The bathroom didn't feel stuffy and suffocating anymore. Brittany made all those stupid little soaps and towels seem suddenly cute and pretty.

What is happening to my brain? Yasmin thought.

"Oh, that's too bad. We could have hung out. I'm so scared of all those boys. Don't tell anyone I said that, okay?"

"I won't," Yasmin swore. Who did she even have to tell?

"See you Monday!" Brittany said, giving Yasmin a little boop on the nose. Yasmin was so baffled she barely managed to say "See ya" back to her. Brittany bounced away, and Yasmin wondered if she should text her dad to come back in an hour. But that would be too weird. Besides, she needed to do her extra-credit lab for AP Physics and finish reading volume six of *The Decline and Fall of the Roman Empire.*

She walked through the parlor on her way to leave. She scanned the room for Brittany and saw her talking to her sister and some other girls. She tried to make eye contact, but the girls were giggling about something and Brittany didn't see her.

Why do I care? she thought. A feeling had come on very suddenly, and Yasmin didn't know what to make of it. She'd thought she was immune to wanting popular girls to like her. But it wasn't about being popular. It was something else. Something weird.

Whatever, she thought. She slipped downstairs past the rowdy boys in the dining room—to whom she was invisible—and out the front door. To her dad's Lexus, to her books, to her life, a world that suddenly seemed much smaller but which at least made sense.

The master bathroom, 9:40 p.m.

Winn knew he was being pathetic. He was sitting in the bathtub drinking an entire bottle of Woodford Reserve, hiding from Corny. He'd thought getting drunk might make it better, but actually it was making it worse.

What have I done?

"Sugarplum?" Corny's little voice called from the other side of the door. Ever since they'd fucked on the football field Thursday night, she'd been calling him that. It was what he'd called her when he'd realized he was in love with her. But once the drug had worn off, he'd felt differently. It was weird. He could replay everything in his mind—Corny's warmth, her extraordinary hotness, her lovingness, her perfection, how he'd wanted to worship her forever. But while he could remember the feelings, he couldn't quite . . . *feel* them. They'd left his system the same time the drug did. He was back to his old self. He wished Scooby-Doo would find out who that creepy drug dealer at the science expo was, so he could get some more of whatever he'd given him.

Corny tapped on the door. It was unlocked, but she would never barge in on him. She always tried to obey Winn's desires, a quality he appreciated and found irritating at the same time.

"Come in," Winn said weakly.

The door squeaked open and Corny came inside. When she saw Winn in the tub, she squealed, "Oh my god! Let's take a bath!" and immediately began shedding her clothes. That was another weird thing—ever since the football field, Corny had turned into a sex maniac. All she seemed to want to do was give Winn blow jobs and tell him how much she loved him. She was so cute and sweet and gave pretty much the best head known to man. Surely he loved her. He'd be a crazy idiot not to love her. And yet . . .

She was taking off his clothes. Winn let her. He'd been trying to come up with a way to tell her that there was no way they could actually have a baby, that the idea had been an insane and drug-induced fantasy. He knew it was going to crush her. Corny had been talking nonstop about how excited she was to get pregnant and have his child. She'd even named it already—Winn Roofus Jughead or something.

They were completely naked now, and Corny was filling up the tub with steaming hot water. She looked so cute when she was naked, with her huge breasts popping out of her little girlish body.

"Are you ready to be the happiest man in the world?" Corny was asking in a dramatic, hushed tone. She leaned over the side of the tub and pulled a small white stick out of her purse. Winn knew instantly what it was. His stomach sank.

Fuck. It's too late.

The whole world kind of stopped for a moment. Winn felt dizzy. He wasn't sure if it was from drinking, or from realizing that his life was over. Maybe he could hide in the forest for ten years, and Corny would forget about him. But when he looked at her bright, adoring face, Winn knew she never would. She'd search for him forever, accompanied by cartoon birds like a Disney princess.

He just needed to stay calm till Scooby-Doo found the drug dealer. Then he could feel those feelings again—feel *love* again—and everything would be fine. He took a swig of bourbon and tried to relax so he could get an erection. Corny deserved more than his pathetic half-boner. He sank into the warm water, wondering what it would feel like to have no thoughts. Probably nice, like being a dog or the ocean. Corny was kissing him.

I love her, he thought, commanding it to be true.

The study, 9:45 p.m.

"Do you have the password?" the voice repeated. Someone was sitting in a high-backed, thronelike chair that had been turned to face the wall. In the darkness, Benny couldn't discern any hint of who it was.

"No."

"I'm afraid that's not the password."

Between the hysteria of DeAndre's impalement and the mysterious nocturnal activities of the golf team, Benny had sort of forgotten about the drug dealer with the password. Not forgotten, but given it a low priority. Now here it was, right in front of him. Feet away. All Benny had to do was get up and walk across the room, and he'd know who he was. But for some reason he was frozen. Whoever it was, it was like he possessed a force field that prevented anyone from coming near him.

"I'll give you one hint," the voice whispered, and the whisper was somehow far more creepy than the growl. And Benny wasn't so sure it was a guy anymore. "The hint is: Who are you?"

Who are you. "I am someone . . . who wants to know who you are."

There was a long, silent moment. "That's not the password. The password is . . ."

Benny tensed. Was it going to be this easy?

"BENNYFLAX!"

A yellow head popped up and the entire chair tipped over. A girl spilled out onto the floor, cackling with laughter. Benny sighed. It was Virginia.

"Oh my god, your face!"

"What are you doing in here?"

Virginia rolled onto her back on the Oriental rug. "Nothing. I was upstairs and I saw you looking in different rooms, and I thought I could beat you here." She started cracking up again. The stiff fabric of her gold skirt had flopped up, revealing the entirety of her legs. Benny tried to focus on her face, but that felt weird too.

"Are you smoking?" He nodded at the cigarette in the ashtray.

"No, not me. Someone left it in here."

"Someone *who*?"

Virginia shrugged. "I don't know, someone. Everyone smokes at parties. Not every single thing is a mystery, Benny. . . ."

Virginia had propped herself up on her elbows and was looking at him. Benny's cheeks heated up, knowing she was assessing him. Had she wanted him to wear the outfit? He'd been certain he'd be able to tell when he saw her face, but now he couldn't. Her expression was totally blank and unreadable. Maybe she'd forgotten about it already. Virginia's mind was kind of unpredictable, Benny had learned. He sat there self-consciously, pretending to be interested in the deer heads on the wall, until Virginia said, "I have a present for you."

She pulled something out of her bag. It was Trevor's phone. She extended her arm, not getting up from the floor. "Look in the deleted pics file. I found it."

"Found what?"

"You'll know when you see it."

Benny swiped the phone open and hurriedly scrolled through the deleted files in the camera app. He didn't like Virginia knowing something he didn't. He wanted to catch up with her as quickly as possible.

What he saw made a chill run down his neck. It was a photo of the golf course. It was grainy and dark. About eight boys were piled into a golf cart, hanging out the sides. A man was lying facedown in the grass, tied to the cart. They were dragging him across the green. It was the caddie.

Benny's mouth fell open. "Jesus . . ."

There had been . . . *incidents* at Winship before. A weird strain of identity confusion existed among the richest boys at their school, who seemed to compensate for the froufrou-ness of their wealth by pretending to be hicks. This resulted in such redneck affectations as eating sunflower seeds, an obsession with hunting and NASCAR, off-roading their pricey Jeep Wranglers, and displays of Dixie pride that verged uncomfortably into white supremacy territory. Graffiti of Confederate flags was rampant on desks and textbooks; Trevor had famously stuck a stem of cotton into a black freshman's backpack once. These incidents went largely ignored by an administration unwilling (or unable) to exert authority over the spoiled sons of the Board of Trustees— Trevor, Craig, Connor Tate, Big Gabe, even Winn Davis to a certain extent. . . . It was a character they played: the good ol' boy, the hayseed in the mansion.

But this wasn't a cotton stem or a doodle of a flag. This was . . . heinous. This was a grown black man being dragged by drunk teenagers across a golf course. Benny felt stunned. Meanwhile, Virginia was on the floor grinning at him like an excited kid.

"Isn't it, like, the jackpot of clues?"

The jackpot. Yes, it was a "jackpot" of a find. But first and foremost, it was terrifying. It felt like a mile stretched between him and Virginia, all of a sudden. Their lives were not the same. Yellow-haired Virginia could see a photo like that without wondering if next time it would be *her* being dragged behind a golf cart. It did something to your psyche, going through life knowing your people were hated—something untranslatable to anyone who hadn't experienced it.

Benny zoomed in the photo, hoping to get a better look at the caddie. Was he dead? It was impossible to tell. The man's pants were smeared with dark stains. The boys in the golf cart were more visible: Trevor Cheek was one, plus a senior whose name Benny didn't know, and two guys whose faces were blurry. Maybe one of them was Craig? They looked bigger than him, though.

"Calvin isn't one of them," Virginia said, as if Benny had asked.

"Are you sure?"

"Pretty sure. He must have left or something."

Benny squinted at the photo. "I don't think Craig is in this photo either," he said.

"He's probably taking the picture."

"I don't understand why Craig is getting the brunt of the punishment. No one could prove he was the photographer, and he's not *in* the photo. . . . He's not in any of the photos. I'm starting to doubt that Craig was even there that night."

"Really?" Virginia sat up.

"He's not in a single picture. . . . Maybe they beat up the caddie and Craig paid him off? Or maybe . . ." Benny trailed off. He couldn't think of anything else. And how was this connected to DeAndre? Normally it wasn't Benny's *modus operandi* to force a narrative, but this was getting frustrating. The two scenarios contained so many parallels: both involved a black male, and an assault relating to Southern recreational activities (DeAndre: hunting; the caddie: golf). Both involved Trevor. Both occurred in darkness. They had to be connected.

On the floor, Virginia was lying on her back with her limbs stretched out like a starfish. She was starting to get bored of this party. She hadn't predicted how disappointing the return of normal Benny would feel. It was like having the possibility that their relationship could actually be exciting dangled in front of her like a cat toy, then yanked away. Maybe she'd imagined the twinkle in his eye. She certainly couldn't see it anymore.

"Do you know what a red pill is?" she asked Benny.

"A red pill? What do you mean?"

"It's something I heard Trevor say to Craig. It was like, 'If you don't leave me alone, I'm gonna take a red pill and kill you.'"

Benny chewed his thumbnail, which he always did when he was thinking. "Well, my mind immediately goes to *The Matrix*."

"Oh, I haven't seen that."

"You haven't? It's really good. I named my dog after one of the characters. . . ."

His voice trailed off, but Virginia's ears had already pricked up at the mention of Benny's mystery dog. She made a mental note to definitely see *The Matrix*. It was the first time Benny had ever recommended something that wasn't, like, a newspaper or the writings of an obscure Zen master.

"Anyway, in *The Matrix*, you get a choice between a red pill and a blue pill," Benny explained. "And the red pill allows you to transcend the simulation and understand true reality. It doesn't really have anything to do with murder, though."

"Maybe Trevor's true reality is that he's a violent animal who likes to kill people."

Suddenly the door slammed open with a bang.

"VIRGINIA!" high-pitched voices shouted. The sound of cheering spilled in from the other room. Big Gabe and another football player appeared in the doorway, and a pair of girls rushed into the room with no shirts on. It was the Montague twins, wearing identical pink bras and their hair in identical pink pigtails with ribbons. They looked like little girls that some pervert had Photoshopped pairs of perfect jiggling breasts onto.

"Omigod!" Virginia yelled, startled.

The twins ran at her, screaming. For a second Virginia thought they were attacking her. They *were* attacking her. But they were shrieking with laughter. Before she knew what was happening, the twins had grabbed her shirt and were yanking it over her head.

"TAKE IT OFF! TAKE IT OFF!" a group of football players shouted from the doorway.

Then a pair of hands grabbed her, and Virginia felt herself being dragged away from the twins. She looked down and saw Benny's maroon-sleeved arms encircling her waist from behind. Her shirt was half-off, hanging around her neck. He had backed against the wall, and was clutching her to his chest. She could feel his heart beating against her back.

He held his hand up like a traffic cop. "Back away!"

Angie stumbled and laughed drunkenly. The boys in the doorway yelled, "BOOOOOOO!"

Virginia twisted around in Benny's arms. His face was so close, she could see a thin sheen of sweat glistening on his forehead. His breaths were jagged. He looked at her, and the expression on his face was so weird that at first Virginia didn't know what was going on. Then she realized:

He's protecting me.

What did Benny think, that the twins were ripping off her clothes so the guys could gang-rape her? At a *fundraiser*? She felt so baffled she didn't know what to think. Was this annoying or amazing? Virginia was used to taking care of herself. No one had ever tried to save her before.

"Benny, it's okay," she whispered. "It's a joke."

He didn't seem to believe her. He didn't let go.

"Omigod! Scooby-Doo is the cutest!" Brittany was squealing. But it felt like she was a thousand miles away.

Virginia squirmed to bring her lips closer to Benny's ear. She didn't know what to say to calm him down. "Benny, it's just body shots. It's for DeAndre. They're not attacking me. They're goofing off."

It was weird to whisper in a guy's ear with your shirt half-off while a bunch of guys screamed at you and a pair of topless twins giggled on the floor. It felt strangely intimate, like she and Benny were alone on a raft in the sea of insanity.

Then she did something really weird. She didn't think about it before she did it; she just did it. She lifted her chin and kissed his mouth. It wasn't a real kiss; in a real kiss the other person kissed you back. This was more like, she put a kiss on his lips with her lips. But it still felt like the most weirdly intense thing she could have chosen to do in that moment.

The crowd around them started to come back into focus. The twins were screaming about how cute Benny was, and more and more people were spilling into the room. Half were guys with red Dixie cups, and the other half were girls with their tops off, showing a variety of pastel-colored bras. Virginia felt a quick hit of satisfaction: she was the only one whose bra was black. She wished Benny would let her go. Everyone would think she was some priss like Constance Bouchelle, traumatized by a body shot and needing to be saved by the biggest nerd in school.

"Benny, I'm okay," she whispered, more firmly this time. As if those were the magic words, Benny's viselike grip on her loosened. His arms went limp.

"SHOT! SHOT! SHOT!" the guys were chanting. Someone was yelling, "Who won the come queen?"— words Virginia assumed she hadn't heard correctly.

Benny stood up, extending his arm to help Virginia off the floor. Her shirt hung around her neck like a scarf.

Benny didn't look in her eyes. He was looking around like he might throw up or something. Virginia could tell he was searching for a way out of the room. The doorway was jammed with people.

"Benny . . . ," she said, reaching for his hand. But in a single, unbelievably smooth motion, he darted to the corner, threw open a large window, and leaped out of it.

"Whoaaa!" all the guys shouted, and the girls cheered.

For a second, Virginia panicked—was Benny dead?—but then she remembered they were on the first floor.

"That was awesome!" a guy was shouting.

"Did you see that? Scooby-Doo just jumped out the window!"

Virginia ran to the window. It was dark outside, except for a pair of blue and red lights down the street. *Is that a police car?*

"Benny! Benny!" she called.

But he was gone.

The roof, 11:00 p.m.
Calvin turned the volume up on his headphones and let the Enya song wash over him. The song was called "Lazy Days," and it was about balloons. When Calvin was a little kid, he'd been scared of balloons. Not of the balloon itself, but of letting it go. The idea that if he let it go, it would fly higher and higher and higher until it exploded. *Good-bye, balloon!* He remembered being six years old at a carnival,

and holding his balloon so tightly that his fingernails broke the skin of his palm, and he bled. He wished he could go back in time and tell himself, *Just let it go.*

Next to him, Craig Beaver was yakking away about something. Calvin and Craig had shared bowls before, but normally Craig would just stay long enough to get moderately high before resuming his life's purpose of following Trevor around like a tongue-wagging dog. But apparently the two of them were having a lovers' spat or something, because Craig seemed antsy and irritable and wouldn't leave.

Calvin reluctantly lifted his headphones. "Are you talking to me or to yourself?"

"I'm just *saying*, if you want to get your body shot from the cum queen, you better do it quick."

"What are you talking about?"

Craig gave an artificial shrug, obviously expecting Calvin to beg him to explain himself. Calvin just rolled his eyes and put his headphones back on. Above his head, mauve-colored clouds floated past the moon. The air felt magnificent. He was excited and nervous to see Virginia. He hoped she liked him. If she didn't, that was okay. But if she did, he wanted to lick tequila off her torso and see what that felt like. He'd already begun writing a poem about it in his mind. He hoped it would feel like an act of carnal worship, a powerful mingling of the debauched and the holy. Basically, he hoped it would feel awesome.

For a long moment, Calvin thought the pretty blue and red flickering lights he saw were only in his mind. The strain of marijuana he'd smoked was known to have mildly hallucinogenic effects. But then suddenly he realized they were real. Two police cars were coming up the driveway. He yanked off his headphones.

"Oh my god. Did you call the cops?" he yelled at Craig. "What the fuck is wrong with you?"

Craig grinned evilly. "Where's your red pill now, Trevor?"

Calvin froze for a second. "What did you just say?"

On the dark lawn below, a male voice boomed: "EVERYBODY FREEZE. PARTY'S OVER."

Within seconds, people were pouring out of the house. Everyone was shouting to each other and running for their cars. Topless girls spilled onto the grass in their bras, not seeming to know where to go. The scene felt like a bust of a teen brothel that catered only to pleasures from the waist up.

"Bang, you're dead. Bang, you're dead."

Craig had pointed his finger like a gun, and was pretending to shoot the topless girls one by one. Calvin felt a strong urge to shove him off the roof and watch him die. Craig deserved to die for deliberately ruining such a beautiful moment of peace. For a second, Calvin actually considered it. He quickly calculated Craig's distance from the edge of the roof, and the degree of force it would require to push him to his doom. But he stopped. He had himself to worry about right now. He couldn't risk a run-in with the police. The thought of getting caught, and his dad being called . . . Calvin shuddered. It was not an option. He had to get out of there.

His heart was pounding. *Calm down,* he commanded himself. He wouldn't do himself any favors by having a fucking heart attack. He started climbing across the roof like a gangly cat. He heard Craig trying to crawl after him, laughing stupidly, saying, "Whoa, I'm really high. . . . Wait, how do I get down? Hey, come back, man!"

Good-bye, Craig!

Calvin slipped around the chimney and located the window that he and Craig had climbed out of. If he could sneak to the second floor, there was a balcony Calvin estimated he could safely dangle from to get to the ground. He was getting better and better at escaping situations. The key was to realize that your life actually depended on it. Every moment was a pass/fail test:

Escape or die.

The driveway, 11:11 p.m.

"Stop touching me," Virginia said, swatting Brittany's hand away. Brittany was trying to braid her hair, and it was annoying.

"It relaxes me!" Brittany whined.

"Well, it doesn't relax me."

All around, people were scattering from the police.

Underage drinking was tolerated to a point at Winship, but once the police were involved, all bets were off. Everyone was panicking, and somehow Virginia had become responsible for the tipsy and topless Montague twins. Which didn't make sense because they were older than her, and they had a billion friends, whereas she just had Benny Flax, who had jumped out a window and vanished from the face of the earth. But they were following her around like little sisters, expecting her to take care of them.

Virginia scanned the lawn for anyone who looked sober enough to drive them out of there. Big Gabe was getting into his Hummer, but he looked so wasted he'd probably immediately drive them into a pole. Then she saw a tall, dark figure dashing toward a black Jaguar.

"Calvin! Calvin!"

She grabbed the twins' hands and dragged them across the street, darting around shirtless girls and drunk boys and a pair of dogs that were barking at everyone.

Calvin barely paused to look at her. He just flung open the back door and said, "GET IN GET IN GET IN GET IN!"

Virginia threw herself in the backseat of the car, and the twins tumbled in after her.

"Fuck," he hissed. "Craig boxed me in. Put your seat belts on."

Virginia scrambled to put hers on, and then Angie's. Brittany was sprawled across their laps, and Virginia couldn't get her to sit up.

SMASH!

The car lurched forward, engine roaring.

"Oh my god!" the twins screamed.

SMASH!

Calvin rammed the Jaguar into Craig's car over and over, violently smashing his way out of the tight space. Virginia barely breathed, her heart slamming in her chest. She felt half-terrified, half-exhilarated. Were they going to die?

SMASH!

Finally there was enough room to maneuver and the car pivoted into the street.

"It's Chrissie!" Angie was yelling, pointing at a stumbling silhouette in a skintight dress outside. "Stop the car! We have to get Chrissie!"

"Cheerleaders stick together!" Brittany chimed in.

Calvin accelerated. "I'm not a cheerleader."

"Neither am I," Virginia agreed. "Go!"

"Chrissieeee!" the twins moaned, as if they would never see her again.

The car sped away, lurching around a dark corner. Virginia wondered if Calvin always drove this insanely, or if it was just the situation. Either way, she felt so excited she could barely stand it. It felt like the seat belt was cutting off her circulation. She ripped it off, feeling a crazy surge of adrenaline. Calvin was wild and it made her feel wild too.

She pushed Brittany off her legs and hurled herself into

the front seat, landing on Calvin's lap and straddling him. Approximately a half second later, her tongue was down his throat.

He slammed the brakes. The tires screeched, and there was a thud as Brittany rolled off the backseat.

"Virginia, stop." Calvin pushed her back, pressing one hand to his chest. She dodged him and kissed him again. He grabbed her by the hair. "Stop it! You're killing me. You're going to kill me."

The next second, there was the sound of breaking glass and metal on metal. Virginia felt a weird sensation in her arm. For a second it was just fuzzy numbness. Then it ruptured into a visceral, hellish pain. It was beyond pain she'd ever experienced, beyond pain she'd ever imagined. She heard a blood-chilling scream. She didn't realize it was her own voice.

Then everything went white.

Then everything went black.

The garden, 11:30 p.m.

Why does no one love me?

Chrissie White was crying. No matter how many times she thought it might be different, this was how it always ended: her phone lost, her makeup ruined, throwing up in a bush and then crying.

She lay in the grass and looked at the stars. They were spinning. Or maybe the earth was spinning. She wished a flaming comet would come and destroy it all. What was the point of a planet with eight billion people on it, if not a single one of them loved her? She cried even harder, pressing her face into the dirt. She didn't understand it. Why didn't anyone *see* her? Her boobs were bigger than the Montague twins', and unlike them, she had four-pack abs. She'd given so many blow jobs last year that the football team had given her kneepads for Christmas. Yet no one had asked her to Homecoming, and no one had bid on her for the auction except for that slimeball Craig Beaver, and Gerard the water boy, which didn't count because he'd bid on everyone.

"Why . . . Why . . . Why . . . ," she moaned over and over. She was so drunk she could barely see. She closed her eyes. The only thing she wanted in the world was to be someone's girlfriend. To be special to someone. Anyone. She didn't even care who it was.

Please God, bring me a boyfriend. I'll be a good person for the rest of my life if you bring me a boyfriend.

"Chrissie?"

Chrissie opened her eyes. Someone was standing over her. A boy. She couldn't believe it. God had listened! God had sent her a boy! She reached out to touch him.

"Are you okay?" He was sitting down on the grass next to her.

"I'm finne, I'm finnne," she said. She sat up dizzily and flopped her arms around his neck. Maybe she really was fine. Maybe this guy was actually the one. He felt skinny but nice. His arms were lean and wiry, and he smelled like bourbon. She liked the smell of bourbon because it reminded her of her grandfather, who had given her a beautiful Tiffany charm bracelet. He was dead now.

She sighed and looked at the sky again. She wished there were more stars. She could only see one. The rest of the sky was the color of a dirty sock. It made her sad.

"That . . . ," she declared, pointing at the star, ". . . is our starm. *Star.*"

"That's a satellite," the boy said.

"Then it's our sat-tuh-lite." She squeezed him tightly.

"Chrissie? Can I ask you something?"

"Anything," she breathed. Except she hoped not a blow job because she thought she might throw up.

"Are you related to Garland White?"

She started crying again. Really crying. She couldn't remember who she was talking to. Then she remembered it was the boyfriend God sent. And before she knew it, she was telling him everything.

Sunday

Piedmont Hospital, 9:10 a.m.

Virginia felt calm. She felt bored but okay with it. Normally when she was bored, she immediately wanted to fix it by doing something interesting. But right now she was content to just look out the window at the Atlanta skyline and replay kissing Calvin Harker in her mind a thousand times. It felt . . . peaceful. It was probably the painkillers.

Her arm hurt. She had a compound fracture, which meant the bone had been crushed and ripped her arm open. Virginia had a vague memory of a white stick covered in blood, and her hand flopping grotesquely. Then she'd passed out. What was with this fainting tendency she was developing? It was annoying. She constantly missed out on the best action of her own life.

She didn't know exactly what had happened. She knew Big Gabe had crashed into Calvin's Jaguar trying to escape the party. The car door had crushed her arm, and Brittany had gotten whiplash. She didn't know what had happened to Calvin. She didn't know if he knew that she was in the hospital, or if he'd tried to contact her. Her room was bare. There weren't any flowers or cards, or teddy bears with heart-shaped paw prints, or any indication that anyone in the world gave a shit that she'd been in a car crash. But instead of making her feel forgotten, it actually made her feel mysterious and cool—a daredevil with no ties, a Jane Doe with a secret past.

She didn't understand why people hated hospitals so much. They seemed pretty interesting to her. They were relaxing but exciting at the same time. It was cool to know that all around her, people were fighting for their lives. It wasn't like everyday life, where people just lay down in the coffin of their office jobs or homework or whatever dumb thing they'd been convinced was important.

An apple-cheeked nurse stood in the doorway holding a pen. "Virginia? The number you gave me? It's disconnected. Does your mom have a cell?"

"That is her cell."

"Well . . . Is there someone else we can call? We need a parent to discharge you. Or at least an adult."

Virginia looked at her arm. They'd let her choose the color of her cast, and she'd chosen black. She'd thought it would look sophisticated, but actually it looked kind of boring and drab. She sighed. She didn't want to call Mrs. Morehouse—the idea of that old hag filling a parental role in her life was too depressing. Dan-Wam was useless, and she didn't have Esteban's new number in Cuba. Maybe

Mrs. Flax would come. Except she couldn't call Benny after that weird kissing thing. Why had she done that? Hopefully it was like the five-hundred-dollar bet: if she never brought it up again, he wouldn't either.

"I dunno. I guess call . . . Mrs. Hope. She's my English teacher."

"Do you know her number?"

"No."

"Then you'll have to stay until we can contact your school or another adult." The nurse shrugged sympathetically, then started to leave.

"Wait," Virginia said. "Um . . . is a guy named DeAndre Bell here? He got, like, impaled by a deer?"

The nurse looked surprised. "The antlers kid? You know him? That boy's in rough shape. I'm not sure he's up for visitors."

Virginia appraised the nurse. Her scrubs had hearts on them. She was wearing lipstick. She probably was in love with some Dr. McDreamy or McSteamy or whatever and fantasized about the day he'd finally notice her and put a baby in her.

"Please let me visit him! We're"—Virginia lowered her voice confidentially—"*in love*. We were supposed to go to the Homecoming dance this Friday. But now that's down the drain. . . ." She tried to look thwarted and romantic.

The nurse pursed her berry-colored lips, deciding. Then she motioned for Virginia to follow her.

DeAndre's room was on a different floor. It looked like the inside of a Hallmark store: poster-size "Get Well Soon" cards, flower arrangements shaped like footballs—all the crap that had been noticeably absent in Virginia's room. DeAndre was lying in a bed hooked up to a variety of quietly beeping machines. Virginia paused in the doorway, suddenly regretting wanting to see him. It was too weird, witnessing this person who once burst with dynamism and sparkle, now weakly clinging to life.

"You have a special visitor, DeAndre!" the nurse chirped.

"Virginia?" his voice croaked. Virginia could barely see his face over the piles of gifts.

"Yeah. Hi . . ."

The nurse leaned close to her and whispered, "Do you know what soul mates are?"

Virginia shrugged. "No?"

The nurse nodded at her black cast, then at DeAndre on the bed. "It's when life decides that two people belong together. And you don't really have a choice in the matter."

She winked at Virginia, and Virginia winked back, even though the idea was actually kind of disturbing. What if life "decided" you belonged with a murderer or a saxophone player or something?

The nurse left. Virginia waded between the bouquets of flowers and sat down on a metal chair by the window. DeAndre looked awful. His brown skin was ashen. There were black circles under his eyes. Virginia realized she'd never seen his face without his signature dazzling grin. Without it, he looked like a completely different person—tired and average. Virginia knew she probably looked just as bad. She was sitting under the same unflattering lights, wearing the same shapeless cotton hospital gown. She didn't know what had happened to her gold skirt. Was it lying in a trash bag somewhere, covered in her own blood? The thought made her want to cry. First the sweater and now the skirt. Both ruined.

"It's so awesome to see you!" DeAndre's voice was weak and unconvincing.

Virginia rolled her eyes. *Wow.* He never let up on the Mr. Congeniality act, did he? Not even when he was lying on his back with half the life stabbed out of him by a pair of deer antlers.

"What are you doing here?" he asked.

Virginia lifted her broken arm. "The nurse thinks destiny brought us together."

"Am I dreaming right now? I'm on a looooot of drugs."

Virginia looked around the room. How did Benny do it? How did he zero in on clues without even knowing what he was looking for?

She reached behind her head and grabbed a humongous "Get Well" card. She set it on her lap and scanned all the inane messages ("We miss you Big D!"; "Get well soon pretty please with a cherry on top!"). She saw Calvin Harker's name. It made her self-conscious, as if Calvin could psychically tell that she was thinking about him. His message was short and written in neat handwriting:

I'm sorry the universe demanded this sacrifice of you.

"DeAndre?" A different nurse appeared in the doorway. "I've got some more visitors for you. A Mr. Cheek and son." He noticed Virginia. "Miss? I think you better get back to your floor."

Virginia felt cold fingers on her hand. DeAndre had snapped out of his daze, eyes now wide. He whispered something barely audible. Virginia leaned toward him, glancing at the nurse in the doorway who was watching them.

"What did you say?"

"Don't leave."

"Miss?" the nurse said loudly.

"Just a minute!" She turned back to DeAndre and whispered, "Why not? DeAndre, why not?"

A booming voice was coming down the hall: "Hail to the chief!"

DeAndre gripped her hand. *"Don't leave me alone with them."*

Benny's house, 9:15 a.m.

Control your dog, son.

Benny was dreaming. He believed in the importance of

dreams—the time when the conscious brain was no longer in charge of the flow of thoughts, allowing the mind to explore new realms and ideas. But sometimes the mind went to dark, forbidden places, and then you were helpless to escape until you woke up.

BANG!

Tank had always been a good dog. He was a six-year-old German shepherd mix, completely devoted to Benny's father. But after the plane crash Tank began acting strangely. He growled at Mr. Flax all the time, as if he no longer recognized his owner. His behavior put extra stress on the family. It was hard enough to keep believing that Mr. Flax was the same man he'd been before and not a stranger, and Tank's irrational aggression didn't help. But at the same time, Benny felt oddly jealous of Tank. At least the dog got to express its natural confusion, while Benny had to hold all of his feelings inside.

I hear you, Benny would say to Tank, scratching his ears and feeling like Tank was the only one in the world who heard him too. But soon even that small solace was taken away.

In the initial months after the accident, the Flaxes would often pile into a wheelchair-accessible van and go on family walks around the park. One Saturday evening there were cops everywhere because of a mugging in the area. Tank was more agitated than usual—nipping at Mr. Flax's ankles in addition to his incessant growling. Mr. Flax seemed to barely notice. Wherever he was in his brain, it seemed very far away.

One of the officers approached them. "Control your dog, son," he said to Benny. Benny would never forget the man's face. His icy blue eyes and stony gaze. The face of a man with zero doubts concerning his own authority. The great, manly protector who never questioned what exactly he was protecting. Benny already unconsciously associated policemen with Nazis; maybe that association was unfair, but what happened next certainly didn't correct it.

"He's just confused," Benny said to the officer. He knew it looked weird, Tank acting so aggressive. But Tank wasn't a bad dog, he just needed time to adjust to the new family dynamic. It was good that the police wanted to protect his dad, but they didn't know the whole story.

"Get your dog away from the elderly gentleman," the officer said, indicating Mr. Flax. He didn't seem to realize that Benny and his dog were part of the family.

"It's *our* dog," Mrs. Flax tried to explain, but the officer wasn't listening. Then Tank snarled and made a small feint at the officer's feet. And before Benny even knew what was happening, there was a loud shot, and Tank was dead on the ground.

Benny was so stunned he couldn't speak. But in his mind he was screaming: *Why did you do that? Why did you do that? Why did you do that?*

Benny had no memory of what happened next. He didn't

remember if his mother had cried, or how they'd dealt with Tank's body. Only much later did it occur to Benny to file a charge against the officer for abuse of power. But when he tried, he found there was no legal recourse to do so. The entire system was rigged to allow police officers to run amok.

So that was life. Benny had always been a sheltered kid, but that shelter contained huge gaping holes now. The people you loved could have an accident and be damaged beyond recognition. The people who were supposed to protect you could turn on you. If only that cop had paused to wonder if there was a *reason* Tank was acting that way. . . . Maybe the cop had a reason too. Maybe a German shepherd had eaten his mother. Which caused him to distrust dogs, which caused Benny to distrust cops—a poisoned gift that kept on giving.

Control your dog, son.

BANG!

Benny woke up on the lumpy living room sofa. For a second he wondered what he was doing there. He felt covered in a residue of dread—Benny always woke up miserable whenever Tank showed up in his dreams. But this wasn't a normal dread. It felt more urgent somehow. And then it all came flooding back: Trevor's party. Virginia in her bra, kissing him. Jumping out the window. An incredibly drunk Chrissie White weeping in his arms about her father's "special plane."

No no no no no no.

He sat up and pushed the quilt off him. He was still wearing his clothes from last night. His glasses were on the coffee table; he grabbed them and shoved them on his face. The room came into focus. Everyone was doing their Sunday morning routine as if nothing were out of the ordinary: his grandma making pancakes and chicken sausage in the kitchen; his mother reading the paper; Rodrigo with Mr. Flax in the dining room, helping him read a book about clouds written for six-year-olds.

"Clouds . . . are too . . . high . . . to touch."

As soon as Benny's mother and grandmother realized he was awake, they both started talking:

"Benjamin, I want to make it clear that this is never, *ever*—"

"Does your girlfriend eat carbs, honey?"

Benny cut them off, "No one talk to me except Rodrigo."

He knew he was being rude, but there was no way he could deal with the women of his household right now. His grandmother was obviously hearing wedding bells, while his mother looked like she would probably set fire to Benny's bed after this. He wasn't sure which was more terrifying.

"What do you need, Ben?" Rodrigo said, looking up from the cloud book.

"Helloooo?" a small voice called from the hallway. Chrissie White tiptoed out of Benny's room, looking completely bewildered. Her dress was the tiniest bit of fabric ever devised to cover a girl in the necessary places. Her face was streaked with makeup, and her long, sand-colored hair hung in tangled bunches. She'd slept in his bed. A girl had slept in his bed. A girl with the tiniest dress in the world had slept in his bed and was now on display before his entire family.

Everyone stared at her. After a long, painful moment, his grandmother broke the silence: "Good morning, honey! Come have breakfast with us!"

Benny glanced at his dad to see how he was reacting to the girlish presence in the house. But Mr. Flax just looked at Chrissie the same way he looked at everyone: like a random stranger.

"Ummm . . ." Chrissie didn't seem to know who to look at. *Don't look at my dad, don't look at my dad.*

"I'm afraid Chrissie needs to get back to her dorm. Rodrigo can drive us." Benny shot Rodrigo a pleading look.

"Rodrigo is not your chauffeur," Mrs. Flax said icily. "Rodrigo is a medical professional."

"I don't mind at all, Mrs. Flax," Rodrigo said, getting up from the table.

Benny's grandmother thrust an overflowing plate of pancakes into Chrissie's hands. "You can eat this in the car, honey."

"Um, thank you."

"It was nice to meet you, Crystal," Mrs. Flax said flatly. Benny glared at her. *Crystal.* It was her way of calling Chrissie trashy.

But Chrissie didn't seem to notice that she'd been

insulted to her face. She just smiled and said in a tiny voice, "Nice to meet you, too!"

Rodrigo's car smelled like cigarettes. Was Rodrigo a smoker? For some reason it made Benny see him differently. Chrissie sat in the front seat looking tense, like she was trying to make her body as small as possible. The plate of pancakes sat untouched on her lap, a huge pat of butter melting into the syrup.

"You should really eat that," Rodrigo said to her. "Benny's gran makes 'em the best."

Chrissie picked up her fork and took a dainty bite. She chewed and swallowed.

"Mmm, good!" She turned to smile at Benny. Benny smiled back weakly. She had better manners than Virginia, who would have wolfed down the whole plate and talked with her mouth full the entire time.

As they pulled up to the Boarders, the house looked empty and abandoned as usual. Benny prayed to God that someone would open the door this time. When they'd come last night, it had been locked, and Chrissie couldn't find her keys. She'd been completely wasted, and as much as Benny wanted to—he'd *really* wanted to—he couldn't just leave her on the porch like a heap of garbage. So he'd told his mom they had to bring her home.

He hadn't thought it was possible for his mother to be less hospitable toward a girl than she was toward Virginia Leeds. But he'd been wrong. It made him want to throttle her. So what if Chrissie wasn't Jewish. So what if she dressed like a hooker. *Deal with it!* he wanted to scream. After what Chrissie had drunkenly told him last night about her father's "special plane," she was literally the last person on the entire planet that Benny wanted in his home. Near his family. Near his *father.* But he'd dealt with it and gotten her to a safe place, because that's what decent human beings did.

Don't think about the plane, he told himself. He could think about it later.

"I'll just be five minutes," Benny told Rodrigo. He shut the car door and walked Chrissie to the porch. But before he could knock, Chrissie touched his hand lightly.

"Thank you for taking me home. No one's ever done that for me before." Her voice was small and kittenish, like she was trying to imitate Marilyn Monroe.

One second later, there were lips on his lips. She was kissing him. After fifteen years of nothing, Benny had now been kissed twice in the last twelve hours. Chrissie's lips were incredibly soft. She tasted like maple syrup, with a hint of vomit underneath. Benny recoiled reflexively.

Chrissie stepped back, smiling at him in a fake, coquettish way. Her makeup-smeared face was confusing; she looked like a little girl and an exhausted, forty-five-year-old woman at the same time.

"You're welcome," Benny said tersely, looking away from her eyes. He knocked on the door. After a long moment, Gottfried the German exchange student appeared.

"*Guten Tag*, Benny Flax," he said. He was holding a bowl full of Lucky Charms that appeared to be topped with Cheez Whiz.

"See you later, Benny," Chrissie purred. She winked at him and then sashayed inside the house.

"You will have de breakfas wid me?" Gottfried offered, holding up his bowl of vile mixture to Benny.

"No thank you. . . . Do you know if Virginia's awake?"

"Veerginia? She is not here."

"Oh." Benny looked at his watch. It was 9:45 a.m. Where else would she be this early on a Sunday?

"She never come back las night."

"*What?*"

Gottfried grinned. "Crazy party."

"No no no," Benny said. "Not 'crazy party.' Jesus Christ. Where is she? Has anyone . . . *looked*? Has anyone called Mrs. Morehouse?"

Gottfried just scoffed and went back inside. Benny understood that the Boarders didn't rat each other out; but they didn't take care of each other either. Everyone was on their own in that desolate, half-empty house, for better or worse. Mostly for worse, it seemed to Benny.

He went back to the car. He sat down in the front seat but didn't buckle his seat belt or close the door.

"You okay?" Rodrigo asked. He had lit a cigarette and was holding it out the open window.

Benny didn't answer. Where the hell was Virginia? Was

she still at Trevor's house? She was probably lying in a heap somewhere, just like Chrissie would have been if Benny hadn't grabbed her. The thought made him feel physically ill. Why had he left her alone? Why had he jumped out the window like a crazy freak the second things got a tiny bit weird?

"So . . . the party went well?" Rodrigo asked, taking a puff of his cigarette. "I assume you're five hundred dollars richer this fine morning?"

"That was a different girl," Benny said with a sigh.

"Oh."

"Scooby. Hey, Scooby!"

Benny looked back toward the house. A curly-haired girl was leaning out the common room window. She was wearing satin pajamas and eating a blue Pop-Tart.

"Are you looking for Virginia? She's in the hospital. Piedmont Hospital, probably." The girl said it casually, then took a huge bite of her Pop-Tart and closed the window.

Benny knew he was tired. He knew he was stressed. But his reaction still took him by surprise. A giant lump formed in his throat. His shoulders were shaking.

Do not cry. Do not cry, he commanded himself. Why was he always such a pathetic baby?

"We'll find her right now," Rodrigo said, turning on the ignition.

Benny nodded. It was a relief not to have to ask. One tear escaped his eye. He wiped it away.

"I hate this place," he said, sniffing. He wasn't exactly sure what place he meant—the Boarders, the entire school, the entire world.

Get me out of here.

Piedmont Hospital, 10:00 a.m.

"It's the fourth down. Fifteen seconds left. It's a perfect snap—the pigskin is in your hands. But all your receivers are tied up! Looks like life handed you a shit sandwich, son. So what do you do? You eat it! Break free and get your ass to the end zone! Break free and . . . eat shit!"

There was definitely something strange going on between DeAndre and the Cheeks. DeAndre was obviously scared—his skin was cold and clammy and he was digging his fingernails into Virginia's hand. But weirdly, Mr. Cheek seemed just as scared of DeAndre. He was talking nonstop, stringing together incomprehensible football metaphors about overcoming adversity. He seemed unable to look at DeAndre for more than two seconds. His eyes bounced all over the room like a pair of racquetballs. Next to him, Trevor stood sullenly, staring at the floor. He looked like he was dying to get out of there. Virginia imagined he would have bolted already if his father weren't there holding him in place by the shoulder.

"You made it this far, son. You made it from Lakewood Heights to Winship Academy. Don't drop the ball now. . . ."

Seriously? Virginia thought. Had DeAndre really "dropped the ball" by getting stabbed in the chest by a deer?

"Well, we had a pretty rip-roarin' get-together last night, buddy," Mr. Cheeks plowed on, his voice way too loud. "It was a real humdinger, wasn't it, Trev?"

"Uh-huh," Trevor answered.

Beep. Beep. Beep. It was one of the machines hooked up to DeAndre.

"The girls got together, and they raised a sweet lil packet for ya." Mr. Cheek fumbled in his jacket pocket for an envelope. He extended it toward DeAndre. DeAndre just stared at him stonily.

Beep. Beep. Beep.

"He can't move right now," Virginia said, reaching out to take the envelope. Mr. Cheek looked at her like he'd just noticed she was there.

Just then a pair of nurses came into the room and examined the beeping machine. One of them injected something into DeAndre's IV. The other began herding the Cheeks out the door.

"DeAndre's body is under a lot of stress right now. You people are obviously too exciting! Only boring visitors from now on, D!"

"You hang in there, big guy! Hail to the chief!" Mr. Cheek called as he and Trevor were ejected into the hall.

Virginia tried to seem invisible as the nurses fiddled with DeAndre. She opened the envelope from Mr. Cheek. There was a check inside. From what Virginia had seen of the body-shot bids, she expected the amount to be one thousand, maybe two thousand dollars. But it wasn't. It was way, way higher. It was such a staggering number, Virginia thought she must have read it wrong.

"DeAndre?" she whispered. He appeared to be falling asleep.

"DeAndre needs to rest now," one of the nurses said. "You should head back to your room, hon."

Virginia leaned closer. "DeAndre. DeAndre! Why is Mr. Cheek giving you two hundred thousand dollars?"

"Hm?"

"This check is gigantic. Why is Mr. Cheek giving you this much money?"

DeAndre seemed barely awake. His voice was soft and halting: "Because . . . he knows . . . I'm not really . . . the chief . . ."

Then the beeping stopped. DeAndre had closed his eyes. He almost looked dead—his face was so drained and lifeless. Virginia put the check back in the envelope, and tucked it into the pocket of her hospital gown, making sure the nurses didn't see.

"You can see him again later, hon," one of them said.

Virginia nodded and left. The hospital was a labyrinth, and it took Virginia a while to get back to her room. When she finally found it, she saw someone sitting on her bed with his back to the door. His shiny, straight hair fooled her for a second. Then she realized it was Benny.

"Benny?"

He whipped around. Then he stood up and crossed the room in two long strides. For a second it felt like he might hug her. But he didn't. His eyes landed on her black cast. He looked furious, like he'd actually rather punch her than hug her.

"What happened to you?" he demanded. "Why did you not call me?"

Virginia sighed. She walked away from him and flopped facedown on the scratchy hospital bed. It was cool that she had a visitor, but not if he was just going to yell at her. He hadn't even brought flowers or anything.

"I was investigating Calvin, and I was in his car, and Big Gabe crashed into us, and I broke my arm," she said into the pillow. "It's not a big deal."

"VIRGINIA!" Benny shouted. Virginia was startled— Benny never shouted. She peeked up from the pillow and saw him kneeling on the floor in front of her.

"WHY DID YOU NOT CALL ME?"

"I dunno! I just . . . It felt weird. Because of . . . the thing." Virginia buried her face in the pillow again.

"Virginia, listen to me. I don't care if you kiss me. I don't care if you burn my house to the ground. I don't care if aliens invade the earth. We are *partners*! You will call me!"

"All right, geez, I'm sorry."

"Virginia, look at me!"

She looked at him. Behind his glasses, Benny's eyes were shiny and slightly red. Had he been *crying*? He was down on one knee, as if this were some bizarre proposal scene.

"Virginia, you will never, *ever* not call me again. Repeat what I just said."

He was obviously serious. He was looking directly in her eyes, which for Benny was rare. He usually glanced around awkwardly or looked at the floor.

"I . . . I will never ever not call you again."

"Good."

Benny stood up. He smoothed his pants and then sat down in the chair beside the bed. Virginia rolled onto her back, carefully lifting her arm out of the way. Neither of them said anything for a moment. Virginia looked out the window at the skyline. It was easy to forget sometimes that they lived in a city. Winship was hidden between a river and a small forest. The surrounding neighborhoods were all mansions and lawns. It was a twenty-minute drive to get anywhere remotely cosmopolitan. And even if you found a cool art gallery or something, it would be right next to some hick barbeque joint or a GRITS (Girls Raised In The South) outlet store. It was Atlanta, not Paris.

"Does it hurt?" Benny asked.

Virginia looked at her cast. "Yeah. Well, I mean, not too bad, considering my arm literally snapped in half."

Benny winced slightly. Then he said, "You know, fifty, sixty years ago, your whole arm probably would have been amputated. It's amazing, the medical advancements we take for granted today. . . . Are you right-handed?"

"Ugh. Yes. I don't know how the hell I'm supposed to get anything done. My arm is stuck in this thing for two months."

"You'll be fine. You're an incredibly adaptable person."

"Really?" Virginia perked up. Benny hardly ever gave out compliments. *Adaptable.* It wasn't the greatest compliment in the world; it wasn't in the same category as *luminous* or *brilliant* or *awe-inspiring.* But she'd take it.

"Adaptability is the greatest survival asset. Greater than strength, greater than speed, even greater than intelligence. It's why the fox will never go extinct. It adapts to any environment, no matter how damaged. I read about a fox that lived in a mall parking lot."

Virginia felt her face heating up. Was Benny calling her . . . *foxy?*

"And anyway," he went on, "learning to be ambidextrous can benefit the mind immeasurably. I've been thinking of doing it myself. It rewires the right and left hemispheres of the brain and increases creative thought. Nikola Tesla and Michelangelo were ambidextrous."

"Cool," she said. *The fox.* Maybe she could get it emblazoned on a jacket or something.

"What's that?" Benny pointed at her pocket. The envelope was sticking out.

"Oh, I wanted you to see this. DeAndre's here, in this hospital. I found his room and talked to him a little. Mr. Cheek and Trevor came in while I was there, and they gave this to DeAndre." Virginia handed him the envelope with the check inside. Benny opened it.

"Whoa."

"I know, right? There's no way in hell they raised that from body shots. And when I asked DeAndre why Mr. Cheek was giving him that much money, he said, 'Because he knows I'm not the chief.' Wait, no, it was, 'Because he knows I'm not the *real* chief.'"

Benny sat thoughtfully for a moment. Then he said, "Do you think you could draw me a map to DeAndre's room? I want to talk to him."

"Why don't I just go with you?"

"No, you stay here. I don't want to attract any attention. And I don't want DeAndre to feel interrogated."

"Well, I don't know how conversational he'll be," Virginia said. "He's really spaced out. They sedated him."

"Perfect," Benny said, standing up. "Sedatives can produce a mild hypnotic state, almost like a truth serum. He won't be able to deceive me."

"Wait, tell me what's going on first!" Virginia demanded.

"I'll be right back. Do not leave this room. When I return, I'll have all the answers."

Critical care wing, 10:30 a.m.

"For I know the plans I have for you,"
declares the Lord,

"plans to prosper you and not to harm you,
plans to give you hope and a future."
—*Jeremiah 29:11*

Benny scanned the messages on the giant "Get Well Soon" card by DeAndre's bed. About half contained Bible verses, some seeming more randomly chosen than others. Benny had received a card like this eighteen months ago after his father's accident, during the tense period when it was uncertain whether he would live or die. The card had contained many assurances that Jesus was looking over his father, and wouldn't make him an angel before his special time. Benny didn't think his classmates had done it to mock him. It just boggled their minds that Benny didn't believe in Jesus. Sometimes they forgot that Judaism was actually a *religion*, not just a set of stereotypes that marked him as socially alien. In a way, DeAndre was probably easier for them to relate to. Even though he was black and lived in Lakewood Heights, he prayed to the same god as them. And that seemed to be what was important.

"Scooby?" DeAndre's voice croaked. "It's so awesome to see you!" Benny could sense the tremendous effort it was taking DeAndre to be enthusiastic.

"Awesome to see you too, man," Benny said back. The word "man" came unnaturally, but Benny thought the conversation would go smoother if he spoke the language of guys. "Hey, can I ask you something?"

"Sure," DeAndre said. He'd closed his eyes, like it was too draining to keep them open.

"How much are you really getting out of this? I can't imagine you sold out for this little." Benny held up the check, pinching it by the corner like it was a piece of garbage.

DeAndre's eyes snapped open. "What?"

"Two hundred thousand dollars? This is *nothing*, DeAndre. This is loose change. Tell me this is the first check in an installment plan. Because if it's not, you're an idiot, and I don't think you're an idiot. So how much are you really getting?"

DeAndre inhaled. "Oh my god."

"You are a client of Mystery Club," Benny assured him. "Everything you say is strictly confidential." He put the check back in its envelope and tucked it in a flower arrangement.

"This is not a game, Benny. . . . This is not for your *club*."

"Do I seem like I'm playing around? Tell me how much you agreed on. Tell me the total sum."

DeAndre sighed. "Three million dollars. Plus medical expenses. For life."

Benny nodded. "That sounds more like it."

For a moment he didn't say anything. It felt surreal to be talking to DeAndre Bell like this. He couldn't recall ever having a conversation with DeAndre that went beyond, "What's up?" and "Not much." But suddenly he knew more about what was happening in DeAndre's life than almost anyone.

Benny picked up a bouquet of yellow roses and pulled out one of the long stems. He inhaled its scent: lush, with a hint of butter. Yellow roses always reminded him of Virginia, partly because of her hair, and partly because during the Mr. Choi investigation someone had left a yellow rose in her locker.

Benny looked back at DeAndre. His face was so tired and expressionless, Benny knew it would be hard to read.

"DeAndre . . . Trevor is violent and dangerous. He belongs in prison."

"What good would that do me?" DeAndre asked flatly. The last glimmer of congeniality was gone from his eye. Benny could feel that DeAndre no longer saw him as a valued constituent; he saw him as a threat.

"It would do the world good," Benny said. "Trevor tried to kill you. Then he lied and pretended it was an accident. Do you not understand that by accepting this money, you're letting an attempted murderer go free?"

DeAndre coughed. "I don't owe the world a single fuck. You white people need to deal with your own out-of-control white people."

"Well, actually, technically, it's debated whether Jews constitute as white, particularly those of Sephardic origin—"

DeAndre held up his hand. "Stop. Just stop. You and me are not the same."

A gulf of silence fell between them. Awkwardly Benny folded his arms and looked out the window. DeAndre's view wasn't as nice as Virginia's. Instead of the glamorous skyline, his room overlooked the parking lot.

"I'm just saying . . . ," Benny started again carefully. "You'll have to see his face every day. And it's going to be harder than you think it will be."

"Shut up," DeAndre groaned. "Like you know anything."

Benny chewed his thumbnail, deciding whether or not to say what he had to say. "Um . . . actually, I do. You know that my father was in a plane crash a while ago? Well, just recently I learned about some . . . *events* that precipitated the accident. I learned that, actually, there's a girl at our school who . . . well, the details don't matter. But I have to look at her now. She even kissed me. This girl's *mouth* was on my *face*. This girl who . . . if it weren't for her, my dad would not be brain-damaged."

DeAndre squinted at him. "What?"

Benny waved his hand. "Whatever, it's a weird story. I'm still processing the facts. Actually, I'm trying to not even think about it right now. But the point is, I will have to look at this girl every day until I get out of this school, and I don't know if I can do it. I think I might . . . explode. And it's going to be a hundred times worse for you."

DeAndre sighed. "I'll transfer to Tate Prep. I'll transfer to Timbuktu."

"Nowhere will be far enough," Benny said. "No matter where you go, Trevor will be out there, polluting the world with his freedom."

"BENNY!" DeAndre growled. His eyes were so full of anger that Benny felt instinctively afraid, even though DeAndre couldn't smush a bug in his condition, much less Benny's face. One of the machines he was hooked up to had started to go off.

Beep beep beep.

"You will not fuck this up for me!" DeAndre hissed. "I am taking this money. I am going wherever I want for college. I'm buying my mom a decent fucking house. One day I will be the president of this country, and Trevor will just be some rich dirtbag whose face I can't even remember. If you fuck this up for me, Benny Flax, I will never forgive you. If you fuck this up for me, *I will haunt you forever!*"

"Okay! Okay!" Benny said quickly. "It's your decision, and I will not . . . fuck it up. I respect your decision."

"What is going on here?" A nurse bustled into the room and started fiddling with DeAndre's IV.

Benny stood up. "I'm sorry—"

Beep beep beep.

The nurse gave Benny a sharp look. "You shouldn't be in here. DeAndre isn't having any more visitors today."

Benny started toward the door.

"Hey, wait!" DeAndre called after him weakly. "Scooby, wait! Are we cool, man?"

Benny turned back. DeAndre's face was full of fear. It made Benny feel bad. DeAndre had enough to deal with without being guilt-tripped for cashing out, and without the anxiety of wondering whether Benny could be trusted.

"We are cool," Benny said. "I swear."

"Get out!" the nurse snapped at him.

Beep beep beep.

"Swear on that Bible," DeAndre demanded, pointing to a Bible amid the clutter of flowers and gifts on his windowsill.

"I . . ." Benny was about to remind him that he was Jewish and the Bible meant nothing to him. But then he decided it didn't matter; it meant something to DeAndre. He went to the Bible and laid his hand on it. "I swear on this Bible that we are cool."

"Get out of here!" the nurse yelled.

Benny scurried out of the room. As soon as he was in the hall, he felt a stinging in his hand and realized he was still clutching the yellow rose. Its thorns were digging into his palm. Benny took a last look at DeAndre, who was being fussed over by the nurse.

Benny wondered how much money he would accept to not report an attempted murder. He'd basically done it for free a few weeks ago. He'd let Zaire Bollo escape to Spain and not given it another thought. Maybe that was the key—he wouldn't do something for money that he wouldn't have done for free anyway. But at a certain point, was there a moral obligation to get dangerous people out of circulation?

No, he decided. He wasn't Batman; he was a mystery-solver. Locking people up didn't make the world a better place; knowledge did. That was the theory anyway. Benny's only obligation was to the truth, and to what DeAndre wanted. What people did with the truth was not his concern.

Recovery wing, room 441, 10:40 a.m.

"Which do you want, tranquility or passion?"

"Passion," Virginia answered.

"Passion it is."

The tea was steaming hot. Virginia took a tiny sip, trying to figure out this gorgeous Hispanic man's relationship to Benny Flax. He was at least twenty-five years old, and he wore a necklace with a tiny gold cross, which meant he wasn't Jewish. Was he Benny's bodyguard? A distant cousin? Virginia was usually good at figuring out people's relationships, but with this "Rodrigo" person, she didn't have a clue. He was very quiet, but she could tell it wasn't because he was shy. He was just being aloof. It was incredibly cool.

Benny appeared in the doorway. "Hey."

"Hey!" Virginia said back. "That was quick."

Rodrigo stood up. "I'll give you two a minute. We gotta go in say, a half hour?"

Benny nodded. "Sure."

Virginia watched Rodrigo leave. She would have expected Benny to seem even dweebier compared to his random gorgeous friend. But actually, Rodrigo's coolness seemed to radiate to include him; Benny must be cool, after all, if this guy wanted to hang out with him.

"Who was that?" Virginia asked as soon as he was gone.

Benny looked at her cup. "Is that tea? You shouldn't be drinking caffeine within twenty-four hours of undergoing anesthesia."

"It's herbal, *Dad*."

Benny flopped down in the metal chair next to the window. He felt weird. He felt . . . nothing. The mystery of DeAndre Bell was solved. Where was the rush of satisfaction? Where was the feeling of triumph?

Relax, he told himself. He was probably just tired.

"So what happened? Tell me!" Virginia demanded. Then she saw the rose in Benny's hand, and reached out and grabbed it. "Wow, thank you!"

"Oh, um, you're welcome," Benny said, feeling guilty that Virginia had assumed he'd brought it back for her on purpose.

She sniffed it. "Mmm. Yellow roses are so much better than red ones. Red roses, like, make me want to throw up. They smell like grandmas."

Benny looked at her. He'd heard her say that about red roses before. It was strange realizing they'd been friends long enough for the conversation to get repetitive.

Virginia stuck her foot out and kicked his shoulder. "So come on, tell me what happened!"

"Well, I couldn't confirm everything before a nurse kicked me out. But I think I know what's going on."

"Tell me!"

Benny took a second to organize his thoughts. "Okay, so . . . obviously I never believed for a second that the impalement was an accident. But Trevor's motive seemed way too flimsy. Revenge for DeAndre winning the election? Trevor is immature, but he's not a four-year-old. I just couldn't believe he was *that* sore of a loser. So I thought Yasmin must have orchestrated it. Or Calvin. But what if it wasn't about being a sore loser? What if Trevor actually . . . *won?*"

"Won what?" Virginia adjusted her arm. It was starting to hurt, but she wanted to know Benny's dirt more than she wanted to call the nurse for more painkillers.

"Won the election. What if he *actually won?* Do you remember when they announced the results, and Trevor made such an idiot of himself, 'succeeding from the Union' and all that crap? I remember him shouting that the election had been rigged. It seemed like it was all a big joke. But what if Trevor was acting out because he'd actually won? It's one thing to lose—you get over that. It's another thing to win and have it taken from your hands."

"Why would they rig the election *against* Trevor? He's, like, Mr. Popular, and his dad's the president of the Board of Trustees or whatever."

Benny was staring out the window. Virginia had noticed this about him before: whenever he was on a serious train of thought, he didn't look at her when he was speaking. It was annoying. It made her feel like a dumping ground for his thought process instead of an actual person having a conversation.

"Winship has . . . a reputation," he was saying. "We're the least diverse private school in Atlanta, did you know that? It's reaching a point where something has to change. And the Board is thinking, what if we just stick a black kid on display at the very top, as the president of the student body. Then maybe we won't have to address the actual *issues* of the student body. The issues of our sons, who think they're living in Dixie Land."

"So wait, you're saying Mr. Cheek stole the election from his own kid? And gave it to DeAndre?"

Benny nodded. "And DeAndre knows. He knows he didn't really win. But he took the position anyway. It wasn't completely selfish—DeAndre *likes* Winship. He has true school spirit. He's a better leader than Trevor, and he knew he'd be a better president, even if he didn't have the votes to back it up."

"If the people wanted Trevor, then they deserved him," Virginia said scornfully. "Idiots."

"This election was probably the first thing Trevor truly earned in his entire life. Imagine having everything handed to you on a silver tray. Then you go out and get *one thing* for yourself, *one thing* that wasn't handed to you. And it's taken away. Trevor toed the line for a long time, hiding his rage under a mask of buffoonery. But the volcano was bound to erupt. It wasn't an accident, but it wasn't premeditated, either. The lights went out, and in that moment of darkness, he just . . . exploded."

"I'd probably explode if my dad stabbed me in the back like that," Virginia said. "That's messed up."

"Mr. Cheek is in a very precarious position right now. He created this situation, and now he's stuck between his volatile son, who feels betrayed, and the boy his son almost murdered, who now has the power to send Trevor to prison. . . . I'd like to get some proof. It shouldn't be that hard. All elections at Winship are conducted through e-mail. The votes are collated and stored in cloud software that's accessible from any administrator's computer. I've broken into the admin software before. It was easy."

"What? When?"

Benny looked at her like he was snapping out of a trance. "Um, huh?"

"When did you break into the admin software?"

"I . . . I don't know. . . . What?"

Virginia cocked her eyebrow. "What is wrong with you? Are you having a stroke?"

"Let's just move on, please."

"Okay, weirdo . . ."

Benny looked out the window. He could feel Virginia staring at him. Then he felt her look away. He exhaled.

That was way too close.

Benny knew he was a bad liar. But he needed to not be *this* bad. A few weeks ago, during the Mr. Choi investigation, he'd broken into the principal's computer to look up Virginia's records. There had been some red flags, and Benny had questions about her Florida origins. Virginia never talked about her home or her family, except for one time when she mentioned a fantastical-sounding stepfather in Cuba. The records hadn't revealed much, except for a restraining order from two years ago between her and a Stephen Kroll in Boca Raton. Benny hadn't been able to determine whether Virginia was the victim or the perpetrator, and he'd felt so guilty about invading her privacy that he'd abandoned the line of inquiry and tried not to think about it.

"It goes without saying that this information stays between us," Benny said, trying to bounce back from his near blunder. "DeAndre wants the money. It's his decision. We can't screw it up by doing anything that would derail his deal with Mr. Cheek. Trevor must remain free. Do you understand? We can't tell *anyone*. After everything DeAndre's been through, we're not going to make his life worse."

Virginia nodded but seemed distracted by something out the window. "Omigod! Do you see that?" She pointed to the sky. Dark gray clouds had formed south of the city. It looked like Mordor from *The Lord of the Rings*. Or like the wrath of DeAndre's neighborhood coming to rain down on them.

"See what?"

"IT'S A BANANA!" she yelled at the top of her lungs.

Benny squinted. Sure enough, one of the dark clouds was an oblong, curved shape that did kind of resemble a banana. Virginia was full-on freaking out, screaming excitedly. Benny stared at her. He'd never met someone who vacillated so unpredictably between a shrewd observer and a weird idiot.

"Please quiet down," Benny said, not wanting a bunch of nurses to flood in and sedate her.

"Bye-bye, banana!" The banana in the sky was being absorbed by the mass of rain clouds, and Virginia waved at it. Then she turned back to Benny. "So does this mean Calvin's cleared? As a suspect?"

"Why, because a banana appeared in the sky?"

"No, because you just said it was Trevor."

Benny shook his head. "There's still . . . *something* with Calvin. I can tell. Just stay on him. And anyway, the golf team investigation is still open. We need to find the caddie they assaulted. Calvin was there. He was involved."

"But he's not like those other guys. He doesn't care about Dixie Land or Southern pride or whatever. He's actually, like, a cool person."

"Virginia!" Benny suddenly felt exasperated. "Are you unable to continue this investigation?"

Virginia looked incredibly offended. "Um, *pardonez moi?*"

"I gave you the lead on this because I thought you were capable of being objective. But if you aren't, you need to give the case back to me."

"What? No way!"

"I don't care how 'cool' Calvin seems. Just stay on him. Except don't get in a car with him again," he stipulated. "He's obviously an unsafe driver."

"It wasn't Calvin's fault. It was Big Gabe," Virginia said, but Benny didn't think she sounded convinced by her own words. This was going to be a problem, he could see already. Virginia couldn't investigate Calvin if she was just going to construe every situation to defend him. But right now wasn't a good time to get in a fight about it. Virginia seemed irritable and on edge. Her arm probably hurt like hell, even though she was acting tough about it.

"Do you think Rodrigo would check me out?"

Benny shot her a look. *Check me out?* Did she seriously want to date a man twice her age whom she'd known for five seconds?

"I need an adult's signature to get out of here."

"Ohhh. . . . Sure, of course."

Outside, it started raining. The gloom seemed inside the room, making everything feel gray.

"Listen, I'm going to be busy this week," Benny said. "There have been developments with my . . . thing."

"Oh my god, what is with you and your *thing*?"

Benny ignored her. "I need to get my grades up four points by the end of the week. That means I'll mostly be studying. I'll follow up with the drug dealer in the bathroom and the election rigging. But you're in charge of Calvin and the golf team."

"Why?"

"Because you're a capable person."

"No, why do you need to get your grades up four points all of a sudden?"

"I just . . . do."

Virginia flopped back on the pillow. Benny was so annoying. The second she pegged him as a truly boring square, he turned out to be more mysterious than anyone. Who the hell was his hot Hispanic friend? What the hell was his *thing* that he refused to tell her? And what was the story with his damn dog? She sipped her cup of tea. Passion tasted suspiciously like artificial raspberry flavoring.

"I hate Sundays," she said. "Will you do my math homework?"

"That would be unethical."

"Pleeeeeeease?"

"Fine."

Virginia sat up, surprised. She hadn't been asking him seriously. She'd assumed it would take much more than a "please" for Benny to take the stick out of his ass and violate his prissy code of ethics.

"Are you ready to get out of here?" Benny asked. The idea of dumping her at the dismal Boarders in the dismal rain—her body literally *broken*—made him feel depressed and useless. But where else was he supposed to take her? It was where she belonged.

The Boarders, 5:55 p.m.

> To: c.harker@winship.edu
>
> From: v.leeds@winship.edu
>
> Subject: (no subject)
>
> Still wanna get Chinsees food? I guss we
> cant drive (oops) but we cn get delivry . . .

She'd sent the e-mail an hour ago and he hadn't responded. Was he mad that she'd made him wreck his car? He didn't seem like the kind of guy who would care about that stuff. But she didn't actually know him very well, did she? The price of that kiss had been incredibly steep: a Jaguar and an entire arm. She didn't regret it, though. Did he?

Chinsees. It was hard to type left-handed. She hoped the misspelling came off as carefree and lackadaisical, but the more she sat there waiting for him to reply, the more embarrassed she felt.

Why am I sitting here like a loser? she asked herself. She didn't want people to think she was the kind of person who sat around waiting for a guy to e-mail her back. Of course, no one was there to see but Gottfried, who was asleep on the sofa clutching a cold piece of pizza like a teddy bear. But the trick to being the person you wanted to be was to be it even when no one was watching. So she shut off the computer and went outside. Ten minutes later she was standing in front of Calvin's house.

The rain had stopped, but the sky was still gloomy and depressing. It was the kind of sky that seemed to be saying, *Go inside and do your homework.* Virginia looked up at it. *No.*

The doorbell was old-fashioned, a Victorian brass key that made a fancy-sounding chime. *Rrrrrring!*

A long minute passed, and then the door creaked open. Virginia inhaled sharply. She'd forgotten how terrifying Headmaster Harker was in person. He was so tall it felt like he could simply lift his foot and squash her like an insect. And the way he was looking at her, Virginia felt like an insect. He didn't even say hello—he just stared at her. His eyes moved coldly from her black cast to her face.

"Sorry to bother you," she said, her voice squeaking. "Um, I'm Virginia Leeds? I'm in tenth grade? Is Calvin home?"

"Calvin is unable to receive guests at this time." The headmaster began closing the door.

"Wait! Is he okay? I was in the car crash with him." She raised her broken arm.

"Calvin is fine. Calvin is . . . grounded."

"For how long?"

"That is a private matter, Miss Leeds." He started to close the door again.

"Wait. Wait! Could you at least give him a message from me?"

He stopped, apparently waiting to hear the message.

"Um, uh, just tell him . . . hi."

"Hi," the headmaster repeated, as if it were the most

asinine word he'd ever been compelled to utter.

"Or, wait, tell him—"

"I'm afraid I don't have time for this, Miss Leeds."

"Just tell him . . . Tell him I had anesthesia, so I was unconscious again? And I wondered if . . . all the world sucked again." It had sounded romantic in her mind, but out loud it seemed so stupid it made her cringe.

"I certainly will give him that message," the headmaster said. "Thank you for stopping by." Then he shut the door in her face.

Damn it.

Virginia bit her lip. She wasn't an idiot; she knew there was no chance in hell that Headmaster Harker would actually tell Calvin that a girl came by and said some thing about anesthesia and the world sucking. She had to try again. She knew she was being pushy, but she turned the brass key anyway.

Rrrrrring . . .

Nobody answered this time.

Monday

The assembly hall, 8:01 a.m.

"What is dignity? What is self-respect?"

These were interesting questions coming from a woman wearing the ugliest pantsuit in creation, and who was so short she had to stand on a box to reach the podium.

Mrs. Jewel paused to glare at everyone in the audience. Chrissie sunk down in her seat. She hated getting yelled at. It made her want to crawl into a hole and cry. Everyone was freaking out that Mrs. Jewel might cancel the Homecoming dance on Saturday. Chrissie wished she would just do it already, and skip the part where she made everyone feel horrible.

"I am appalled by the behavior that many of you showed this weekend. In my ten years as principal at the Saint Mary's School in Connecticut, I never saw as much troubling conduct as I have seen in my two weeks here at Winship. Two of your fellow students spent yesterday in the hospital, one with a broken bone and one with whiplash. Those of you who attended the so-called fundraiser at the Cheek residence—and you know who you are—have disgraced your school, your parents, and most important, you have disgraced yourselves."

Chrissie felt her eyes stinging with tears. *Please don't cry. Please don't cry,* she begged herself. Why did Mrs. Jewel have to be such a mean old lady? She was probably just jealous, because no one in their right mind would ever do a tequila shot off her troll body.

"The young women of this school are long overdue for a lesson in self-respect. Do *self-respecting* ladies auction their bodies like chattel? Do young men show their respect for ladies by *buying* them to use as vessels for alcoholic beverages that are being *illegally* consumed? No, they do not. And to answer the question I know is burning in everyone's minds, no, I am not canceling the Homecoming dance."

There was a collective sigh of relief, and a few people even clapped. But Mrs. Jewel wasn't finished.

"However, as of this moment, I am declaring all dates heretofore arranged to be void. The women will be in charge. This is not a request. This is not optional. The Homecoming dance is now girls-ask-boys."

Everyone groaned loudly. There had been one official girls-ask-boys dance in Winship history, and it had been a disaster. In the end, everyone had mostly gone stag. It wasn't that the girls were scared of boys. It was that there weren't enough crush-worthy guys to go around, and none of the girls wanted to be selfish and grab the good ones, which would screw over their friends. Girls stuck together at Winship, especially the cheerleaders. Didn't Mrs. Jewel understand that? It just worked better if the guys were in charge.

Chrissie scanned the sea of heads for Benny Flax and spotted him in the front row. Chrissie had always assumed Benny was with Virginia Leeds; they even had those ugly matching rings. But apparently Virginia was dating that weird vampire Calvin Harker, and Chrissie was glad. She'd never considered Benny Flax dating material before; he wasn't in her social circle at all, and Chrissie usually only went for athletes. She liked manly guys. But maybe this whole time she'd been going for the wrong kind of manly. Benny wasn't a football stud, but he was strong in a different way. He reminded her of her grandfather, who had been an important Georgia senator. She'd always loved him and imagined that if he'd been alive, he would have stood up for her after what happened last Fourth of July, instead of blaming her like her father had.

Did I tell Benny about . . . the plane? Chrissie couldn't remember. She hoped not. She knew she tended to say a lot of random stuff when she was drunk. But hopefully she hadn't said . . . *that.*

"Fuckin' Yankee midget tellin' us how to do our business," a guy behind her was muttering. All around, everyone was whispering and complaining.

"Enough," Mrs. Jewel said. "You know, when I was at

Radcliffe, an exceptional woman said to me, 'As a woman, there's no greater power than the power you give yourself.' And that woman's name was—"

"Hillary Clinton," everyone groaned. Mrs. Jewel had already told her Hillary Clinton story five thousand times. But at least she wasn't yelling anymore. Chrissie fiddled with her charm bracelet. She was anxious to hear what Brittany and Angie thought about the girls-ask-guys situation, so she could know what to do.

Did I blend my makeup all the way? She'd forgotten to check her face in natural light before she left the Boarders. What if everyone could see the big blob of concealer on her cheek? She wished Mrs. Jewel would wrap it up so she could go look in a mirror. Chrissie had a weird relationship with mirrors. She constantly wanted to check her face to make sure it looked perfect. Which it never really did. Which just made her want to check the mirror even more. Truly beautiful people probably never looked in mirrors, because their beauty came from within. People like the Native Americans, or Maria from *The Sound of Music*.

People like Benny Flax.

The girls' bathroom, 9:00 a.m.

Benny's reflection surprised himself. He looked about thirty years old. There were dark circles under his eyes. He hadn't slept well since Saturday, and this morning he'd gotten up at 5:30 a.m. to be at school the second Rick the janitor opened the administrative annex. While Mrs. Jewel's secretary was making coffee in the lounge, he'd snuck into the office to log into the admin software. He was hoping to resolve the remaining Mystery Club cases as quickly as possible so he could concentrate on studying. Usually Benny skated on 90 to 95 percent grades, but right now that wasn't good enough. Right now he needed to be perfect.

Except things weren't going perfectly. Mrs. Jewel's computer was different from the last principal's, and it was password-protected. Benny had made some guesses, including "hillaryclinton," but nothing worked. So that had been a bust.

Next he'd gone to the library to look up unsolved homicides and missing persons reports for black men of slim build on the Georgia Bureau of Investigation website. But none of the dates matched the midnight golf game closely enough for any of the victims to plausibly be the nameless caddie.

So now Benny was in the girls' room, hoping he could at least wrap up the identity of the mysterious drug dealer. This case had involved way too many trips into the girls' bathroom. But he couldn't ask Virginia to do it with only one arm in working condition.

The room was brighter than it had been the last time. Benny looked up. The missing fluorescent bulb had been returned to the light in the ceiling. Benny jumped onto the sink excitedly. If the bulb was back, it meant someone had come to retrieve the X10 controller wired into the fixture. And as long as they hadn't spotted the small camera in the crevice of the ceiling, in five seconds Benny would know who the drug dealer was.

"Oh my god! What are you doing in here?"

Benny jumped, almost falling off the sink. A girl was standing in the doorway, looking at him like he was an escaped mental patient. It was a girl he recognized from the Boarders, Lindsay something.

"I'm—I'm assisting Rick with some electrical issues." Benny stealthily grabbed the camera and popped the plastic light covering back into the ceiling.

"Are you, like, an assistant janitor?" Lindsay said, a smirk forming on her face.

Oh my god, Benny thought. This was going to be one of those things that followed him to his grave. It wasn't enough to be Scooby-Doo; from now on he would also be known as a janitor's apprentice. Benny sighed. There was nothing to do but go along with it.

"Yep," he said, hopping off the sink. "But it's all taken care of now. Enjoy your . . . bathroom time."

"Whatever, Janitor Junior," Lindsay said, barely suppressing her grin.

Benny squeezed past her and left. He found a secluded spot in the hallway and sat down. He turned on the camera. The icon showed that there were two photos on the memory card. The first shot was of a hand: an abnormally long, pale hand with bony fingers. Benny felt a surge of validation.

I knew you had something to do with this!

The second photo showed Calvin's face. He was looking directly at the camera and smiling slightly. There was a small piece of paper in his hand with two words written on it:

Hi Benny

The cafeteria, 12:30 p.m.

One great thing about her ugly black cast was that at least no one was trying to sign it. Virginia really didn't need to stare at a bunch of Neil Young quotes and Bible verses and doodles of hearts for two months. Maybe Calvin would paint one of his poems on it in Wite-Out. Virginia scanned the cafeteria for him. He was a pretty easy person to spot, but she didn't see him anywhere.

Everyone was talking about Trevor's party and how Benny Flax had jumped out a window when the cops showed up. Except the story had ballooned from Benny simply stepping out of a first-floor window to Benny making a death-defying leap through a *third*-floor window like James Bond. It made Virginia feel jealous. *She* was the one with the broken arm. *She* was the one who'd almost been killed by Big Gabe's huge yellow Hummer. But no one was talking about that.

"Is this Scooby's table?"

Virginia turned around. Winn Davis was standing behind her, looking tired and confused.

"I guess so. . . ." Virginia was pretty sure Benny didn't believe in cafeteria territory. But it was the place he usually sat.

"Sorry I'm late," Benny said, appearing out of nowhere and sitting down with a tray piled with textbooks and a sandwich. He gestured to the chair across from Virginia. "Winn, please sit down."

Winn plunked down and sunk his teeth into a chicken wing. Winn was less overtly Neanderthal-ish than some of his friends, but you could still see by the way he ate his meat that this guy could tear anyone apart if he wanted to. No one knew this better than Virginia—she'd witnessed him beating Min-Jun to a sputtering pulp a few weeks ago, throwing punches like Min-Jun was made of butter. Virginia wondered what it would feel like to be that strong.

She looked around the cafeteria. It was kind of cool, Winn Davis sitting with Mystery Club. It gave her a little buzz, disrupting the social order. Everyone was looking at them, but Winn didn't seem to notice or care.

"I'm pleased to inform you that Mystery Club has ascertained the identity of the person in the bathroom the night of the science expo," Benny said in a low voice. He slid a piece of paper across the table. Virginia squinted to read the name on it:

CALVIN HARKER.

Her eyes widened. Then she felt Benny looking at her, and she tried to make her face blank. *He's checking my reaction,* she realized. It made her feel vaguely offended, like Benny thought she was suspicious or something.

"Thanks, man." Winn tucked the slip of paper into his pocket.

"I helped," Virginia piped up.

Winn gave her a nod. "Y'all are pretty cool." He ripped off another piece of chicken with his perfect white teeth.

"Can I ask you one thing?" Benny asked. "Strictly confidential."

Winn nodded.

"What is a 'red pill'?"

Winn stopped chewing for a second. Then he swallowed and said, "I dunno. I took the blue one."

"And what was that?"

"I dunno," Winn said again. "It was . . . happiness."

There was a short silence that felt long. Then Benny said, "Sounds like ecstasy."

Winn nodded. "Yeah. That's a good word for it."

"No, I mean the drug ecstasy. It creates a sensation of euphoria."

"Oh."

"But the red pill was something else? An amphetamine, perhaps. Something that heightens aggressive behavior."

Winn shrugged. He was looking over his shoulder, obviously ready for the conversation to be over. Benny waved his hand, as if waving the question away. He reached into his backpack and handed Winn an envelope. "Would you mind filling out this client satisfaction survey? Just return to the locker number on the front."

"Uh, sure."

"We aim for the highest-quality investigative service."

"Okay." And with that, Winn picked up his tray and went to sit down with his friends.

Virginia felt Benny staring at her. "What?" she said.

"I told you it was Calvin."

"You did not! You said he was a banana-peel-dropping psychopath."

"Well, he's a drug dealer. That's not much better."

Virginia scoffed. "Since when do you care what people do? We've let two attempted murderers go free, but god forbid Calvin gives drugs to consenting people?" She was trying to seem blasé, but on the inside she was freaking out. Calvin was a drug dealer? She was having a hard time wrapping her head around it. Drug dealers were supposed to be scary sleazebags, not poetic, pants-ironing headmaster's sons.

"Whatever," Benny said brusquely, opening one of his textbooks. "I need to study."

"What is wrong with you?" Virginia said, poking his arm with her fork.

"Nothing."

"I don't believe that."

Benny sighed and closed his book. He pulled a camera out of his pocket and turned it on, frowning as if its very existence offended him. And as soon as Virginia saw the image on its tiny screen, she understood why.

"Oh my god!" she squealed. "He called you. He like, *called you*, Benny Flax."

"He's a joker and a drug dealer and an unsafe driver. I don't think you should hang out with him anymore."

Virginia balked. "Um, ex-squeeze me?"

Benny opened his book again. "I really don't have time for this conversation. I need to study."

"Well, what am I supposed to do?"

Benny didn't look up from his book. "Do what you want. We still have two open cases. Mrs. Jewel's computer was password-protected, so I couldn't get proof of the election rigging. And I haven't had any luck with the identity of the caddie the golf team assaulted. If you insist on seeing Calvin again, I suggest you make use of it and get some answers out of him."

"Okaaaay . . ." Virginia waited for Benny to say something else, but he just stared at his book as if she were invisible. She was used to Benny's random mood swings, and normally they didn't bother her. But suddenly she wished she could go back in time and relive that brief, weird moment on the golf course where things had felt different between them. Benny with his shiny hair and twinkling eyes, and that smile she'd never seen before or since.

You don't have five hundred dollars.

You have no idea what I have.

Virginia sighed. Whatever that moment had been, it was dead now. She buried it in a grave, mourned it for five seconds, then picked up her lunch tray and moved on.

Friday

The administrative annex, 3:15 p.m.

Something was going on with Benny Flax, and Yasmin had a bad feeling about it. He'd turned in four extra-credit projects that week, which was incredibly alarming. Benny never went the extra mile with school stuff. Teachers even lectured him about it. One of the best moments of ninth grade was when Yasmin overheard the college counselor saying to Benny, "I want to see you push yourself. Yasmin Astarabadi is a good example—Yasmin never stops pushing. That's a girl who's going somewhere. Where are you going, Benny Flax?" Praise from teachers was like crack to Yasmin. It was the only thing that made her feel good, and she'd do anything to get it.

She was sitting on the bench outside Mrs. Jewel's office, nervously picking at her cuticles until they bled. There had been a memo on her locker to report to the principal's office after school, and she didn't know what it was about. She knew she couldn't be in trouble. What could she possibly be in trouble for? But she was still so anxious she felt slightly ill.

I didn't see anything, I swear.

She practiced saying it in her mind, in case this was about that spooky thing with the Harkers. Every time she thought about it, it gave her a little chill: the headmaster standing silently with his hand around his son's throat. Both of them looking at her like she was an intrusive cockroach.

Something else was bothering her too. All week Yasmin had been hyperaware of wherever Brittany Montague was in the hallways between classes. It made her feel creepy. What if Brittany had reported her to Mrs. Jewel for being a stalker? But it's not like Yasmin ever *followed* Brittany. She just . . . *noticed* her. She noticed everything about her. Her hair. Her skin. How adorable she managed to look in the neck brace she had to wear from getting whiplash. And Brittany would smile and wave when she saw Yasmin, which felt good for about half a second before she smiled and waved at someone else. Brittany smiled and waved like it was her job. Yasmin wished she could stop thinking about her. It was taking up too much space in her already maxed-out brain.

"Yasmin?"

Mrs. Jewel opened her door and invited Yasmin inside her office. Yasmin sat down on the vinyl chair, carefully positioning her copy of Hillary Clinton's book on her lap so Mrs. Jewel would notice it. She'd memorized a variety of quotes from the book to insert into the conversation wherever possible.

"I'm afraid I have some bad news, Yasmin. I wanted to

tell you personally because, though I've only been here a short while, it's very evident to me that you are a serious student who cares deeply about academic and civic achievement. Oh, is that *Hard Choices*?"

"Hm? Oh, yes . . ." Yasmin had prepared to launch into a glowing review of the book in her lap, but suddenly her mouth felt dry and she couldn't speak. *Bad news?*

Mrs. Jewel tapped her stubby fingers on the desk. Her nails were short and unmanicured. "Well, anyway. We all expected you to be attending the leadership luncheon in December. You know that the governor has invited the top two students from each class. Calvin Harker has maintained the number one position, and until today you were number two. But I'm afraid that Benny Flax has overtaken you, and the invitation will now be extended to him."

For a moment Yasmin felt stunned, like she'd been punched but for some reason couldn't feel pain. *I knew it,* she thought. *I knew that fucker was up to something.* But the tiny amount of validation was instantly drowned by a flood of panicked disbelief.

"What?" she heard herself saying.

Mrs. Jewel looked uncomfortable. "I'm sorry. I was warned that you might take this a little hard. But you're a strong young woman. You will rise above this."

"Benny Flax?" she sputtered. "This—this isn't fair!"

"I'm afraid it is," Mrs. Jewel said. "He pulled up his GPA

rather miraculously. We have to give the spot to him."

"Well, I'll pull up my GPA even further! Give me an extra week!" she begged.

Mrs. Jewel shook her head. "Today was the deadline. Participants need time to prepare their presentations. I'm not happy about this either, Yasmin. You were the only female on the list. Guess who we are now sending to the Governor's Mansion? Eight *boys*." She spat the word with contempt normally reserved for words like *terrorists* or *puppy killers*. She went on, "What kind of message does that send to the young women of this school?"

"It's—it's not my fault!" Yasmin said, feeling an immense lump forming in her throat.

Mrs. Jewel frowned. "There's a mistake that women make when they get to the top: they forget to look down. They don't see the men coming to drag them back to the dirt. Never, *ever* let a man steal something you earned."

Leave me alone! Yasmin wanted to yell. She scanned her mind for a Hillary Clinton quote that was the equivalent of "Fuck mean bitches who like to kick girls when they're down." She bit her lip to keep from screaming.

"I will certainly keep that in mind," Yasmin said evenly. Then she picked up her bag and her copy of Hillary Clinton's useless-ass book and left.

As soon as she was alone in the empty hallway, Yasmin knew she had two options: she could melt down and cry, or she could keep pushing.

I can still do this, she thought. Not because Mrs. Jewel's guilt trip had been so inspiring, but because Yasmin had something on her side that no one else did. And it wasn't brains or conviction or women's empowerment.

It was the Shark.

The Boarders, 5:30 p.m.

To: c.harker@winship.edu
From: v.leeds@winship.edu
Subject: (no subject)

What's up? I guess you're still grounded.

Hey I have a question. Can you sneak onto your dad's computer? It's for Mystery Club. I'm trying to get proof that the prez election last spring was rigged. Benny says the electronic voting records should be on the admin cloud software.

Sorry that question was so boring. I have other things I could ask you but Im not sure if you're checking your e-mail anymore. Well, I guess I'll say bye now.

Bye!

Virginia read the e-mail for the thousandth time. She'd sent it on Monday and there'd been no reply. Had she been too business-like? Maybe she should have said, *Dear Calvin,*

Sorry I Frenched you and made you wreck your car. Is it true that you're a drug dealer? Xoxo!

Virginia flopped onto the ratty common-room sofa. It had been such a boring week, she wanted to throw herself off a bridge. Calvin hadn't shown up to school at all. She'd heard a messenger was handing in all his homework. And Benny had been basically a blur, rushing between classes with his nose in a book, barely acknowledging her when they passed in the hallway. She had two e-mails from Min-Jun about wanting to meet soon to "talk business," which made her so nervous she'd just deleted them both without answering.

The two Mystery Club cases were still open. Virginia had no idea how to find the name of an unidentified beaten-up black man, and she had no idea how to get into an administrator's password-protected computer. She'd always resented Benny's bossiness, but now she was realizing that, without him, she didn't have the first clue how to conduct an investigation. Plus her arm hurt constantly—a relentless, throbbing ache that made her feel irritable and tired.

Mrs. Jewel's proclamation that the Homecoming dance was now girls-ask-guys had created the most boring pre-dance week in history. To ensure that no one's feelings would get hurt, the Montague twins had organized a box in their homeroom where all the girls could anonymously submit the name of the guy they wanted to ask, and if a guy's name was in the box more than once, it meant no one was allowed to ask him at all. It was the exact kind of thing that drove Virginia crazy. She envied male friendships and the way boys gave each other space; girls were always stifling each other, and holding each other back with their suffocating togetherness.

The upshot of the twins' box system was that only guys on the fringe and guys no one else wanted were fair game to ask. It didn't really affect Virginia. She preferred going to dances alone anyway; it opened the night up to more possibility. If she was honest, the thing that was really bugging her was Chrissie White. Apparently Chrissie had had a magical love connection with Benny Flax at Trevor's party, where he'd saved her from her own sloppy drunkenness by riding in on a unicorn or something. And now Chrissie wanted to ask him to the dance if she could get up the courage (which, knowing her, she probably couldn't). The insane part was that, according to her, she'd had breakfast with Benny's entire family *at his house*. It was beyond unfair. After all the countless hours Virginia had spent being Benny's servant for Mystery Club, he wouldn't even invite her to his synagogue for Chinese food. Meanwhile, Chrissie spent *one* night with him and managed to make it something to brag about.

Whatever, she thought. If Benny just wanted a secretary to help him solve mysteries, she'd be such a good secretary she'd blow his mind. She pulled Trevor's phone out of her bag. Maybe if she stared long enough at the photo of the golf team dragging the caddie, a clue would magically present itself.

Figure this out, she commanded herself. *You don't need Benny Flax. Benny Flax needs YOU.*

The photo didn't even shock her anymore. It was freaky how quickly her mind had adjusted to the reality of things: that the golfers were violent racist bullies, that Trevor Cheek was an attempted murderer. It wasn't even that surprising. Trevor had always been a Neanderthal who liked pushing people around. It was only a matter of time before his bullying went too far, and probably only a matter of time before it would happen again. But Benny didn't seem to think that was their problem. He didn't believe in interfering, Virginia had long observed. Mystery Club only went in after the blood was already on the ground.

She zoomed the photo on the caddie's face, a blurry blob of facial features contorted in pain. The weird thing was that the more Virginia looked at it, the more it seemed like he wasn't actually screaming, he was *laughing.* Then she'd zoom out, and it would look like a scream again. Then she'd zoom in and feel certain it was a laugh.

Then she noticed something else. A tiny bit of hand that wasn't the right color, like it had been cut and pasted onto the wrong body.

Oh my god. Oh my god.

Suddenly Virginia knew exactly who the caddie was. She jumped up from the couch and lunged for the phone. She was dialing Benny's number when she noticed the computer. A new message had appeared in her in-box. She set the phone down and opened it.

To: v.leeds@winship.edu
From: c.harker@winship.edu
Subject: (no subject)

DO NOT RESPOND TO THIS MESSAGE.
Account is possibly being monitored
   got on my dad's computer. Voting data for student body prez has been deleted. Data from other elections (prom theme, Homecoming Queen etc.) is still on the cloud, so looks like someone intentionally deleted prez files. Hope that is helpful
   so sorry about almost getting us killed. Are u going to the dance? Look at your Rx and if it's Percocet or anything w "oxy" or "codone" in the name plz bring all of it. Also bring a passport if u have one.
   Sry I can't write more, no time. But to answer your question,
   YES

Benny's house, 6:00 p.m.

The governor was on the news again. He was addressing allegations that his personal conflict with the lobbyist Garland

White had resulted in the loss of four thousand jobs for the state. He was "apologizing." Benny put the sound on mute and studied the governor's face. He was a robust and red-blooded Southern man. But there was a disturbing lack of depth behind his eyes, as if he were a cardboard cutout who would tip over if faced with an actual thought. They were the eyes of a man who no longer possessed a soul. How did it happen? At what point in a man's life did he wake up and find himself as hollow as a drum? A beat still pounding in the absence of a heart.

It is my wish that the world should know everlasting peace.

Benny always did his aikido exercises in the living room during the news while his mother made dinner in the kitchen. He felt it was beneficial for his father to observe this ritual in whatever foggy capacity he was able to. The translation of aikido meant "the way of unifying with life energy." It was a martial art based on purely defensive action. The aikido fighter was trained to evade and redirect attacks in such a way that caused harm to no one, not even the attacker. The idea was that everyone is deserving of empathy and compassion, even those who seek to destroy you. It didn't require physical strength or brute aggression: only focus and awareness, and the desire to understand your enemy rather than hate them.

It is my wish that the world should know everlasting peace.

He said the mantra again, but the words felt empty. Benny looked at his dad, who was gazing mutely at a spot on the floor. He had the face of a dazed old man. It was hard to remember sometimes that this person was his father and not his grandfather or even *great*-grandfather—one of those old Holocaust survivors you encountered every once in a while at temple. Usually when Benny looked at his dad—really looked at him—he was filled with a kind of aggravated despair that was hard to describe. But right now he felt nothing, except for a vague alarm at his own numbness. Had it begun for him? The hollowing-out of his soul?

Stop being dramatic, he told himself. He felt as exhausted as a sled dog. He needed to sleep for twenty hours before attempting to unify with life energy. It had been a rough week. Benny had never worked so hard for something in his life. He'd aced three tests and pulled four extra-credit assignments out of thin air. He'd done bonus labs for chemistry, and read the entirety of *Moby Dick* in three days so he could turn the essay in early. He'd slept a total of eight hours since Monday. He was so tired he barely felt human. But he'd done it. The invitation to the Governor's Mansion was his. And now he had an entire month to plan what to do with it. Plotting and scheming was not "the way," Benny knew. But somehow he'd been able to push that out of his mind. He'd pushed a lot of things out of his mind this week.

"I'm going to bed," he announced to no one.

Rrrrrrring!

It was the phone. His mother picked it up in the kitchen. "Flax residence. . . . One moment, please. Benjamin," she said, holding out the cordless phone to him. Benny could tell from the tone of her voice that it was Virginia. Benny avoided his mother's eyes as he took the phone.

"Hello?" he said, going into his room and shutting the door.

"Benny?" The voice wasn't Virginia's. It was small and girlish and hesitant.

"Yes?"

"Um, it's me. Chrissie?"

"Oh. Hi," Benny said, caught off-guard. He wasn't great on the phone; he knew that about himself. He'd developed a fairly comfortable rapport with Virginia, but it didn't really translate to other girls.

"I was just wondering . . ." Chrissie's voice trailed off, obviously requiring encouragement to go on.

I can't deal with you right now, he said in his mind, wishing he had the courage to say it out loud. "Yes?"

"Are you going to the dance tomorrow?"

"Yes," Benny said. "I always attend school events."

"Because, you know, it's girls-ask-guys. . . ." There was a long pause. Then Benny realized: *She wants to ask me.* His stomach twisted with dread.

"Are you going?" he prompted dutifully, wishing he could just hang up the phone. Awkward social pressures were his kryptonite; if he wasn't careful, he'd end up going to the dance with Chrissie just to be polite and to put this phone conversation out of its misery.

"Um, I'm not sure. . . ."

Oh my god, Benny thought. She was trying to get him to ask her, which not only put him in an impossible position, but defeated the entire purpose of Mrs. Jewel's women's empowerment scheme.

"Well, I'll definitely see you there," Benny said, trying to sound kind but firm at the same time.

"Do you want to know what color my dress is?" Chrissie asked.

Benny rubbed his temples. Why on earth would he want to know the color of her dress? Was this kindergarten? "Um, sure," he answered.

"It's Carolina blue. So . . . a yellow corsage would be really pretty. Maybe a yellow rose?"

A corsage? Benny wished he could die. "Got it. Okay. I have to go. I'll see you there. Bye."

He hit the "End" button. Then he buried his face in his pillow, taunted by visions of corsages. *Carolina blue?* Was that different from regular blue?

Rrrrrrring!

Benny groaned into the pillow. Then he picked up the phone, not wanting his mother to answer it first. "Yes?" he said, knowing how rude he sounded and hating himself for it.

"Guess what?" The voice wasn't Chrissie's. It was Virginia's. *Thank god,* Benny thought. The anxious knot in his stomach loosened. He started taking his shoes off and flopped onto his bed.

"What?"

"There is no caddie. The caddie doesn't exist."

"Huh?"

"There is no caddie!" she repeated, and then started rambling a hundred miles an hour about a white hand and smudged pants and how the golf team were all psychopaths.

"Virginia, stop. What are you talking about?"

"I know who the caddie is!" she shrieked. Benny held the phone away from his ear.

"Okay, then just tell me," he said. *"Slowly."*

"The caddie . . . is . . ."

"Oh my god, not that slow."

"It's Craig. That's why you can't see him in any of the pictures. The caddie *is* Craig!"

Benny sat up, trying to focus on what she was saying. "What do you mean, the caddie is Craig?"

"If you look closely at the photo, you can see that he's *laughing*. And his hand is *white*. Remember the smudges you pointed out on the caddie's pants? You thought it was blood, but it wasn't. It was *paint*. They painted Craig black. Isn't that, like, horrifying?"

"They painted Craig black," Benny repeated.

"Yeah. So they could drag him around. Like, as a gross joke."

"That's—that's—" Benny couldn't think of a decent word.

There was no decent word. It was . . . indecent. It was foul.

"Those guys are crazy," Virginia was saying. "They made Craig their punching bag. And he *liked* it."

"Craig likes attention. He doesn't care how he gets it."

Benny didn't know what else to say. He felt stunned. Who were these people? They thought this was *funny*? He tried to wrap his mind around it. It wasn't an assault; it was a *joke*. Somehow the former had been easier to comprehend. These were his classmates. He saw their faces every day. They all lived in the same city as him and had the same teachers. They wore literally the same clothes. But the way their minds worked was utterly baffling, as if they were aliens. Or maybe Benny was the alien.

"It's, like, pathological," Virginia was saying. Benny was pretty sure she didn't understand what that word meant.

"Racism isn't a pathology," he corrected her. "It's a prejudiced point of view. You can't take a Xanax and stop being racist."

"Whatever. Those guys are insane."

"It's not productive to dismiss people as insane just because they think differently. . . ." Benny trailed off. He felt too tired to have a philosophical debate about a bunch of assholes whose brains would probably explode if they examined themselves for five seconds. *You have everything!* Benny wanted to scream at them. *Why are you so threatened by people scraping to get the tiniest bit for themselves?*

"So what do we do?" Virginia asked.

Benny closed his eyes. He unzipped his pants and slid them off, getting under the covers. "What do you mean?" He yawned.

"Craig only got suspended for two weeks. Trevor didn't get punished at all. It doesn't seem fair."

"Punishment isn't our concern."

On the other end of the line, Virginia made a frustrated noise. "Well, what's the point of this, then? What's the point of Mystery Club if we just let everyone get away with everything?"

"I don't know," Benny said lifelessly. They'd had this argument before. Normally he would have launched into a speech about the power of knowledge, and how understanding was the goal, not judgment. How all human beings were flawed. No one could presume to know what was right for anyone else. But Benny didn't have the energy to stand behind his own credo at the moment.

"I have to go to sleep," he said. "It's been a really long week."

"Yeah, I barely saw you. . . . Did you get your magical four points?"

"I did," Benny answered. *Four points.* It was telling that Virginia remembered the exact number. Obviously she expected an explanation for his sudden interest in his grades. But he wasn't prepared to give her one.

"Is this about that lunch at the Governor's Mansion?" she asked out of the blue.

Benny's heart thudded. She'd caught him. She always did. Virginia was better at this stuff than she realized. People's facades didn't fool her. He looked at the phone in his hand, considering how to proceed. Then he pressed it back to his ear.

"Can I give you some advice?" he pivoted. "About investigating?"

"Sure." Virginia sounded annoyed.

"If you have a question like that, never ask over the phone. You need to see someone's face to know if you're getting the truth."

There was a long pause. Then Benny said, "I really need to go to sleep. See you tomorrow at the dance."

"Should we meet out front and go in together?" Virginia asked. Benny could sense a current of interest beneath the casualness of her voice. *She knows Chrissie asked me,* he thought. *But she doesn't know if I said yes.* He'd been noticing this about Virginia lately: she was learning how to use information. How to dangle it to get what she wanted, rather than using it as a bludgeon. It was a little unsettling, witnessing someone evolve before your eyes.

"Let's meet inside."

For a crucial second she didn't say anything. Then she said, "Okeydoke. Well, bye then."

"Bye. I lo—" Benny stopped himself. *Jesus.* That had been way too close. He'd almost just said "I love you" to Virginia Leeds. Surely it wasn't some big Freudian slip. It was only a habit from always saying it to his mom on the phone.

"Did you just say something?" Virginia asked. "Oh my god, I'm having *déjà vu* right now. This is so weird. . . ."

Benny turned off the lamp and pulled his comforter up to his chin. "Did you know there are three forms of *déjà vu*?"

"God, you sound tired. Are you in bed right now?"

"Yep. . . ." It struck Benny how weirdly intimate it was, talking on the phone in bed. It was basically being in bed with someone.

"You're like a ninety-year-old man, going to bed this early."

"That's me."

"Well, good night, old fogey."

"Good night. I lo—" *Jesus!* He almost wanted to laugh, it was so ridiculous.

"What do you keep stuttering?"

"Nothing. Good night."

"Night."

There was a pause as each of them waited for the other to hang up. Then Benny heard the dial tone in his ear. He pushed end and dropped the phone onto the floor. He was so excited to go to sleep, it almost made him feel energized again. But he dreaded waking up in the morning. Without exhaustion to numb him, he'd have to feel his feelings. Without studying to distract him, he'd have to think his thoughts. Benny had always been a very mentally organized person. But the last week had been too overwhelming. His school was controlled by racist oligarchs. Virginia continued to get into cars with criminals. Chrissie White had unloaded some very weird information on him, which—if true—basically meant that Benny's entire life as he knew it was a lie.

Don't think about it, Benny ordered himself. He knew that if he thought about it, he wouldn't be able to sleep, and if he couldn't get some sleep, he was going to fall apart. *I'm going to fall apart anyway,* he thought miserably. He wasn't sure if Chrissie even understood the full implications of what she'd told him that night. She seemed incredibly, almost insufferably oblivious. And now Benny would have to buy her a yellow rose—*Virginia's* flower—and spend an entire evening with her in her Carolina-colored dress, whatever that entailed.

Dewdrop, let me cleanse in your brief sweet waters . . . These dark hands of life.

He'd forgotten his idea to touch the dew on the grass in the morning. It came rushing back to him now, like a much-needed hug. He could almost feel the cold, beautiful droplets on his fingertips. It was going to be okay. Everything was going to be okay. Benny was asleep before the good feeling could evaporate. The way dew always did.

Saturday
Calvin's house, 7:30 p.m.

It was like looking in a mirror—a horrible, cursed mirror that showed the future. Calvin's face had never felt like his own; he shared all his features with his father. Same dark brow, straight nose, hollow cheeks, green eyes. His father was himself plus thirty years, and looking at him felt like a threat from life: *Behold your fate.* Calvin stood still, waiting for their miserable father-and-son ritual to be over.

"I'm not high," he said hoarsely. Mr. Harker was gripping his throat, almost strangling him. He stared into his son's eyes, looking for signs that he was lying: sclerotic redness, glassiness, puffy lids, unusually dilated pupils. He didn't believe anything Calvin said anymore.

Calvin took shallow breaths. His dad was cutting off his windpipe. It was purposefully cruel. Mr. Harker had Marfan syndrome too—it was inherited—and he knew his son bruised easily. But Calvin had no choice but to meet his dad's eyes, which were boring intensely into his own. It was uncomfortably intimate. At this point, the two barely felt like father and son anymore; it was more like jailer and inmate. What had begun as a normal disciplinary skirmish *("Go to your room!" "No!")* had escalated into an all-consuming battle of wills between the two Harkers.

Father: *You will submit.*

Son: *I will escape.*

Calvin felt nervous, even though he knew he didn't have a reason to be. He was definitely, definitely not high. He hadn't introduced a single intoxicant into his system for six days. He felt like his old self again. Dead inside, uninspired, trapped.

After he crashed the Jaguar, Calvin's lockdown had gotten truly serious. Mr. Harker had reinstalled the lock on the basement and enforced it with two extras. He made sure Calvin only did homework, nothing else, and checked his progress every few hours. His mother and sister stayed out of it, which somehow hurt worse than anything.

The week had been a mind-numbing blur of math and *Moby Dick* and catching up on all the overdue projects he'd been blowing off lately. He'd been allowed ten minutes of Internet a day on his dad's computer in order to e-mail assignments to teachers. No music, no poetry. His mind felt so blank he couldn't have written a poem anyway. At night he dreamed of the sky above his head and the ground beneath his feet. In the morning he woke up on a cot amid four blank, windowless walls.

The only thing that had kept him moving forward was

the dance. His dad had promised that if he got his shit together and maintained his solid number-one position in the sophomore class, he could go to the Homecoming dance. His drug stash was completely wiped, but freedom would be enough of a high after the week he'd had. And if it wasn't, hopefully Virginia would have some Percocet.

Mr. Harker finally dropped his hand. Calvin took a deep breath of air.

"You know the rules," Mr. Harker said. His voice was gravelly and severe. "You will not leave the gym. You will be home by ten o'clock, and you can expect a Breathalyzer and a urine test. Olek will be watching your every move."

Mr. Harker gestured to the stony Slavic man who'd been lurking in the corner this whole time. He was like no man Calvin had ever encountered in real life. His head was shaved and he wore a gaudy Tag Heuer watch. Calvin could see the tiniest hint of a neck tattoo peeking out of his collar. Thick biceps strained the sleeves of his shirt. Where on earth had his dad found such a man? Certainly not at the Beau Ideal golf course or the Harvard Alumni Association. Calvin tried not to feel intimidated. It didn't matter if this guy could crush his skull with his fist. Calvin didn't need to fight him; he only needed to outsmart him.

"If you take drugs tonight, Olek has been instructed to remove you from the dance and return you to my custody. If you *give* anyone drugs tonight, I will call the police."

No you won't, Calvin thought. If the homework prison

downstairs revealed anything, it was Mr. Harker's fanatical desire for his prize brain of a son to achieve academically. There was no honor roll in juvie, and his father knew that. They were both inventive men: Mr. Harker would invent ways to keep Calvin in school; Calvin would invent ways to get away.

"This is a test," Mr. Harker continued. "If you ever want to leave the house again, you will behave yourself and give Olek no cause for concern. Trust is earned, not given."

"Yes sir," Calvin said.

Mr. Harker nodded toward the front door. "Enjoy your evening."

Calvin went to the door. Olek mirrored his movements, as if connected to him by an invisible tether. Calvin imagined how it would look, entering a high school dance shadowed by a babysitter plucked from the Russian mafia.

Then something caught his eye out the window. A man was walking in a circle around the dented Jaguar in the driveway. Not a man—a boy. But he looked like a man. He was wearing a sophisticated gray wool suit instead of the sloppy khaki pants/blue blazer/random tie combination that was *de rigeur* among Winship boys.

It was Benny Flax.

"Ve vill go?" Olek asked behind him. Calvin could feel his eyes boring into his back.

"Just one minute."

He watched Benny circle the car twice, then stare intently

at the massive dent in the driver's side. *What are you up to?* Calvin wondered. He liked Benny and found him mildly interesting. But Benny was a product of the world. He was always staring at the ground, searching for clues. Didn't he understand that the true clues of life were in the stars? This world was a speck in the universe. The mysteries here didn't matter. Benny was on the wrong track, and always would be.

The parking lot, 8:00 p.m.

This would probably end up being the worst decision of his entire life. Craig was aware of this on some level. But he'd made up his mind—or at least what constituted a mind after five shots of Woodford Reserve and a Miller High Life. He was drunk. He shouldn't have been driving. But what did it matter? His car was already wrecked, thanks to that asshole freak Calvin Harker, who'd destroyed the fender *and* the bumper at Trevor's party. It was humiliating, having to drive around in this dented hunk of garbage. Calvin hadn't even apologized.

"Yull be sorrrry," Craig slurred to himself. He was slumped in the driver's seat, typing out increasingly garbled drunk-texts to Trevor Cheek.

Dude com outside u cant hide from me

He wasn't sure exactly what his plan was. He just wanted someone to fucking apologize. Trevor for letting Craig take the fall for the golf team when the whole thing had been *his* idea. Calvin for destroying his car with his big gay Jaguar. Winn Davis for being so popular without ever having to work for it. The whole school for being a piece of shit and never appreciating him.

You'll all be sorry, he thought. It was in his power to bring them all down; all he had to do was open his mouth. It was more power than he'd ever felt in his life. Greater than the power of being Trevor's wacky sidekick and getting invited to parties. Greater than the power of making people laugh with his dumbass YouTube channel. This was the power to annihilate and destroy. He'd felt it when he called the cops on Trevor's party, and he wanted to feel it again. The only catch was that he'd have to destroy himself in the process. But he didn't care. It'd be worth it to see the looks on their faces. The entire golf team: expelled. Winship's reputation: down the toilet once and for all.

He got a text. He squinted at the words, which were going in and out of focus. It wasn't from Trevor; it was from Skylar Jones.

Dude, AV closet is locked. What the hell u want anyway?

Damn it, Craig thought. He really should have planned this better. He'd come up with a vague idea of getting Skylar, who worked in the audio-visual lab, to project the picture from the golf course onto the wall of the gym the second they announced Homecoming King and Queen. That would have brought the evening to a nice grinding halt! Craig rubbed his temples, wishing he hadn't gotten so drunk. His thoughts felt sloppy and slow, and he was having a hard time coming up with a new idea. Maybe he could just grab the microphone when the King and Queen were announced and make a shocking confession.

"Ladays and gently-man," he practiced. "Shit." There was no way he could deliver a coherent confession in this state. He racked his drunken mind. There had to be another way.

That's when it hit him. *The gun.* The shiny silver Beretta he'd borrowed from his dad to use at the science expo last week. He checked the glove compartment, fumbling a little with the latch. Sure enough, it was still there. It wasn't loaded, but Trevor didn't need to know that. Craig felt a surge of violent glee as he imagined the scene: Trevor, gun to his head, confessing everything to the entire school.

"Say it," Craig practiced saying. "Tell them what you made me do." *He made me do it,* he thought, revising the memories in his mind. *It wasn't my fault.*

He had a small, nagging feeling that maybe this idea was a little too extreme. But it already felt too late to turn back, as if the idea had a will of its own, and was running on full steam, and Craig was just its pawn.

Bullets don't kill; velocity kills.

The gym, 8:10 p.m.

Virginia loitered by the punch bowl, sipping cup after cup of too-sweet red swill. So far the dance had been . . . weird.

Some genius in the senior class had sent out a mass e-mail that morning declaring that it was Opposite Day, so the boys could swoop in and restore order instead of everyone going stag. On the one hand, it was degrading to witness how eagerly the girls of Winship had relinquished the power to choose their own dates; on the other hand, given the general quality of the boys, it was equally degrading to think that was a power worth having in the first place.

And now the Opposite Day thing seemed to be taking on a life of its own. A group of rowdy guys were dominating the dance floor, fast-dancing during the slow songs and slow-dancing during the fast songs. Maybe Virginia should have been pleased by the chaos—she was always complaining about how boring Winship was and how nothing interesting ever happened. But deep down, she knew she relied on the school's usual monotony so she could seem more interesting in comparison.

She felt bulky and awkward with a cast on one arm and a purse hanging from the other. No one wore purses to dances. Either you put your stuff in your date's pockets, or you tucked it into your bra. But Virginia was carrying a passport and two sizable pill bottles, which made the purse necessary.

Bring a passport if u have one.

Every time she thought about it, Virginia felt a rush of exhilaration. A *passport*? Were they running away together? The idea was so crazy, she tried not to get too excited.

Calvin probably just needed a government-issued ID to confirm her identity for some reason.

Virginia looked around. The gym was tastefully decorated with blue streamers and strings of lights. It didn't magically resemble a ballroom the way dances did on TV shows. But it was a far cry from how it had looked last Thursday at the science expo. It felt pretty and romantic, or at least it would have if the buffoons on the dance floor would chill out and stop being obsessed with Opposite Day.

She scanned the gym for Benny. For some reason she felt nervous about seeing him. Maybe it was the romantic setting. It had been easy to push their weird kiss under the rug in the dismal environments of the hospital and the school cafeteria. But what if tonight it felt like a date? Or worse, like it was Chrissie's date and Virginia was the pathetic third wheel?

I don't care if you kiss me. I don't care if you burn my house to the ground. She kept thinking about those words. Wasn't it strange that he'd equated kissing with committing a crime?

"Dudes, Opposite Day! I'm using a plate as a cup!"

Virginia turned and saw Skylar Jones dumping a ladle of punch onto a small cake plate. Of course it sloshed everywhere, splattering across the floor. In a way, Virginia was glad she didn't have Zaire's expensive clothes anymore. What did it matter if Skylar spilled punch on her shitty Target dress? But at the same time, it was depressing. She missed the feeling that wearing Zaire's clothes had given her. The feeling of dignity.

One of the teacher chaperones walked past, carrying a plastic case containing the Homecoming crowns: a delicate tiara for the queen and a thick, pointy gold helmet for the king. The tiara didn't make Virginia feel the remotest bit covetous. Who wanted to be the queen of a bunch of high school sheep? She had bigger dreams.

She hadn't even bothered to e-mail her vote. It was pretty much written in stone that the golden couple Corny Davenport and Winn Davis would win, despite being juniors. The senior class was a particularly boring one that year, with no standouts like Corny and Winn. Amid cheers and applause, they'd be lifted into the horse-drawn carriage for a victory ride around campus. For Virginia it represented just how pointless it was to be popular: riding around in a circle, feeling special but not actually going anywhere.

She saw Benny across the gym. He spotted her immediately and started walking toward her. He looked . . . amazing. He was wearing a snappy suit that fit him perfectly. There was something in his hand. As he came closer, Virginia could see that it was a rose corsage. A yellow rose, just like the one he'd given her in the hospital. Maybe he'd decided not to come with Chrissie after all.

"Hi," he said.

"Hi!" Virginia said back. The DJ was playing an embarrassing Tim McGraw love song, and a handful of guys were square-dancing to it clownishly. Their dates were giggling at the edge of the dance floor. The whole thing felt like fifth grade. Virginia straightened her posture, hoping she looked as grown-up as Benny. She knew she probably didn't. Compared to him, she was sure she looked like a ten-year-old who'd broken her arm on the swing set.

She noticed Benny eyeing her cast. He was probably worrying that the corsage wouldn't fit on it. It didn't matter. She could just wear it on the other wrist.

"How exactly did that happen?" he asked. He didn't sound curious. He sounded suspicious.

Virginia cocked her eyebrow. "What, my arm? I told you. Big Gabe crashed into us."

"Why were you in the driver's seat? You can't drive."

"Um, I—"

Benny cut her off. "And even if, for some bizarre reason, you had attempted to drive, why would that result in your *right* arm being broken? It should be your left."

Virginia folded her arms instinctively, as if she could somehow hide the cast. Her mind whirred, trying to come up with an explanation that contained the basic elements of the truth without actually being the truth. Admitting that she'd essentially caused the crash by jumping into Calvin's lap and ramming her tongue down his throat was not an option right now. Not the way Benny was looking at her.

"Whatever," she said finally. "I'm not required to tell

you every single thing about my life. It's not like you tell me anything."

"What's that supposed to mean?"

Virginia stared at him for a second. "Benny, who do you think you're talking to? I know everything. About everyone. Did you know Corny Davenport is pregnant?"

Benny looked baffled. "Excuse me?"

"I know that Chrissie White went to your house."

Benny didn't respond. He was looking past her at something. Virginia glanced over her shoulder. There was a man loitering at the doors of the gym. He looked like a guy in a mob film who gets shot in the first scene and is credited as Gangster #1. He was too young to be anyone's dad, and he definitely wasn't a teacher.

"Friend of yours?" Virginia asked.

"What? No." Benny sounded annoyed.

Virginia scowled. How the hell was she supposed to know? He'd shown up at the hospital with that dreamboat Rodrigo—for all she knew, Benny had a whole collection of older guy friends to trot out at random times.

"He has a gun," Benny said. "Concealed under his arm. He's watching Calvin."

"Calvin's here?" Virginia followed Benny's eyes. She spotted Calvin in a dark corner talking to Skylar and Sophat. Her heart raced and she looked away, not ready to make eye contact with him yet.

"This guy looks . . . serious," Benny said. Then he

turned back to Virginia. "Listen, do what you want. But I advise you to stay away from Calvin tonight. That man could be a drug dealer. Or a cartel enforcer. Whoever he is, he has a gun, and Calvin led him here."

"Oh my god," Virginia breathed. It was so thrilling she could barely stand it. This definitely explained the passport thing. Calvin was fleeing a hit man! And he was taking her with him! She opened her mouth to tell Benny but stopped herself. He'd think she was insane to want to go along. Fifteen minutes into the dance and she'd already reached her peak tolerance of Benny's judginess. If she wanted to do this, she couldn't expect Benny to cheer her on.

"I'll see you later," she said curtly, setting down her cup of punch.

"See you later," he mumbled back.

She made a point of taking the long way around the dance floor so Benny wouldn't think she was running straight to Calvin, which she wasn't. Virginia was a better tactician than that. As she strode into the lobby, she turned to take a last look at the refreshments table, feeling a tiny twinge of guilt for leaving Benny alone so abruptly. But he wasn't alone. Chrissie had materialized out of thin air, as if she'd been hiding behind the punch bowl, waiting to pounce on Benny the second Virginia left. She watched them for a moment. Chrissie looked like a wide-eyed kitten. She was touching the lapel of Benny's suit, obviously awed by it. Benny was staring awkwardly at his shoes. He hated compliments. Didn't Chrissie know that about him? He held out the yellow rose corsage and Chrissie seized it excitedly.

So it wasn't for me anyway, Virginia thought. She'd been feeling weirdly undecided about Benny for a while now. But the corsage pretty much settled it. It wasn't for her.

The hallway, 8:45 p.m.

"You want the red pill this time?"

"Nah. I definitely want the blue again."

"Good. 'Cause I definitely want the red."

The conversation made Winn uneasy. He wasn't sure if it was such a great idea for Trevor to have another red pill. Hadn't he nearly killed DeAndre Bell when he took one of those last time? *Whatever,* Winn thought. He had bigger problems, and it was impossible to reason with Trevor anyway. Ever since Winn had told him that he knew who the mysterious drug dealer was, all Trevor could talk about was getting more pills so he could "Hulk out" again. The Incredible Hulk was Trevor's favorite Avenger. Winn's favorite was Thor, even though it was confusing because Thor wasn't in the Bible.

They sat side by side against the lockers in the dimly lit corridor. Trevor's phone buzzed for the hundredth time. He pulled it out and started messing with it.

"Damn it," he said. "I can't figure out how to block people on this thing. I want my old phone back." Trevor was famous for having the junkiest phone on earth, which he never upgraded as a point of pride. But he'd lost it last Friday and been forced to get a decent one because they didn't make his old model anymore.

"Here, give it to me. Who are you trying to block?"

"Fuckin' Craig."

Winn took the phone and scrolled through the barrage of messages. "What does he want?"

"He's trying to sneak into the dance. I'm like, dude, you're suspended. Go home and play video games and leave me the fuck alone."

Poor Craig, Winn thought. He was the latest toy that Trevor had played with and discarded. Trevor did that with everyone. He'd broken so many of the cheerleaders' hearts that he had to date Tate Prep girls now because none of the Winship girls would go near him. He just used people until he got bored and threw them away. In fact, the only person he didn't pull that shit with was Winn. They'd been best friends since they were five, even though they barely liked each other half the time. Trevor thought Winn was a bummer; Winn thought Trevor was an asshole. But they were used to each other, and besides, who else was there to be friends with?

"I heard you knocked up your girl," Trevor said, elbowing him in the ribs.

"Yeah . . . ," Winn replied.

"Nice."

It still didn't feel real. Winn and Corny: together forever.

FOREVER. It was a little terrifying. Probably the only reason they were together in the first place was because they had the same first three letters of their last names, so they'd been thrown together constantly in the alphabetized world of middle school. Corny said God made it happen because they were soul mates. But to Winn it seemed hopelessly random, that his entire life's path was being determined by the fact that his name was Winn Davis and not Winn Jones.

"There he is," Trevor said. "Hey, Cal! C'mere, buddy!"

Trevor was always doing that, acting all chummy with people he barely ever talked to. As Calvin Harker approached them, a weird feeling came over Winn. He was used to being the tallest guy in the room and always looking down at people. But Calvin was at least four inches taller than him. Winn knew he could snap the guy like a twig, but he still felt strangely intimidated. There was also the fact that Calvin had been part of his and Trevor's class growing up. He'd been held back after his heart cancer thing or whatever, so now he was a sophomore. But Winn still felt a vague proprietary feeling toward him. Calvin was a weirdo, but he was *their* weirdo. Except he wasn't.

"What's up?" Calvin said. Winn noticed him giving a quick glance over his shoulder. There was an incredibly weird-looking bald guy lurking in the corner of the lobby, watching them. He made Winn nervous. What if he was a cop, and they were all about to be arrested? But Calvin didn't seem to be bothered by his presence at all.

"You got some more of that cool stuff?" Trevor whispered.

Cool stuff. Sometimes Trevor was such a kid, it made Winn remember why they were friends. He wished he could go back in time to when they were seven years old and life was just cool stuff like playing with G.I. Joes and going hunting with their dads and eating hot dogs at football games.

Calvin looked at them for a second, obviously debating whether to deny that the secret drug dealer at the science expo had been him. Then he shrugged, apparently deciding it wasn't worth it. "Sorry," he said. "I'm totally out right now."

"But you have some of the blue pills, right?" Winn asked, hearing the pathetic desperation in his own voice.

Calvin shook his head again. "Sorry, man. And even if I did, you can't take that stuff all the time. Like, once a month, max."

Once a month? Once a MONTH? Winn felt his stomach sink. His plan was to take it every day! How else was he supposed to deal with having a baby? "Wait, are you serious?" he asked.

"Yeah, I mean, it's ecstasy. You have to be careful. You'll end up with serious brain damage if you take it too often."

"But—except—well—I—" Winn stammered helplessly, wanting to explain that he'd rather have brain damage than face his life right now. In fact, brain damage would probably make it easier.

"I really can't be talking about this," Calvin whispered.

"It's a very sensitive time for me." He nodded toward the bald guy staring at them from the corner. Then, without another word, he walked away.

"There goes my night," Trevor said glumly. He kicked the locker, and the sound echoed down the dreary hallway. Winn covered his face with his hands.

There goes my life.

The refreshments table, 9:00 p.m.

"So, what do you like most about playing the flute?"

Benny gritted his teeth. *Be polite,* he ordered himself. Chrissie seemed to have read an article in a women's magazine about how to make conversation on a date. He looked around the gym for Virginia. Where had she gone? Chrissie was nice and she looked very pretty, but she didn't seem to understand that Benny didn't come to dances to chitchat; he came to Be There. It was hard to concentrate on his surroundings with her hanging on him and distracting him. He wished Virginia would come back and run interference on her or something.

"I totally love your suit," Chrissie was saying for the eighth time. "Is it Italian?"

"I don't know. It's my dad's."

Benny couldn't say exactly why he'd decided to wear it. He was just tired of looking like an idiot all the time. He didn't want to be the hideous nerd Virginia saw him as, but he didn't want to be the blow-dried, pink-Polo-wearing country club phony either. He wanted to be himself. A capable, intelligent man: a Flax. Last week he'd been too afraid to even touch the suit, like he thought he didn't deserve it or something. But it was time to stop behaving like a seventh grader with low self-esteem. An invitation to become a man wasn't going to arrive in the mail—that fact was suddenly obvious. So he'd put the suit on. It was his now. And all the things he'd been afraid of—that his mother would be offended, that Virginia would make fun of him—they just melted away.

"Do you want to dance?" Chrissie said in her tiny voice.

Benny looked at the dance floor, which was empty except for a handful of unruly guys making a mockery of things. Everyone else was milling around outside and in the lobby, waiting for the Opposite Day joke to die so they could start taking the dance seriously and actually enjoy themselves. The scene was utterly emblematic of how things operated at Winship: a bunch of immature guys at the top forcing everyone to tiptoe around them until they got bored enough of acting like ogres for everyone else to have a decent evening.

Benny squinted out the doors into the lobby. Calvin Harker had just ducked into the boys' bathroom, followed by the tough-looking goon with the gun.

"Hey, can you give me a minute? I'll be right back."

"Where are you going?"

Benny didn't answer her. He swiftly crossed the dance floor, narrowly avoiding Skylar and Sophat doing the

Macarena to a Taylor Swift song. His heart was pounding.
Was Calvin Harker about to get shot by a cartel enforcer?
In the boys' bathroom? At a *Homecoming dance*? Benny listened at the bathroom door for a second. Then he pushed it
open with his foot, peering inside.

Calvin was washing his hands in the sink. The bald
man was standing by the urinals with his muscular arms
crossed, not doing anything. It was weird. The two obviously knew each other, but they weren't speaking, and
Calvin seemed to be pretending the bald man was invisible.

"Hi, Benny," Calvin said, noticing him in the doorway.

HI, BENNY. Benny's jaw clenched, unsure whether the
pointedness he heard in Calvin's voice was real or only in
his mind. He stepped inside, not wanting Calvin to think
he wasn't in control. "Hi," he said back.

"So far so weird, huh?" Calvin remarked.

"What?"

"This whole Opposite Day thing."

"Right . . ."

Then Calvin seemed to notice Benny glancing at the
guy by the urinals. "Oh, don't mind Olek. He's my date!
Aren't you, Olek?"

The man, evidently named Olek, made a short grunting
sound.

"We're having a very romantic evening. Think they'll
play our song, Olek?"

Benny narrowed his eyes at them. He didn't believe

Olek was Calvin's "date" for a second. But who the hell was he?

"Anyway," Calvin said, shaking the water off his wet hands. "Don't bother spending your Mystery Club resources on me tonight. I am clean as a whistle."

"No red pills?" Benny said, testing Calvin and Olek's reactions. Both of their faces were expressionless.

"No pills of any color in the rainbow." Calvin grabbed a paper towel from the dispenser.

"It's your fault, what happened to DeAndre," Benny accused him. Calvin's blasé attitude was getting under his skin for some reason. He wanted to see Calvin flinch.

"Excuse me?" Calvin seemed genuinely confused.

"You gave Trevor the drug that wound him up. Then you caused the blackout, which gave him the opportunity to attack."

"The blackout was necessary. My dad is a prison warden and I needed to escape the bathroom without being seen. I didn't know there would be such a high price."

"So you admit that you're partly responsible?" *Why am I pressing this?* Benny wondered. Calvin's cool demeanor was making him feel more and more agitated.

"Trevor's a monster. He would have done it anyway. Or something worse."

"You can't be sure of that," Benny argued. "*You* set all this in motion. *You* gave Trevor drugs. *You* put him in a violent state of mind."

Calvin shook his head. "Drugs don't change who we are. They *reveal* who we are."

Benny didn't know how to continue defending his point. When it came to drugs, he was completely straight-edge. The sip of bourbon from Rodrigo was the most illicit substance Benny had ever consumed in his life. He didn't feel equipped to debate the philosophy of drug-induced states with Calvin, who was obviously a drug aficionado. Benny glanced at Olek. He couldn't tell if the man was listening to them particularly closely, or if he even understood English.

"Well, what about what happened on the golf course?" Benny challenged, switching his line of attack. "Do you feel bad about that?"

Calvin held up his hands. "I was just there to golf. I did not participate in . . . *that*."

"But you didn't stop it."

He met Benny's eyes in the mirror. "I'm not in charge of those guys. You couldn't have stopped it either."

"I wouldn't have been there in the first place."

"Well, *that* is certainly true."

This time the pointedness of the remark was unmistakable. Benny said nothing, and a tense moment passed.

"I'm sorry," Calvin said finally. "I didn't mean it like that. I mean, maybe I did. But you're being very judgmental and it's making me defensive."

"I'm not *judging*," Benny said. "I'm just . . . I'm just . . ." The sentence hung unfinished in the air.

Calvin balled up his paper towel and tossed it in the trash.

"I was wondering," he said, his tone suddenly brisk and casual, "is Mystery Club accepting new membership right now?"

Oh god. "Of course," Benny forced himself to say. It was against his ethos to exclude people, but the idea of Calvin Harker invading his club made him feel panicked.

"Virginia told me about your investigation into the student-body president election. Very very interesting . . ."

"Very," Benny said back, like a dumb parrot.

"How do you use that sort of information?"

Benny looked at Calvin in the mirror. "What do you mean, how do we use it?"

"I mean, what do you *do*?"

Calvin turned from the mirror and looked right at Benny. The wild green of his eyes seemed to be dialed up about ten notches. *Do not stare into the eyes of your opponent: he may mesmerize you. Do not fix your gaze on his sword: he may intimidate you.* It was one of the principles of aikido. But Calvin's eyes were so intense, Benny couldn't make himself look away.

"We . . . We don't do anything."

There was a pause. Then Calvin smiled. "That's what I thought. Okay, let's go, Olek. Don't want you to miss one magical moment."

Calvin brushed past Benny and sailed out the door. The apparently mute Olek followed him, leaving Benny alone. The fluorescent light above his head buzzed irritatingly. Benny looked sourly at his reflection. Why had that encounter been so frustrating? Because Calvin didn't seem to care what Benny thought of him? No one ever cared what Benny thought; why should that suddenly bother him now?

He left the bathroom, unsure where to go next. He didn't want to be alone with his reflection anymore, but he didn't want to go back to sipping endless punch with Chrissie either. He went to the lobby doors and stepped outside. The crowd had thinned as everyone finally started to head to the gym. Only a few stragglers remained, guys leaning against their cars and waiting till the very last minute to put on their ties. The air felt cool and wintry. Benny took a deep breath.

I am calm however and whenever I am attacked. I have no attachment to life or death.

Something rustled in the bush next to him. "Hello?"

A person tumbled out, landing at Benny's feet. Benny jumped back instinctively. The person tried to stand up but stumbled on himself and fell down again.

"Craig?"

He made a second attempt to stand up, propping himself up on the bush.

"Are you drunk?" Benny asked, though the answer was plainly evident. Craig didn't seem to have heard the question anyway. He pointed himself toward the door and lurched forward.

"Whoa whoa whoa," Benny said, stepping in front of him. "You shouldn't be here. You're suspended."

Craig scoffed, looking at Benny like he was just now noticing he was there. "Move, freak," he said.

Benny didn't move. "Craig, get out of here. I'll call a teacher if I have to."

"Call a teacher, you lil pussy," Craig slurred. He gave Benny a push.

"Hey!" Benny said. "Don't touch me."

Craig reached out and rubbed his hands sloppily on Benny's face. Benny swatted him away, catching his glasses before they fell off. *"Don't touch me!"* he repeated.

Craig stepped back and looked Benny up and down. "What the hell are you wearing?"

"Go home, Craig."

"You look like a mini-man. Are you a mini-man?"

"Shut up!"

"Move!" Craig stepped to the right, but Benny blocked him. Then Craig stepped the other way, and Benny blocked him again. Something was coming over him. Usually Benny didn't care what people did—it was his ethos not to interfere in "the way" of life. But he felt his fists tightening with anger. It meant nothing to Craig that he was suspended; it meant nothing to him, what he'd done. A sequence of images flashed in Benny's mind: the mutilated deer head, the pool of blood, "HI, BENNY," Craig's black-painted face. All of them laughing, everything a joke.

"You're not welcome here," Benny said. "Get out."

What happened next happened very quickly. Craig swung his fist, and Benny grabbed it and used his momentum to slam Craig's entire body on the ground.

"Fuuuuck!" Craig groaned.

"Whoaaa!" people were shouting behind him. "Fight! Fight!"

Craig jumped to his feet and launched himself at Benny. Benny dodged him, and Craig ran face-first into a wall. It was like a cartoon, only there was no funny sound effect ("BONK! BOINGGGG!"), only Craig crumpling to the ground with blood running from his face.

Something shiny had skidded out of his pocket onto the grass. It was a gun. Benny stared at it for a long second, stunned. *That's a gun,* he told himself, disbelieving his own eyes. It didn't occur to him to call for help. His loner/detective instincts kicked in, and he dove down and grabbed it, quickly tucking it into his pants. People were all around now, but Benny barely saw them. He braced himself for further attack. Craig had pulled himself up and was baring his teeth like an animal.

"I'M GONNA FUCK YOU UP, KIKE!" he screamed. He hurled himself at Benny, but Benny leaped out of the way.

Aikido is not used to fight. It is the way to reconcile the world and make human beings one family. It was a saying by O'Sensei, the founder of aikido. But Benny didn't want to be a family with human beings like Craig. He wanted to punch human beings like Craig in the face.

THWACK!

Craig tipped back like a felled tree. The two seconds between Benny's fist making contact and Craig's body hitting the ground felt like a long, infinite eternity. Benny dimly registered the sound of applause all around him. They weren't cheering for him, he knew. They were cheering for violence—for the triumph of barbarity over civility. They'd be clapping just as loudly if Craig's punch had been the one to land instead of his own. Suddenly Benny felt dizzy.

Oh my god. What did I just do?

The girls' bathroom, 9:20 p.m.

Virginia wasn't hiding. She was just . . . *laying low.* That's what she told herself anyway. She was so nervous to see Calvin it was giving her butterflies. And without Benny to talk to, she didn't feel confident enough to go back into the gym and just stand around awkwardly. *This is what it must feel like to be Chrissie,* she suddenly understood. But the thought didn't fill her with compassion; it just made her hate herself for sinking this low. She looked in the mirror and messed with her hair for the millionth time.

Get it together, she commanded herself.

She could hear shouting coming from the lobby. It took her a second to realize that it was actual *shouting*, not just general excitement. Something was happening out there.

She abandoned her reflection and raced out the door. A huge crowd was gathered at the doors.

"What's going on?" Virginia asked the first person she saw.

"Scooby-Doo killed Craig!" a hysterical ninth-grade girl shrieked.

"What?" Virginia shouted. Without waiting for an answer, she squeezed her way to the center of the crowd. An ambulance had pulled up next to the white horse and carriage. A pair of EMTs were wheeling a stretcher into the back.

"What happened?" she asked someone else. "Is Craig really dead?"

The guy just shrugged. Virginia noticed a splatter of blood on the concrete at her feet. She whirled around, looking for Benny.

"YOU'LL BE SORRY! YOU'LL BE SORRY!" someone was screaming. It was coming from the ambulance. It was Craig. He sounded like a lunatic. It felt like the end of a horror movie where the guy gets dragged away in a straitjacket. *What the hell is going on?*

Finally she spotted Benny a ways off, talking to a man and a woman. She recognized them immediately. It was that pair of detectives who always showed up whenever anything at Winship got weird. She started walking toward them. Then she felt a hand on her wrist.

"Virginia."

She turned around, startled. It was Calvin. The red lights from the ambulance flickered on his pale face. His eyes were completely focused on her, like he didn't notice the craziness around them at all. Or maybe he just didn't care. She tried to think of something to say, but he spoke first:

"It's almost time. Are you ready?"

The courtyard, 9:45 p.m.

I have a gun. I have a gun.

He kept thinking it over and over while Mr. Rashid and four other teachers plus the two detectives made him explain what had happened for the eighth time:

"I saw him, and he was obviously intoxicated. I tried to prevent him from entering the dance. He fought me, and I fought back in self-defense. I didn't mean to injure him so severely."

Now would be the time to mention the gun, if he were going to. But he didn't. Why would he help these two idiot detectives? It still felt weird, lying. But it was only the anxiety of being immoral, not the anxiety of actually getting caught. Adults didn't know anything—that was suddenly very clear. They didn't have X-ray vision. They weren't psychic. They weren't going to strip-search him. He was the *good guy* here, after all. He'd saved the dance from a drunken, suspended interloper! No one had caught him when he pulled the fire alarm, and no one was going to catch him now. It was a spectacular illusion, the authority of adults.

Only Detective Disco didn't seem to be entirely buying it. He gave Benny a suspicious look and said, "I'm getting pretty used to seeing your face, Benny Flax. Wherever I am, you seem to appear."

"Maybe we're soul mates," Benny said back, feeling mildly astonished at himself. He'd never been sarcastic with an adult before. He'd been raised to be respectful.

The detective's female partner snorted. "Let's get out of here, Disco."

"You're a good man, Benny Flax," Mr. Rashid said, slapping him on the back in a way that made Benny feel more like a good dog than a good man.

Suddenly a huge, cheering crowd surged out the lobby doors into the courtyard. For a second Benny thought the cheering was for him. But then he realized no one was even looking at him, which made him feel foolish and egotistical. They were cheering for someone else. They were cheering for . . .

Calvin?

"God save the king!" people were shouting. Calvin towered in the middle of the crowd, smiling hugely while they herded him toward the horse and carriage.

Benny felt a soft hand on his wrist. He turned around, hoping it was Virginia. It was Chrissie. She kissed him on the cheek—a quick, incredibly soft and graceful kiss.

"I heard what you did!" she breathed. "You're amazing."

"What's going on?" he asked her, shouting over the noise. "What are they doing with Calvin?"

"He's Homecoming King!" she squealed.

Benny watched as Calvin was hoisted by the crowd into the carriage. Was this for real? In what universe was *Calvin Harker* the Homecoming King?

Chrissie was clapping and giggling. "Isn't it funny? It's Opposite Day!"

Benny shook his head. "He . . . he must have rigged it."

"What did you say?" Chrissie shouted.

"He rigged it!" Benny shouted back, not sure why he was even explaining this to her. "Why would he do that?"

Chrissie shrugged. "Maybe he just wanted to be a king for a day. Wouldn't you?"

Benny shook his head. "No. I believe in democracy."

"You're just like my grandfather!" Chrissie said, which at first Benny assumed was an insult. It was like Virginia calling him a ninety-year-old man. But when he looked at Chrissie's face, her wide eyes were full of . . . *awe*. Apparently it was a compliment. She sighed deeply and leaned against him. Benny adjusted himself so that she wouldn't feel the gun in his pants, which she seemed to take as an invitation to plaster herself even closer to him.

In the carriage, Calvin extended his freakishly long arm toward the crowd. As if she weighed nothing, a girl was lifted up in the arms of the crowd. Benny watched as her small hand was engulfed by Calvin's long, bony fingers. It was Virginia.

"God save the queen!"

"Long live Opposite Day!"

Look at me, Benny pleaded with her in his mind. But he was lost in a sea of people, and she wasn't searching for him. She was laughing—not the mean, smirking laugh he was used to seeing. Her smile was radiant, and her pale skin shined as if glowing from within. On top of her head sat a delicate silver tiara. It looked perfect, nestled in her thicket of curls. Calvin's crown looked goofier, plunked on his gaunt head like he was the king of the skeletons. But his smile was so genuine and warm, it was hard to mistake his handsomeness. The two waved together, and Benny noticed a corsage of red roses tied around Virginia's cast.

She hates red roses, you idiot.

They looked like a bizarre pair of newlyweds. Benny felt a pain in his chest like someone was hitting him with a metal pipe.

"It's so romantic," Chrissie said, nuzzling her face into Benny's shoulder.

As the carriage pulled away from the curb, the cheering swelled to a new height. Calvin's grim Russian friend was standing at the edge of the crowd, watching the hoopla with a surly expression. Evidently Benny and Olek were the only ones who were not amused by the spectacle. Everyone else was smiling and hugging and laughing. Benny saw Corny Davenport giggling with her friends. Even *she* thought this was funny, even though the crown on Virginia's head belonged, by all rights, to her.

The carriage grew smaller and smaller as it traveled down the road. Then, just as the horse was about to circle back, there was a loud collective gasp from the crowd.

As if alighting onto a soft cloud, the King and Queen leaped from the carriage. Benny watched, slightly stunned. Virginia stumbled. *Don't hurt yourself!* he screamed in his mind, watching her arm. In a swift motion Calvin swooped down and helped her up. Then they were running into the forest.

Olek swore loudly in Russian, *"Tchyo za ga`lima!"* Then he took off running.

The realization hit Benny like a truck: Calvin had rigged the election and made himself king so he could use the carriage ride to escape. Virginia had handed him the idea on a silver platter when she told him about DeAndre and Trevor.

"Oh my god." Benny slid out of Chrissie's arms and sprinted after Olek. Within seconds he had overtaken him. The two ran down the dark road toward the distant carriage.

"Opposite Day forever!" The shouts behind them grew distant.

The pounding of Olek's feet slowed, then finally stopped. Benny stopped too, his lungs burning. He bent over, out of breath. His eyes met Olek's across the darkness, and for a weird moment it felt like he and this Russian stranger were on the same team. The losing team.

Benny squinted toward the edge of the forest. He saw a tiny blur as Calvin darted between two trees and disappeared. Virginia followed him into the shadows.

She was gone.

Two weeks later
Piedmont Hospital, recovery wing, 5:00 p.m.

It was the same room, and DeAndre was the same person. But everything felt different. Before, it was like all the flowers in the room were floating. Or maybe he'd been the one who was floating. Nothing was floating anymore. The snug, warm cloud of painkillers had evaporated and dumped everything back down to the ground.

Every breath was painful. Every movement was agony. The doctors had advised him not to go off the morphine drip so soon. But morphine was basically heroin, and DeAndre didn't want to be on drugs a minute longer than absolutely necessary. DeAndre's neighbor was a heroin addict, and DeAndre had seen firsthand the way drugs could hollow a person from the inside out. The way people lost control of their lives, handing the reins over to crack or meth or whatever their thing was. Except now DeAndre was just handing the reins over to pain. The pain was all he could think about. Constant, mind-numbing, unreal pain. Was this really better than drugs?

The antlers had pierced his lungs, abdomen, and spinal canal. The extent of the damage was still uncertain. He'd never play football again. He might not be able to walk for months. And the pain. The *pain*. The doctors all said the pain was a good thing; it meant he wasn't completely paralyzed.

I want my heroin back, DeAndre thought, regretting his stupid arrogance thinking he could deal with this torture. But he still had too much pride to call for the nurse. He'd made his choice, and now he had to stick with it. He tried to imagine Cary Grant lying in a hospital bed in this pitiful condition. Would he still be flirting with the nurses and cracking rakish jokes? Would he somehow manage to look debonair in his drab hospital gown?

I can do this, DeAndre told himself. *I can do this.*

His bleary gaze landed on a white envelope tucked into a bouquet of roses next to his bed.

From the Cheeks and all your biggest fans! Get well soon, champ!

DeAndre knew what was inside. A check for two hundred thousand dollars. And that money was just the beginning. While he was swaddled in the sweet cloud of morphine, the choice had seemed easy: a rich cripple or a poor cripple, which did DeAndre want to be? A rich one, obviously.

But now that DeAndre was back on earth—the hard, cruel ground—he wasn't sure anymore. How much was his

pride worth? Three million dollars had seemed like a perfectly adequate number while he was high on morphine,
before he fully comprehended what the Cheeks were truly
paying for. Which was not just his silence but his dignity.
Money or pride? If DeAndre played the Cheeks' game, he
had to choose one.

But what if I didn't?

Suddenly another option opened in DeAndre's mind, as
if a guardian angel had appeared to clear the brush away
and reveal a hidden path. For a moment all of DeAndre's
pain melted away. He felt excited for the first time since the
attack. Money *and* pride.

I choose both.

There was a phone on the table next to the flowers.
DeAndre picked it up—slowly, painfully—along with a
copy of the Winship private directory. He flipped through
the pages until he found the number he needed.

"Hello?" a male voice answered.

"Benny Flax? This is DeAndre Bell." DeAndre was
shocked by the hoarse, weak sound of his own voice.

"DeAndre? Hi. How . . . um, how are you?"

"Worse in some ways, better in others," DeAndre croaked.
"Listen. I changed my mind. I'm not taking the Cheeks' deal.
I'm making my own deal. But I need your help."

There was a pause on the other end of the line. DeAndre
felt nervous. Maybe he was wrong to trust Benny. He barely
knew the guy, after all.

"What kind of deal?"

"No. You're either in or you're out," DeAndre said. "Tell me now, or I hang up the phone."

"I'm in, I'm in. . . ."

DeAndre could feel Benny thinking.

"There's something you can do for me, too," Benny's voice said finally.

"Like what?" DeAndre asked.

"No. You're either in or you're out."

DeAndre tried to laugh, but it was too painful. He'd laugh later.

"Yeah," he said. "I'm in."

acknowledgments

All my gratitude to Liesa Abrams and Stephen Barr for making me a better writer; and to Nico Carver, Nic Stone, and Chanel Parks for making me a better person.

about the author

Maggie Thrash grew up in the South. She is the author of the graphic memoir *Honor Girl* (a *Los Angeles Times* Book Prize nominee). *Strange Truth* and *Strange Lies* were inspired by her experiences at an exclusive prep school in Atlanta, where everyone had secrets.